Other Books by AJ Adaire

Friend Series

Sunset Island - Book 1

The Interim (a novelette)

Awaiting My Assignment - Book 2

Anything Your Heart Desires - Book 3

One Day Longer Than Forever

by

A J Adaire

Desert Palm Press

One Day Longer Than Forever
by AJ Adaire

© 2014 AJ Adaire

ISBN-13: 9781499354157
ISBN-10: 1499354150

Desert Palm Press
1961 Main Street, Suite 220
Watsonville, California 95076
www.desertpalmpress.com

Editor: Sue Hilliker
Cover Design: AJ Adaire
Cover Art:Colin Cramm
(http://www.dreamstime.com/noedelhap_info) I Dreamstime.com

Printed in the United States of America
First Edition June 2014

DEDICATION

This book is dedicated to my readers, especially to my first readers. Over time, first readers have come and gone as the demands of life have intruded on their time. Most steadfast have been my partner and our friend Pat. Thank you both for your encouragement and support.

This time, I picked up a couple of new readers from my Facebook friends. Thank you M-C H, TW, and CK for your feedback and encouragement. Michelle Boehlen, despite having challenges and constraints to the amount of time she has available, read the first, second, and third drafts in search of typos and inconsistencies in the plot. Her help and feedback were invaluable.

As always, thank you Sue Hilliker and Lee Fitzsimmons for your edits and suggestions. To my partner, thank you for your patience and understanding.

To my readers, thank you for your interest in my books. I appreciate your continued support of my work and thank those of you who have written reviews online, or have taken the initiative to write personal notes to tell me that I've touched you in some way. I've enjoyed hearing that you've been surprised, or moved to tears, and have, at times, laughed out loud as you've read my stories. I hope I will continue to entertain you.

One Day Longer Than Forever

Section 1 – Kate and Max

CHAPTER 1

KATE MARTIN JUNIOR YEAR OF COLLEGE 1985

THE REVELATION CAME JUST before the end of Kate's junior and Marie Claire's senior year. Marie Claire came home from an evening out dancing with some friends at a local bar. It was apparent she'd consumed more to drink than she should have as she unsteadily made her way down the hallway towards Kate's room. Kate stirred from sleep, still groggy, as Marie Claire entered her room and knelt next to her bed. The breath she exhaled carried the sharp aroma of the alcohol she'd consumed. "You awake?"

"Um hum." Marie Claire's hand felt cool as she brushed Kate's short soft curls off her forehead. The illumination from the ceiling fixture in the hallway caused Marie's mane of shiny light brown hair to glow in the soft light.

"I need to tell you something," Marie Claire whispered in the thick-tongued speech characteristic of one who'd consumed too much alcohol. Marie leaned over to place a soft kiss on Kate's mouth. It wasn't much of a kiss as kisses go, since Kate was too shocked to kiss her back. Still, it marked the first time Kate knew for sure that she could physically respond to another woman.

Marie Claire's breath brushed Kate's ear raising goose bumps. "I love you," she whispered, and then she was gone.

Alone in the dark, Kate felt disoriented, almost unsure whether she had dreamed the whole experience. The feeling was reinforced when her roommate didn't make any acknowledgement of the event the next day.

Several weeks later, just before the end of the semester, she and Marie Claire were alone for a long weekend in the tiny, off-campus apartment they shared with their roommate, Kelly.

Feet to feet, Marie Claire and Kate were stretched out on the sofa. "It's nice that we're alone. It's quieter without Kelly here," Kate observed.

Marie Claire nodded and placed her finger in the book she was reading. "I know. It's amazing that someone so small can make so much noise. It's been like a library here since she left for her parents' home this afternoon when classes ended. It'll be nice having the place to ourselves for the weekend." Following the brief exchange, they returned to their reading.

Studying for the next week's final exams, each woman had a textbook propped on her knees. Sensing Marie Claire's eyes on her, Kate looked up. Meeting her roommate's warm chocolate brown gaze, she felt an immediate physical response. Marie Claire was golden, one of those people who seemed to have a perpetual tan. Kate watched the slow and deliberate path as Marie Claire's pink tongue emerged to moisten her plush lips. Kate loved her expressive eyes and the way her lips curved up at the corners even when she was deep in thought. Nearly as tall as Kate, she had full breasts and a shapely derrière that filled out her jeans perfectly. Kate could hear Marie Claire's nervous swallow as Kate continued to hold her focus.

Unable to stand the silence any longer, Marie Claire asked, "What?"

Kate gathered her courage. "Did you mean it, MC?"

"Mean what?"

"What you told me that night a few weeks ago, you know, that you love me?"

Marie Claire looked away, her gaze resting everywhere but on the source of her discomfort. At last, her eyes returned to Kate's open, unwavering gaze. A flood of moisture glazed MC's eyes at her whispered acknowledgement. One tear spilled over to track its way down the contour of her cheek, eventually disappearing into the corner of her mouth, causing her to lick her lips again.

Kate slid across the sofa to sit facing her roommate. Gently brushing away the evidence of the tear's path, she said, "Don't cry. I love you, too." Later she would wonder where she got the courage to lean over to place a kiss on those tantalizing lips. Their contact was tentative at first, but when MC pulled her closer, the kiss deepened. The attraction that had smoldered between them for months burst into flame.

"Oh God, Kate. Your lips are so soft and you taste so sweet."

"Umm. You taste salty. Kissing you is amazing. Kiss me again, MC." Kate had experienced her fair share of kisses with the guys she'd dated over the years, even a quick but unfulfilling tussle when she lost her virginity in the back seat of Keith's car. Despite all that, she'd never before felt her body respond as it did to the tentative touches of this woman.

MC slipped her fingers under Kate's pajama top, slowly sliding it up her torso and lifting it off over her head. She paused long enough to allow her eyes to leisurely roam over newly exposed breasts. "You're beautiful." She reached out to touch the smooth skin. Slowly, her fingertips traveled down Kate's chest, lightly brushing across the swell of her breast, leaving a trail of goose bumps in their wake. The closer MC's fingertips came to Kate's nipples, the harder they contracted.

"Oh my God!" Kate arched into MC's touch when her fingers finally reached their destination. MC bent and sucked an erect nipple into her mouth as Kate closed her eyes. If this were her last breath she'd die happy and fulfilled. Like a woman possessed she reached out and pulled MC to her, inhaling the sweetness of her skin in the hollow of her neck. Without hesitation or doubt, Kate stripped MC's pajamas off before quickly divesting herself of her own remaining clothing. "I can't get close enough to you," she murmured into MC's neck as they struggled to adjust their positions so they could slide their fingers into each other. A few short strokes later they lay entwined, a tangle of arms and legs, each trying to restore her breathing to a normal level. Once recovered, they began again to explore each other's bodies and find what gave the most pleasure.

Sunday afternoon, snuggled in bed, Kate stirred as her lover tossed the covers back and slipped from bed. "Where are you going?"

"To get us some food. Aren't you hungry?"

Kate's eyes glinted with desire as she responded. "I hate to let you go even for as long as it takes to make a sandwich. I'm having too much fun."

On Sunday evening, Marie Claire gently touched Kate's face drawing her attention to the seriousness of her words. "This weekend was wonderful. Sweetie, you know tonight will be the end, right? I'm leaving for at least six more years of school in California, and you have a minimum of five years here in Philly, more if you specialize."

"I know." Tears welled in Kate's eyes, threatening to spill over. "Maybe I can transfer."

"Be realistic. I don't like it any more than you do. I can't think of any other options. We have to accept it. There's just no way. I'm glad we had this weekend though, and I'm glad my first time with a woman was with you."

"First time?" The thought had never crossed Kate's mind that she might be homosexual. It was impossible to believe that either of them would do this again with another woman or that there would be a next time with someone else. "Do you think we're lesbians or just attracted to each other?"

"I don't know. I've been so focused on you, I've never thought about wanting anyone else. What about you?"

"No, I've never really felt like this about anyone else. I don't want anyone other than you."

Marie Claire cradled Kate. "I know. Think about it, though. We have to face reality. You've got one more year of pre-med with vet school and possibly specialization after that. I'm farther along than you, and I'm not even close to being ready to settle down. With me attending school in California next year and you in school here in Pennsylvania, we'll be on opposite sides of the country. We have no chance, Katie. There's no more time for us, just tonight. So come here and love me one more time."

"Doesn't what we've found mean anything to you? Don't you want us to be together like this?"

"Katie, be real. It means something, but not everything. I can only give you now. I can't give you forever. I'm sorry."

Kate blinked back her tears and buried her face in Marie Claire's neck. Never before had she been so happy and so miserable all at the same time.

CHAPTER 2

DR. KATE MARTIN

DOCTOR BRACKEN DECIDED TO expand his veterinary practice in 1992. Dr. Kate Martin was the last of the three candidates to be interviewed. Doctor Bracken greeted Kate warmly. "Call me Doc, or Doc B. Everyone does. Only my mother calls me Nathaniel." They shook hands and he pointed to a chair opposite him. "Have a seat. May I call you Kate?"

"Please."

"I've reviewed your application. Let's start with you telling me a little more about your background." Dr. Bracken set the clipboard with Kate's application on the table and gave her his full attention.

Kate adjusted her position and exhaled a nervous breath before she began. "In addition to my basic degree in general veterinary medicine, I specialized in large animals. I also volunteered at my local wildlife rescue and refuge center throughout college and whenever I could during my years of vet school as well."

"Your background will mesh well with the type of work we do here in this practice. A substantial proportion of our clients are the local farmers and their livestock, including cows, pigs, sheep, and horses. Both of my assistants and I volunteer at the refuge center a few hours a week where we provide services to sick animals. Additionally, we provide emergency care to the refuge for injured wildlife.

Unfortunately, many of them, especially the deer, owls, and other raptors, too often have unfortunate run-ins with vehicles. As a group, we donate as much time as we can to their facility. They do good work." Doctor Bracken made some notes on the interview sheet secured to the clipboard on the table. "Tell me a little more about your experience."

Kate, feeling more relaxed, elaborated on her coursework and her training. The interview was informal, and there were several instances of laughter as they shared some of their more humorous experiences dealing with animals and their owners.

"You're quite young to have so much training and experience."

"I skipped a grade in elementary school, so I graduated high school at sixteen. In high school, I took several advanced placement classes. Those courses, plus the fact that I took classes during summer school sessions enabled me to finish my undergrad just after I turned nineteen. Vet school and specialization after that. Seems I've been in school forever."

"Impressive." He flipped through her file. "Your transcripts confirm that you were an excellent student, and your letters of recommendation are extremely strong." He returned to his list of questions on the front of his clipboard. "Well, that's the last question I have. Is there anything you'd like to ask me?"

Kate smiled. She felt comfortable enough with her potential boss to respond with, "You mean other than are you going hire me?" She was pleased when Doctor Bracken laughed at her response.

"Yes, I think I am. Let's talk about the details over a cup of coffee, shall we?"

"Make it tea, and you have a deal."

***

Kate relocated and started her new job. A few months later, she bought a house and became a permanent part of the community. As she and Doc B worked cooperatively over the next four years, the practice grew. During that time, one-by-one the large, mostly family owned, farms sold to developers, and the rural nature of the small Pennsylvania community began to change. When she started work, the total population of the town was around three thousand, while another eight hundred and some lived on the surrounding farms.

Kate and Dr. Braken met each morning to divide the work, taking turns on office hours and farm visits. They split their day so that one of them was always in the office during regular hours.

"Good morning, Kate." Doc B reviewed the day's schedule. "You have quite a few house calls this morning."

"Yes, I'm about to leave. I just finishing loading all the vaccines and other supplies I'll need today." Kate snapped her bag closed.

"Did you see the Johnson farm is for sale?"

Kate nodded. "Yes, noticed the sign on my way in. It seems that almost every month another farm in the area is put on sale. I can't believe how quickly things have changed."

As local farmers reached retirement age and learned that their children and family members were uninterested in continuing in their vocation, one long-term farmer after another had no choice except to put their farms up for sale. As each farm sold, their fertile fields gave birth to a crop of large developments. Each group of houses was filled with young families who commuted to high paying jobs in Philadelphia or New York City.

"Yes." Dr. Bracken replaced the schedule book on the reception desk. "Our practice is changing too. Notice it? We're seeing many more family pets now. The population of the community has swelled to over five thousand in the few short years since you came here. Fewer farms mean a reduced need for our large animal services."

"I've noticed the change. We're the only practice around who still specializes in providing services to the larger animals. Still, with all the people moving into the developments there's an increase in the number of clients with house pets. Our small animal practice is flourishing."

"You know, Kate, if the practice continues to grow, and we want to continue our specialization on horses, cows, and other large animals, we may need to entertain adding another vet. Right now, some days, it feels like there aren't enough hours in the day to meet all the need."

***

Several months later, Dr. Bracken and Kate agreed they could no longer handle the demands of the busy practice on their own. "Kate, I think it's time to hire another vet. Will you sit in on the interviews with me?"

"I'd love to."

They interviewed and settled on a young vet straight out of school, Dr. Maxine Mountebank. At lunchtime on Maxine's first day of work, between patients, Kate stuck her head into the exam room and announced, "I'm ordering lunch. Want me to order something for you? Here's the menu."

"Thanks. I'm starving. I skipped breakfast this morning. I have another patient coming in a minute, so just get me the biggest salad they have with chicken on it. Let me know what I owe you."

They settled in the staff room during the lunch break. "Man, I'm so hungry I could eat a horse," Maxine said as she unwrapped her bag and slid payment for her salad across the table to Kate.

"Maybe that's not a good sentiment to express in a practice that still caters to large animals." Kate chuckled.

Maxine looked over each shoulder before she whispered, "I won't tell if you don't."

"Deal." The aroma of fried onions permeated the small room as Kate unwrapped her cheese steak sandwich.

"I'm glad you offered to get me lunch. Thank you. I'm staying at the motel out on the main highway. I didn't know where to get something for lunch this morning. You saved my life, figuratively and maybe even literally." Max squeezed the dressing from the plastic envelope onto her salad. "I need to get a place to live as soon as possible. I can't afford to stay in the motel longer than a few more days. Where would you suggest I look to find inexpensive accommodations?"

Kate lowered her sandwich long enough to ask, "Do you want a house, an apartment, or a room?"

"House? Ha! I can't afford that or an apartment right now for that matter. I'm going to have to settle for a room or a share, at least for a few months, until I get some money put aside."

Kate thought for a moment before she offered. "Look, I have a house with a spare bedroom. Why don't you rent that for a little while until you have time to explore the area and can find something more satisfactory? At least you'll be able to get a feel for the town and figure out where you'll feel most comfortable."

"That's very generous. I appreciate it."

They agreed to meet after work at Kate's house to allow Max to see the room and to work out the details.

***

As the practice flourished, so did Max and Kate's friendship. What they intended as a temporary solution to Max's need for a place to live stretched into several months.

"This place is really dead. I'm going down to Tappy's." Max was used to more nightlife than their small town offered. She hung out at the local tavern most Friday evenings where a small band played and the audience danced to country western songs. "Come with me. Please." The phrase had become her mantra every time she left to go out for an evening.

Kate steadfastly resisted. Finally growing tired of making up excuses and feeling comfortable enough with Max, she confided the reason she wasn't interested in hanging at the local bar on Saturday night. "I'm sorry, going there is just not my thing. Listen, I hope this won't impact our friendship. I have something to tell you. I'm uh, a lesbian."

Max blinked, giving no additional visible reaction other than to arch her eyebrows. "Really? How did you know you were gay?"

Kate's mind quickly flashed back to college. She wondered how much she really needed to divulge of her past.

"Hey, where did you go?" Max touched Kate's arm, snapping her mind back from her memories and refocusing her in the present. "You don't have to tell me how you knew if you don't want to. It really doesn't matter. I was just curious."

"No, it's okay. Your question just made me think of an old memory. I don't mind telling you. It took me a while to figure it out, the fact I was attracted to women, I mean. The realization first occurred to me during my junior year in college when I had a very short affair with my roommate." The recollection of that the weekend-long affair, if one could even call it that, made her smile. "I wasn't yet nineteen. I had no clue I was attracted to women until she kissed me and everything became clear. After that, I had two relationships in vet school, each of which ended when the woman I cared about graduated and moved on while I remained to finish my training. I hate to sound sorry for myself. The truth is I've never been involved with anyone who made me a priority. In fairness, I've never been willing to sacrifice my goals for anyone else either."

A look of puzzlement flashed across Max's face. "I don't understand, don't you want a husband, children, pets, stability?"

"A husband, no. Children, not any more." Kate shook her head. "I've missed that boat. I already have a dog, a good job, own a home—that's stability in my estimation." Her brow furrowed. "You think I'm not stable?"

In response, Max waved a hand in dismissal. "No, of course not. I do wonder though, what about love? Don't you miss having someone love you?"

"How can I miss something I've never had?"

"It's just not fair." Max brushed her hand slowly along Kate's forearm up to her elbow before returning to her starting point, only to repeat the journey. "You deserve more. You're a wonderfully warm and caring person. You deserve to be loved."

Kate's skin warmed at Max's touch. "Well, perhaps that's true. Do you see anyone volunteering? I don't"

After a pause Max replied, "Not yet. I'll keep you posted if anyone comes to mind." Max abruptly changed the subject. "So, let's go pick out some paint. This place is depressing. If you expect me to stay here, we need to spruce it up a bit. We're starting here in the living room. My room is next." She softened her criticism with a smile and a warm squeeze of Kate's hand before she stood, pulling Kate up after her. "Come on, get a move on."

CHAPTER 3

KATE MARTIN AND MAX

AS TIME PASSED, MAX and Kate grew steadily closer. After living with Kate a little more than four months Max stopped going to the bars to meet men. She hadn't dated anyone since she'd moved in with Kate because, when not working, she and Kate were enjoying dinner at their favorite Italian restaurant, catching a movie, or working on the house.

"Max, please don't misunderstand me. It's not that I don't enjoy spending time with you. It's just that you should be getting out and meeting people."

"No, I like when it's just the two of us doing things on the house, having dinner, talking. I'm happy with that. I only miss one thing about not going out. I love to dance and I never get to do that any more." She paused, pursing her lips in thought. Almost as an after thought she added, "That's about it."

Even though Kate enjoyed her time with Max, she also enjoyed a variety of other activities including sharing her life with friends and family. She was overdue to see her best friend, Kyle, with whom she usually visited regularly, if not once a week, at least several times a month. A few additional times during the year Kate acted as Kyle's 'date' for the deeply closeted lawyer's work related dinners and social functions. It didn't hurt Kate's reputation to be seen on the arm of the handsome attorney either, she admitted to herself. Kyle was fond of saying, "The town you live in is just large enough that not everyone knows your business, just those who count." It had been nearly a month since she'd seen him, a combination of his demanding job and her own focus on the improvements she and Max had been making on the house.

Max had proven that she knew what she was talking about when it came to home repairs. Kate's craftsman style cottage was originally constructed in 1905. As they worked, it soon became apparent that there had been several renovations after the house was first constructed. The original and beautifully grained oak emerged as layers and layers of different colored paint were stripped from the woodwork in the living room.

Kate looked forward to hearing Kyle's deep voice as she dialed his number.

"Hello, Kate. It's good to hear from you."

"Hey there, long time, and all that. How have you been?"

"Hey Babe! I'm good, and so glad you called. You were on my list of people to contact today. Great minds, right? We're overdue for a get together. Can you manage lunch later, maybe around oneish?"

Kate quickly reviewed her calendar. "Make it one-thirty, don't call me babe again, and you're on. Same place as usual?"

"Okay. Sure. I'll see you there, Sweet Cheeks."

Kate was still laughing when she hung up. She was working a split shift, with three on-site visits that morning, followed by office hours starting at four. Hurrying to get out the door, she uttered a silent prayer that the visits would go smoothly so she could get home to shower before she met Kyle. Her mind was in overdrive as she reviewed the jobs scheduled for that morning. Her happy conclusion was that they shouldn't be too dirty, just vaccinations for Marge Jacobson's small flock of prized sheep, a health check on the cow Mr. Brown just bought, and a visit to check the wound and remove the stitches from the leg of the Gunther's stallion that she had sutured on her previous visit. An easy morning if all went as expected which, of course, it never did.

The sheep proved to be uncooperative, as did the stallion. Fortunately, things improved when Kate arrived at the Brown's. When Kate finished her exam of the new cow the Browns bought the weekend before to breed with their bull, Kate pronounced her healthy. "She has about the sweetest disposition of any cow I've ever treated."

"Thanks, Kate. You're right, she is a sweetie." Jim Brown beamed as the vet complimented his ability to pick good stock.

Cindy Brown waved as she joined her husband and his companion at the fence. "How about some tea?"

Checking her watch for how much time remained, Kate begged off. "I promise I'll take you up on your offer next visit. I'll even bring the donuts next time. I'm sorry, I have to decline today because I have a lunch date. If I hurry I have just enough time to get home so I can clean up before I go. It'll make me a much better dining companion, I think."

"That's likely true," Cindy said. Her husband nodded his head in agreement.

"Gee, thanks a lot." They returned her cheerful wave as she drove away.

Kate hummed an upbeat tune as she sailed through the shower. She dressed in tan slacks, a white turtleneck, and a navy colored cotton crew neck sweater. Enough time had passed that her hair had reached 'critical mass,' the perfect state of dampness where it was still moist enough to style yet wouldn't take too long under the heat of the dryer. She liked her thick, naturally wavy hair short and had worn it that way since high school. She didn't even mind the streaks of silver running through it. A couple of sprays of musk, quick dusting of powder, and a stroke or two of mascara completed her primping. She was whistling cheerfully as she hustled out the door to meet her friend.

"Hi, Kate. Sit here at the table in front of the window. Is Kyle coming?" Louisa smiled as she placed two menus on the table. Kate, habitually punctual, arrived at the restaurant first and the club soda with lime she'd ordered had already been delivered when, through the window, she saw Kyle striding up the walkway. He glanced up and Kate offered a wide smile and a jaunty wave.

Kyle was tall and well built, with sandy hair, and deep-set blue eyes. His sincere smile, when he saw her, indicated he reciprocated the love Kate felt for him. They had been friends almost from the minute she'd relocated to Farmington. Feeling lonely shortly after she moved there, Kate made the trip to the gay bar/restaurant named 'The Wheelhouse.' It was located in a city an easy forty-five minute drive away from her home. Because she'd gone alone Kate opted to sit at the bar, planning to have her meal there, instead of eating alone at a table. It was still early for dinner, and the only other patron in the bar area had been Kyle. She recalled how easily their friendship had developed.

The handsome young man at the bar glanced over. "Hi, mind if I slide over so we can chat? It appears we're the only two people here. Are we that early?"

"Please. Sometimes I feel like…" Kate glanced left and right. "I guess I don't have to explain. Single life can be pretty lonely sometimes. I'd be glad for the company."

After introductions, she and Kyle had chatted over drinks, lamenting their lack of a gay social network, Kate's because she was new to the area, and Kyle's because he was living a closeted life. "I rarely come here," he admitted. "I'm only here today because I was in need of a conversation with a kindred spirit, so to speak."

"If you are craving companionship of a romantic nature, you are obviously barking up the wrong tree." Kate raised an eyebrow and gave a shrug.

"Pot calling the kettle names, I dare say. I'm not here looking for love today. A more pressing need is to have some good conversation and friendship in my life. It's lonely in the closet." After over an hour of lively and interesting conversation, Kyle asked, "Join me for dinner? My treat."

"Only if I can pick up our bar tab."

By the time they were settled in the dining room, the pair felt like they'd known each other forever. Dinner conversation included gentle teasing, true confessions, and an agreement to meet the following Saturday for dinner and a movie. They shared a history of their relationships that had not lasted and a mutual desire to find someone with whom they could share a 'forever.' It was an auspicious beginning to a close and enduring friendship.

Louisa dropped off a basket of fresh baked bread. "Your friend is late. This should keep you alive until he gets here."

"He's here. I just saw him coming up the walk. He probably stopped to wash his hands." Kate waited, eager for Kyle to make his way to the table so she could catch up on any new developments in Kyle's life.

The hostess led Kyle to where Kate was seated. "I hope I haven't kept you waiting." He leaned over to give her a quick kiss before taking his seat opposite her at the table. "You look fabulous, Sweetheart. I still can't believe nobody has snapped you up. What's the matter with the women in this area?"

Kate felt her skin warm as she blushed at the compliment. "You're too kind. You know that I don't make it any easier than you do to meet someone. My busy work schedule, and your being in the closet, we're quite the pair. At least you're dating someone. I was just thinking about when we met. It was my lucky day."

"Mine too." He reached across the table and squeezed her hand. After nearly ten years of friendship, they had no secrets between them. "So what's got your knickers so happy?"

"I told you Max is living at my place. We've been doing a lot of repairs. I'm enjoying fixing up the house with her. We're having a lot of fun. By the way, I came out to her."

"Really? How'd she react?"

"She seems okay with it."

"You said that she's straight, right? You sure?"

"Yes, and before you start, I'm well aware of that." Kate looked away for a moment before drawing her eyes back. "I'm trying to keep that fact in the forefront of my mind." She paused and exhaled a sigh. "I could be in trouble here. I'm developing feelings for her that could go beyond platonic. She's easy company, and being with her makes me happy."

"Be careful, Kate. Getting involved with her has heartache written all over it. You've always said you want a relationship that will go the distance and don't want another one that will end with the woman leaving you for something more important to her."

Kate glanced away, over Kyle's shoulder as she had a quick flash of how none of the women she'd dated had ever thought her worthy of a relationship longer than it took them to move on to the next phase in their lives. She gritted her teeth against the memories.

She quickly drew her attention back to Kyle when their favorite server reappeared bringing Kyle a draft. "Thanks, Louisa. I'll have my regular, the well done burger and salad with Russian on the side."

"Me too, Louisa, I'll have the same thing." Kate smiled. "How's your family?"

"Very well, thank you for asking." Louisa tucked the menus under her arm. "We'll be bringing Bucky in for his shots next week, so you'll be able to see the kids in a few days. You won't recognize Julio. He's grown at least four inches since you saw him last." Pointing at her own front teeth with two fingers separated into a V shape, she added, "Anna lost both of her front teeth. She's embarrassed. I think she's adorable." Louisa glanced up at the clock. "You two in a hurry?"

In unison, both Kyle and Kate shook their heads. "No, not today," Kate replied.

"Okay, let me get your order in. Save room for dessert. We have a great homemade apple tart with a maple glaze. Yum!" A quick wiggle of Louisa's eyebrows before she hurried away made Kate and Kyle laugh.

"I'll go save you a couple of slices."

Kyle reached for Kate's hand. "Okay, enough about you, it's my turn. You aren't the only one with news. Mike and I are talking about moving in together. We've been dating for almost a year now, and we're both equally tired of the shuffle between our respective apartments. Since he's more open about being gay than I've ever been, I'll need to adjust my thinking if we decide to move forward. If I come out, there's still a possibility it could cost me my job. There are no legal protections for us here in Pennsylvania, so I'm lucky that I work across the river in New Jersey where I can't be fired for being gay. Despite the laws, being out still can mean subtle discrimination. You know, no clients referred my way, other colleagues not wanting to work with me." Kyle shrugged. "I'm fortunate that I can always open my own practice if I have to. As an estate-planning attorney, I'm sure there would be options. I have a buddy, an investment advisor, who has previously expressed an interest in forming a partnership with me. It could be a good opportunity for me." Kyle took a sip of his beer.

"Are you seriously considering it, going into business for yourself, I mean?"

"Well, as an architect, Mike makes decent money. He's willing to shoulder the financial load until I can get established, if my friend and I open our own practice. So, that's not a problem. It's just that it's a whole different mindset for me. Mike's out to his entire family and expects us to function openly within my own family as well."

"That would be a big change for you, wouldn't it?"

"Yes, for sure. I know it will take some adjustment on my part. I feel ready to do it. I'm already forty-one years old, and I'm tired of hiding who I am. If Mike and I take our relationship to the next level, I'll definitely have his support for the next steps I need to take."

Kate raised her glass and Kyle joined in her toast wishing him happiness. "I like Mike a lot. I'm sure you'll be happy as a couple."

Louisa delivered the food and brought Kyle another beer. The two friends spent the next hour catching up on news, laughing at shared memories, and after finishing their burgers, enjoying the apple tarts with a huge scoop of vanilla ice cream.

"Kyle, Max wants to go out dancing. Do you think I should take her to The Wheelhouse? My other option is to get you and Mike to take us to the local tavern. What do you think?"

After finishing the last swallow of his coffee, he shrugged. "Would she be comfortable at a gay bar?"

"I'm not sure."

"Well, you two figure it out. We could use a fun night out. How about Saturday night? We'll pick you up at nine."

Kate smiled. "Make that eight o'clock and dinner is on me."

"In that case," Kyle said reaching for the check, "lunch is on me today."

Hand-in-hand they walked to the parking lot where they exchanged a quick hug and kiss. "See you Saturday," Kyle said, before closing Kate's car door.

After a quick wave goodbye, Kate started her car. She had two days to decide where they would go for dinner and their night of dancing. More importantly, she needed to analyze her feelings for Max and decide how to proceed.

CHAPTER 4

AFTER LUNCH, KATE RETURNED to the office, finished her patient hours, and made the twenty-minute drive home. It had been a long day. Thankfully, Max had already walked the dog. Kate changed into sweats and joined Max in the living room for a glass of wine while Penny napped in her bed in the corner.

"This wine really hits the spot," Kate sighed, finally relaxing. As she settled Penny stood up, stretched, and relocated to curl up at her side. Kate nodded at Max. "Thanks." Stifling a yawn, "Long day," she confessed.

The roommates reviewed the day, sharing information about which clients had appointments, and what ailments each had including a brief overview of the treatment each patient received. As time passed, conversation settled into a companionable silence. Kate took a swallow of her wine, and fortified by the alcohol, decided to forge ahead. "Do you have plans for Saturday night?"

"Nope. What do you have in mind?"

"Um, you have two options. We can have dinner in town, or we can go to a restaurant that Kyle and I like called the Wheelhouse. It's in a gay bar about forty-five minutes from here. They have a great band on the weekends, and Kyle and Mike both love to dance. I should probably call for reservations wherever we decide to go, so what are your thoughts?"

"I've never been to a gay bar before...let's do that."

***

Dinner with Kyle, Mike, and Max was a great success. By the time they got to the restaurant, everyone was comfortable with each other and Max was asking questions. "Kate tells me that you picked her up here at the bar, Kyle."

"Really? That's not how I remember it, Kate. You plied me with liquor before you forced me to buy you dinner. You'd better be careful, Max. She can beguile."

Max glanced over at Kate. "I'm learning that. She's definitely a charmer."

While she enjoyed watching her friends get to know each other, Kate remained reserved. After dinner, they moved to the dance area located on the lower level of the building. A great DJ played music from the sixties to current day, mixing in fast and slow numbers. Not wanting to make her friend uncomfortable, Kate didn't ask Max to dance. Kyle and Mike danced several dances with each of the women. At the end of the evening, Mike and Kyle danced several dances with each other including the last two slow dances, as Max and Kate watched from their table. On the way home everyone agreed it was a fun evening that they all wanted to repeat again soon.

Kate and Max enjoyed a cup of tea after the guys left. Perched on the stools at the kitchen counter they shared their recollections of conversations and events of the evening. Eventually, Max grew quiet.

"Is something bothering you? You just went silent."

"I don't know. I guess I was wondering why you didn't ask me to dance."

"You know why Max. You're straight. You could probably dance with me and not have it mean anything. As a lesbian who finds you very attractive, a slow dance with you would be uh—difficult for me. I mean it would make me want something more with you that I know isn't possible. So as the saying goes, believe me when I say it's me, not you."

"You find me attractive?"

Kate laughed. "Of all that I just revealed to you that's what you focus on? Yes, I do find you attractive. No doubt, if you weren't straight we wouldn't be out here sipping tea. However, since you are, I think it's time I put this discussion and me, to bed. I'll see you tomorrow. Have a good night."

Kate took a quick shower before sliding naked between the smooth sheets. Forcing her mind to remain blank, it only took a few minutes for her to start to drift off into sleep.

An hour later, Max settled her weight on the edge of the bed. The blankets pulled tight across Kate's chest restraining her arms beneath the covers. The ceiling fixture in the hall provided enough light that Kate could see a slight smile curling the corners of Max's luscious mouth. Max put a hand on either side of Kate's shoulders, leaned down, and placed a soft, slow, sensuous kiss on Kate's mouth.

"Max."

"Shhh." Max stilled Kate's protest by kissing her again, not stopping until Kate began to respond.

Again, Kate tried to protest. "Max, wait. This won't work, you're straight."

"Am I? If I'm so straight, why do I lie in my room every night struggling for all I'm worth not to come in here to you. Why can't I get you out of my mind when I'm working, and why can't I wait to get home to you, or have you come home to me every night? Tell me why I want to put my hands on you every chance I can." Max kissed Kate again. This time when Max's tongue sought access Kate allowed it, moaning softly as her long stifled passion surfaced. Max stood and stripped off the covers, surprised to find Kate naked. She paused, allowing her eyes to caress Kate's body. "My God, you're even more gorgeous than I'd imagined."

Kate reached out her hand pulling Max toward the bed.

"Wait. I need to feel you against my skin." Max stripped off her nightshirt and slipped into bed with Kate. She settled onto Kate, smooth skin sliding over smooth skin, and adjusted her weight to fit the contours of their bodies to each other.

Max buried her nose in the hollow of Kate's shoulder to inhale Kate's fresh soapy scent. "You smell so good," she murmured before she traced her tongue up Kate's neck, outlining the shape of her earlobe with her lips before she pulled it into her mouth.

Unable to stand it any longer, Kate flipped Max over onto her back. Their mouths met, hot, and wet. Kate pulled back giving Max one last chance to change her mind. "Are you sure this is what you want?"

Max answered with her body. Kate had never had a lover so responsive to her touch, or so vocal in appreciation of her efforts. When Kate entered her, Max wasn't shy in conveying her needs, directing Kate with moans of appreciation and whispers of "harder," or "faster." Max came and barely rested a heartbeat before she began her own eager exploration of Kate's body with her lips, teeth, tongue, and hands.

To Kate, it felt like Max was everywhere at once. "That's wonderful, right there. Umm. I've never felt so desired, nor so thoroughly loved." Eyes closed, Kate savored being touched. She gasped, "Max" when she climaxed.

Max freely explored Kate's body. Even after they had exhausted their desire for each other, Max's hands roamed the curves of Kate's breasts and the planes of her stomach. She trailed her fingers through the soft curls at the apex of Kate's thighs.

"Tell me what you're thinking. Are you really okay with this?" Kate asked, a lump of fear lodged in her throat that Max would change her mind now that she'd experienced their shared intimacy.

Max kissed Kate before adjusting her position to rest her head on Kate's shoulder. "Why wouldn't I be? Making love with you was amazing."

"Yes, for me too." Kate had a vague sense of disquiet. "You didn't answer my question though."

"I loved making love with you, and I love being with you the time we spend together is perfect. I just…"

Kate slid out from under Max's weight and sat up in the bed, leaning against the headboard. "You just what? Was this just an experiment for you?" Her abrupt disconnect from their embrace and tightness in her voice caused Max to sit up as well.

"No, Kate. Please don't be angry. I just can't say I'll be able to do this right now."

"Do this? This what? Have sex? Have a relationship?

"I don't know. I do want you. Can't you see that?" Max ran her hand through her hair. When she looked up, she sought Kate's eyes. "I've already told you that I love the time we spend together. I love working with you. I'm just not sure I can be, you know, a lesbian." The last two words Max uttered in almost a whisper.

Kate slid out of bed and grabbed a robe from the chair. "I think you'd better go back to your room. This definitely won't work. You can't even bring yourself to say the word. Please, Max. Just go."

Max lowered her head into her hands and began to sob. Raising her tear stained face, she begged Kate, "Please don't send me away. I couldn't bear it. I think I'm in love with you."

Kate sighed, closing her lids against the need in Max's eyes. Against her better judgment, she approached the bed, retrieved Max's nightshirt and waited for her to slip it on. Only then did she sit next to

Max on the bed.

"Max, sex isn't all there is to 'it', to being a lesbian. I have feelings for you and...

"I'm sorry. I don't mean to interrupt you. I just don't understand what I'm feeling." Max adjusted her nightshirt and leaned back against the headboard. She inhaled a deep breath before she opened her eyes. "It's not you I doubt, it's me. I don't know if I'm strong enough to live openly as a lesbian."

Kate remained silent. Max was obviously struggling to organize her thoughts and Kate waited patiently, giving her the time she needed.

Max sniffed one final time before she continued. "Here with you, making love, no problem. Out there in the world where people disapprove, I'm not so sure. I hope I will be able to one day. I hope I'll be brave enough and strong enough to live what I feel for you. Can you give me some time? What I'm feeling is so new. I can't get my head wrapped around it. The only thing I'm sure of is that I want you. I can't bear that you might send me away." She grabbed Kate's hand and pulled it to her lips. "Can you give me some time? Please?" Max ran her hand up Kate's arm, across her shoulder, and cupped it around the back of Kate's neck. She pulled gently, tugging Kate toward her until their lips met.

Kate resisted the kiss at first, but when Max's tongue probed, she moaned and gave in to the sensations. They made love until they couldn't stay awake any longer and fell into an exhausted slumber.

Kate awoke first, just a few hours later. She slipped from the bed and made her way to the kitchen. She let the dog out before making herself a cup of tea. She sat drinking the warm liquid, mulling her options. She knew she'd never cared for anyone before, not like this. During her past affairs, she'd never felt the intensity of caring that she had for Max. The closest she came to what she was feeling for Max had been with Marie Claire. There had only been two others after that who had mattered at all. It seemed that each time she was ready to commit her heart to someone, despite the developing feelings, the next chapter in their educational programs took them away to a different state. Although she was afraid of being hurt, the opportunity to have exactly what she'd always wanted was a possibility with Max. The physical attraction for Max had always been there. The fact that Max was also someone she enjoyed being with out of bed as well as between the sheets made it hard to resist going where her emotions were pulling her. They had many shared interests in common and had always enjoyed interesting conversations and fun times together. *I'm older now and know more about what I want from life,* she reasoned. *I want to be with her. Would it be possible to give Max the time she needs without investing so much of my heart that I'd be devastated if she broke things off?* Her conclusion was that it was worth trying for a bit. *I'll hold back just a little until I'm sure.*

The sound of Max's footsteps pulled Kate from her thoughts, and she turned towards Max as she entered the kitchen. Max acted as though it was the most natural thing in the world to walk over and kiss Kate. Wrapping her arms around Kate after the quick kiss, Max rested her head on Kate's shoulder as she pulled her into an embrace.

"You doing okay this morning, sleepyhead?"

"Mm hum. I think so." Max pulled away and went to the stove to reheat the teakettle. She made a cup for herself and another cup for Kate. The silence between them was comfortable.

Max pulled up a chair opposite Kate. "I've actually been awake for a while. I've been doing some thinking. What you and I have is special. I've never felt this way before for anyone. I fully expected to fall in love one day, to marry, and have kids. You know, the whole picket fence thing. You, being in a relationship with a woman...it's not something I ever expected and I don't know how I feel about people knowing about us, about me."

"We don't have to shout it from the rooftops. I've never really been a flag bearer about being gay. This is new to me, too. I've never had the potential for a relationship like this before, one that I feel can last. I've always wanted a relationship that I felt would continue for a lifetime, and it's always eluded me. The affairs I had in college were probably more physical than emotional and they probably never were begun with the hope of more than a short time together. This, what we have, scares me. Because if you decide this isn't for you and you leave me, it will break my heart on many different levels." Kate wanted to give Max one more chance to back away. "I'm not sure how to undo what we've done. Do you think we should try to put the genie back in the bottle until you're sure?"

Max paused a few seconds before answering. "No, not if you can just be patient with me. Give me some time to get used to the idea of us before we talk about telling anyone, okay?"

Kate tried to silence the alarm bells clanging in her head with an internal dialogue of calming, reassuring phrases. Despite a sincere effort, she couldn't quash the tentative feeling that dogged her. "I hear what you're saying, although I think we need friends who know about us. I at least need to tell Kyle. And I want my family to know I'm happy." Max held firm, and despite her desires, Kate agreed to what Max asked.

At first, being completely closeted wasn't a huge issue. Most of their spare time was spent working on the house, watching television, or reading at home. However, the passage of time saw numerous discussions about Max's need to be completely closeted. After one particularly heated discussion, tears filled Max's eyes. "I'm not what you say. I'm not ashamed of us. I...I just can't face people who know."

Kate blinked, trying to comprehend Max's reasoning. "You make no sense. You say you're not ashamed, but you can't face people."

"You just don't understand." Max stood up. "I can't talk about this with you any more." Despite all of Kate's powers of persuasion, she refused to discuss it any further.

During another attempt at a resolution to the issue about six months after the first time they made love, Kate again brought up the topic. "Max, I don't understand why you're so against me telling my family. I want them to know I'm happy. Please. We need a support system of some sort. You asked for time, but I don't see you making any progress at accepting my need to tell a few select people."

Max closed her eyes and shook her head, a habit she had that infuriated Kate.

"Kyle and Mike love us. They're in a deliriously happy relationship. Please, can't we tell them? If you let me tell them, I'll stop bugging you about anyone else. I need someone to share us with, Max. I'm begging you."

"You know I love you, Kate." Max looked directly at Kate, her gaze steady. "Okay, Mike and Kyle and nobody else. Ever. I am sick of this discussion. I've given you what you want."

"Not really, but it's a start."

"No. It's the end of the discussion. Don't bring it up again. I mean it."

Telling Kyle and Mike and socializing with them at least gave Kate hope that with time Max might realize she was losing out by not living their love more openly. Time slipped by, and as the focus of the veterinary practice continued to shift from larger animals to more domestic pets. They became increasingly busy at work. Their private life fell into a routine that, for the most part, met their needs. Two years later, in 1999, when Doc decided to retire, Kate and Max went into debt and bought the practice in partnership. With less travel involved to see patients, they decided not to replace Doc, opting instead to split his hours between them. The increased workload kept them even busier. They maintained that pace for three grueling years, until the demands of the growing practice became so burdensome they finally decided to hire in a third vet, Dr. Kevin Rosen, and another vet tech. They expanded their hours on the weekends and arranged to offer ophthalmology and dermatology services by contracting specialists, each scheduled to work with them one day a week. As their practice thrived and flourished, their relationship, which lacked the nourishment and support of friends and family, began to wither.

Over that time, Kyle came out to his family and although he never made an issue of his sexuality at work, he stopped using Kate as a cover. One day, Kate received a phone call from Kyle. "I have some exciting news," he said, excitement evident in his tone. "Can you meet me for a drink after work?"

Kate agreed and they arranged the place and time. As he and Kate sat at the bar, she said, "Well, spill it. I've been wondering all day the reason for our get together."

"I'm going to take a chance. I'm opening my own practice with my friend. We hope to begin to specialize, to build a gay clientele. Regardless of our goal, we certainly won't discriminate against anyone interested in our services. We plan to focus on helping gay and lesbian couples protect themselves and their assets legally by using medical and financial powers of attorney, wills, and trust documents."

"Good for you, my friend." Kate raised her glass, clinked it against Kyle's, and kissed him on the cheek. "I have no doubt that you'll be successful. You're a hard worker and an honest man. I wish you the best. How are you planning on developing a gay clientele?"

"Workshops, speaking at gay organizations, advocating for equality for gays and lesbians, and word of mouth. Hopefully, some of my current clients will opt to come with me and through their referrals our client list will grow." In the moment, Kyle was taking a huge risk, giving up a dependable income with potential for advancement in exchange for being able to be true to who he was.

Kate and Max continued their friendship with Kyle and Mike, seeing them regularly. In reality, that was their only social outlet due to Max's insistence they remain so closeted. Even that one friendship was limited due to Max's steadfast refusal to attend any social gatherings or parties the guys invited them to attend. Max consistently denied Kate's requests to join her, stating in one form or another, "I can't become identified as half of a lesbian couple."

"Honey, everyone there will be gay. They're just like us."
"No. I'm sorry, Kate. I just can't."

***

Holidays had always been an issue between them. "Come home with me, Max."

"You know we always spend holidays separately. I always fly home to see my parents in Oregon for Christmas. It's the only time I see my parents all year."

It was a bone of contention and was the subject of the fight they'd had the night before Max was scheduled to leave for a week to attend the 2003 Veterinary Conference in Florida. "Max, I don't understand why I can't tell my family about us. I want them to know I have more in my life than my job."

"We've been over this time and again. You know how I feel about it. As far as I'm concerned, the subject is closed." Max crossed her arms in front of her chest, her expression unyielding.

Kate's frustration and anger reddened her face. Max's continued refusal to allow Kate to divulge their relationship to her family caused Kate to lash out. "My God, Max! My family lives three hours away and in a different state, and your family lives on the other side of the country. I don't get it. Is it shame? Are you so ashamed of us that you fear them knowing about us?"

Tears welled in Max's eyes. Her failure to deny Kate's statement hurt them both. The strain of their core issue was taking its toll on their relationship. They bickered constantly about things that were not the real issue. Kate eventually admitted to herself that they were obviously coming to a crisis point in their relationship. Neither of them was happy. However, after eight years as a couple, six years of which they'd been business partners, their lives were so intertwined between their personal and their business relationships that they seemed trapped in a limbo of their own design. For the first time ever, Kate really began to consider the possibility that they were not going to survive as a couple. Could they dissolve their personal relationship and continue to work together? Her life was a mess. Kate put her head in her hands and cried as the enormity of that thought struck her. She felt sick to her stomach at the prospect of it. I have nobody to blame for this disaster but myself.

Kate, after allowing herself a brief time for self-pity, decided to make one more attempt to reach her partner. She fixed them a nice meal and

27

opened a bottle of wine. After dinner, she raised the issue they'd been bickering about for over a week. "Max, you have to give a little on this. I'm starving here, living in this vacuum. I can't go on like this."

"You knew how I felt from the beginning, and nothing has changed." Max opened her mouth as if to add something then simply shook her head. "I've been telling you for years this is a closed issue. You are the most persistent person I've ever met. Sometimes 'no' means 'no,' Kate. When will you believe me?" Max stood up, carried her plate to the sink and turned towards her lover. "I'm done, Kate. Never, and I mean never bring this up again," she spat out before turning to walk into the bedroom to pack for her trip to Florida.

Early the next morning, Kate was alternately drifting in and out of sleep while Max made final preparations to leave for the airport. Max sat on the edge of the bed, her weight tugging on the blanket caused Kate to stir. She opened her eyes and smiled. "All ready to go?" Still only half awake, Kate reached her hand out to grasp her lover's.

"Yes, I just came to say goodbye before I leave."

"I hope you have a good time at the conference."

Max looked away briefly. "I'm certain I will."

Kate's attempt to pull Max into an embrace met with resistance. "Don't get me all wrinkled," she admonished. "I just finished ironing this blouse." She grasped Kate's hands in her own and placed a chaste, dry peck on Kate's lips before abruptly standing up. "I'll call you when I get there," she promised, tossing a quick wave in Kate's direction before closing the bedroom door on her way out.

Kate snuggled back under the comfort of the covers seeking to warm the chill that she felt after her exchange with Max. A long sigh did nothing to relieve her disquiet. There were obviously problems with their relationship, nevertheless Max steadfastly resisted giving any ground on their primary issue. What once was a happy and loving relationship now left Kate feeling empty and continually lonely.

Section 2 – Lee and Kendra

CHAPTER 5

LEE FOSTER – 1966

BILLY LEE FOSTER SAUNTERED up to the counter in the new school he was transferring to, his mother trailing behind him. His mother addressed the secretary. "I need the papers to register my son. Here are his transcripts. He's in his junior year of high school, transferring from Texas."

"Fill in this form, please. I think I saw his transcripts come in a couple of days ago. I'll check."

Billy Lee began attending classes. He was different from all the other boys in the north Jersey suburb his family moved to when his father accepted the job promotion offered by his company. Billy Lee soon earned a well-deserved reputation as a 'bad boy.' His dark-haired, brown-eyed good looks garnered a lot of female attention, while his athleticism attracted a cadre of male friends. He had a magnetic personality, quick wit, and a killer southern drawl. His only flaw was that he was meanness personified. Not the run of the mill, dull kind of mean, he was the smart, subtly mean sort—the dangerous kind of mean. Billy Lee rarely carried out his evil deeds himself. Generally, his minions carried out his bidding. He was clever, manipulative, and smart enough to pull the strings without getting blamed for his misdeeds.

Billy Lee sauntered into study hall and surveyed the room before he chose his seat. "Hello, Darlin'," he drawled. "My name is Billy Lee. I'm new here." He shot the attractive young woman a dazzling smile.

"I'm Sandra. Sandra Billings. Where are you from?" With that innocent conversation, Sandra's life was destined to change dramatically and her fate sealed.

Sandra Billings loved Billy Lee exclusively. He started dating her after they sat next to each other that day in study hall. Despite her reluctance to give in to his demands for a sexual relationship, he continued to date her.

Sandra's best friend had serious reservations about Billy Lee. "Sandy, I don't know what you see in him other than the fact that he's handsome. He tells you he loves you yet we all hear that he sees other girls. You know the type he likes."

"I don't believe all the gossip about him. I've asked him and he says it's not true. He loves me and I love him."

The night of the senior prom, Billy Lee spiked the punch bowl. "Here, Sandra. Here's some punch. Drink up. We'll have some fun later." Solicitously, he made sure Sandra had a steady supply of punch throughout the evening. Later, when he made his advances, Sandra was in no condition to resist.

Roughly two months later, following the fireworks on July fourth, they were in the back seat of Billy Lee's car. They had just made love. "Billy, you know I'm crazy about you, don't you? Do you love me?"

"Sure baby, you know I do."

"I have something to tell you. I think I'm pregnant. I missed my second period."

"So? What makes you think it's mine?" He pushed away from her.

Tears welled in Sandra's eyes. "Billy, you know I don't do this with anyone else. You're the only one. I love you. What are we going to do?"

"We? What do you mean we?"

Their parents became involved when Sandra confessed to her mother what happened. Succumbing to pressure from both families, they were married by the end of the month. Billy Lee got a job working for a mason instead of going to college as he had originally planned. The backbreaking labor did little to improve his temper. It didn't take long for Sandra to realize her hope for a happy life with the guy she loved, and the hope that once their baby was born things would improve, were nothing but a dream.

Unfortunately, if anything, conditions became even worse. The birth of their daughter Lee, served only to further annoy Billy Lee. He complained that she cried too much. "Make her stop that caterwauling," he demanded. When Sandra couldn't get Lee to stop, Billy stormed out of their tiny apartment slamming the door behind him as he departed. Sandra finally got the baby to sleep. When Billy Lee came home drunk and demanding sex, he woke the baby. "Shut that squalling brat up."

Frustrated, and without thinking, Sandra flung back, "You woke her."

That was the first time he hit her. Sandra's self confidence shriveled under the glowering presence of her husband.

Friday night, Billy Lee came home after cashing his check. "Come on, let's go get some pizza." At the pizza restaurant, the server, Bobby, brought them menus. "Hi Billy Lee. Sandra." He chucked Lee under the chin and touched her head with his palm, a gentle touch. "She's beautiful, Sandy."

"Thanks, Bobby." Sandy blessed him with a dazzling smile in appreciation of his kind acknowledgement of what Sandra considered her greatest achievement in life, her daughter.

Bobby took their order and headed back to the kitchen.

Billy Lee's lip curled and his voice held menace. "Maybe Lee is his. He certainly looked kindly on her. Y'all are pretty friendly."

"Please don't start, Billy. We've both known Bobby since high school. He was just saying she's pretty, that's all. It had nothing to do with me." She dreaded going anywhere with him because he was insanely jealous and would accuse her of flirting with the waiter. At the food store it was the produce guy or the cashier, and while at home the mailman.

Lee, first as a toddler and later as a young child, created additional tension in the home just by her mere existence. Like most little girls, Lee wanted her father's attention. "Daddy," she would yell as she ran across the room towards him holding up her arms. Depending on his mood, sometimes he'd pick her up. Just as often he'd ignore her.

On one such evening, Billy Lee pushed his daughter away, causing her to fall on her diaper-padded backside. The frightened little girl began to cry despite the fact that no real harm had been done.

"Shut that bawling brat up," Billy screamed, his face red with anger.

Sandra rushed to scoop the little girl into her arms. "Come here, Sweetie." She comforted the child and put her into her swing before facing her husband. "Don't you ever manhandle her like that again—she doesn't deserve that."

Billy grabbed Sandra by the hair and slapped her hard. "Listen, you bitch. Don't you ever talk to me like that again, or I'll kill you.

Understand me?"

By the time her daughter was six years old she had seen her mother beaten more times than Sandra cared to recall. When Billy Lee's anger became focused on their daughter, Sandra would deflect it away from Lee by drawing his ire to herself. Always choosing to protect Lee over her own safety, Sandra had taken a number of blows originally intended for Lee.

Both Lee and her mother learned to disappear into the background and not make waves. When Billy Lee was due home from work, Sandra would get Lee involved in a quiet activity. "Come here, Lee. Draw mommy a picture. Your father will be home soon and we need to keep out of his way and not annoy him." She took the little girl by the hand and led her to the small desk in the corner of the living room where she kept her paper and drawing pencils. "You know your mommy loves you, don't you?"

Lee nodded. "I'll draw you a pretty picture, Mommy." Lee knew her mother loved her, and when her father was not home they always had fun, no matter the activity.

"I love all your pictures. If you finish your picture I'll read you a story later. Okay?" Sandra loved to read to her daughter and continually praised and encouraged her love of drawing. When Lee got too old to be read to, Sandra let Lee read to her.

***

Less fearful for her own safety than she was for her daughter's, Sandra made every effort never to leave Lee alone with her father especially after the summer before her eleventh birthday, when Lee started to develop early. Not liking the way Billy Lee sometimes looked at his daughter, Sandy remained very vigilant. One Saturday morning, when she caught him peering through the bathroom keyhole while Lee was bathing, she confronted him. While Lee was still in the tub, she heard her mother screaming, "If you so much as breathe heavy in her direction, you bastard, I swear I'll kill you."

Billy Lee's initial reaction was to laugh. However, he soon sobered when he saw the look on his wife's face. He responded deliberately, "Yeah, you and what army?"

Sandra replied in a calm and icy voice that conveyed the intensity of her feelings. "Just me. I don't need an army to take care of the likes of you."

Something in her tone defused him. It was the first time she had ever successfully stood up to him. The situation would normally have resulted in him slapping her around. Instead it ended with him calmly drinking himself into a stupor and then staggering into the bedroom to fall asleep.

Sitting at the kitchen table, Sandra could hear Billy Lee's snoring through the open bedroom door. Her hatred for her husband boiled inside her. Her stomach churned and her heart beat fast as her hands clenched, nails digging into her palms. "You've threatened and terrorized us for the last time. I'm not taking this shit off of you any more." The venom in her own voice shocked her. Something in her had changed. Their last exchange had freed a new resolve within her. She called her parents' number and spoke in a calm and quiet voice with her mother about what she'd observed.

"That man is not fit to continue to walk this earth," her mother said. "Don't say anything to your father about this, Sandra. I do believe he'd kill him if he touched that little girl."

"Mom, I need to think about what I'm going to do. He's told me before that he'd kill me if I leave him." Sandra exhaled a weary sigh. "Can you come pick up Lee and keep her with you for the weekend?"

Lee's mother objected strongly to Sandra's determination to remain at home alone with her husband. "Sweetheart, please come with us. At least your father will be able to help protect you if he comes after you."

Sandra's father tried desperately to convince his daughter to come back home with him and her mother. "You'll be safe with us honey. I'll see to it. You know I'd never let anything happen either to you or to my granddaughter."

Sandra was adamant. "No, not this time, Mom and Dad. I've made up my mind. I'm not taking any more of his crap. I'm going to stand up to him, and it won't mean anything to Billy Lee if Daddy is standing there protecting me. I need to do this on my own. If Lee isn't here I won't have to worry about her getting hurt. Please don't worry about me. I'll be fine, I promise. He's not going to hurt me, or my daughter, ever again. Now, please go." She kissed her parents and her daughter goodbye. As they pulled away from the curb Sandra walked up the steps and entered her home.

Once her daughter was safe with her grandmother, Sandra went straight to her kitchen to make a cup of tea. Her anger and hatred for her husband festered as she listened to Billy Lee snore. She'd suffered so many indignities at his hands. Standing up after taking the last sip of her tea, she walked to the sink to wash and dry her cup and spoon. When Sandra opened the kitchen drawer to put her teaspoon away she saw the butcher knife resting there. Ever so slowly her hand reached out to pick it up. She saw her weary eyes reflected back as she stared at its shiny surface. Her index finger traced the sharp edge of the blade to the finely honed point as her mind flashed back to the insults, beatings and Billy's many other transgressions. She ended with her fears for her daughter's safety as she recalled the glint in his eye, earlier that day, as he watched his daughter. A sigh trembled from her lips. The longer she stood there staring at her reflection, the more emotion roiled within her. The anger grew until something snapped. "It's one thing for him to abuse me..." In a barely audible voice, she vowed, "But he's never going to touch my daughter."

A few minutes later, Sandra dialed the number for the police where the voice on the other end asked, "How can I help you?"

"I'd like to report a death," Sandra replied calmly.

"Okay. Who died?"

"My husband," Sandra reported calmly.

The policewoman questioned Sandra in an effort to understand what had happened. "Was your husband ill?"

"Well, that's probably a matter for debate. But no, not in the way you mean. I stabbed him."

"The police are on the way." The dispatcher continued to give Sandra instructions designed to insure Sandra's as well as the officers' safety.

The trial garnered a lot of attention and debate about the proper punishment for the abused woman on trial. Upon hearing the details of Sandra and Lee's life with Billy Lee, the jury did sympathize with her plight.

At the conclusion of the deliberations, the judge asked, "Has the jury reached a verdict?"

"We have your honor. The jury finds the defendant guilty."

The judge polled the jury. "Sentencing will be in two weeks." He banged the gavel, sealing Sandra's fate.

A murmur spread through the courtroom. Shouts of "Not fair," and "The bastard got what was coming to him," could be heard above the general din of the courtroom.

The next day, a few of the jurors agreed to an interview. The commentator interviewed the foreperson of the jury after the trial concluded. "Obviously there were many people watching this trial who felt the killing was justified. Apparently the jury felt differently since you found the defendant guilty."

"Honestly, I don't think there was a person on the jury who didn't feel for and empathize with Mrs. Foster. However, it was because of her calm and measured manner with the police, and her making arrangements for her daughter's well being before the killing that Sandra ended up being charged with and convicted of murder. Had she stabbed him while he was peering through the keyhole, there would have been much less question. That would have clearly been a crime of passion. The fact that she called her parents and arranged to have Lee cared for gave too many members concern that the crime was premeditated, thus the murder conviction. Regardless of the fact that a lot of us felt the killing was justified, we had to follow the instructions from the judge. We did recommend he go easy on her in the sentencing."

Despite the jury's recommendation for leniency, Sandra was sentenced to twelve years in prison, of which she served a little over ten years. Lee was already in college when Sandra got out. Once released from prison, Sandra returned to the home of her parents to live. Finding a job was not easy. Fortunately, the woman in charge of the local women's shelter remembered what had happened and gave her a job.

Lee was a bright young woman with a love for bookish things. She was sure her grandmother would have been appalled had she known that Lee had overheard her on the phone telling her mother, "At least her father gave her his looks and brains, and not that miserable disposition of his. Thankfully, she inherited your kind heart and gentle way with people, instead."

CHAPTER 6

LEE FOSTER - 1980

LEE WAS AT HER DESK in her bedroom when her grandmother came in to see her. "What are you doing, honey?"

"Finishing up a picture for my art class, Gram."

"Oh, it's beautiful." The older woman placed a kiss on her granddaughter's forehead before she bid her a good night.

As a child, drawing provided Lee a haven from the upheaval of her family life. By the time she was in high school her natural ability to draw anything she saw had grown into a real talent. Her sense of perspective seemed to be a natural gift. Lee's grandparents encouraged her artistic skills by paying for private drawing lessons. An avid interest in photography caused Lee to rarely be seen without a camera in her hand. Academically, she was fascinated by and excelled in science and math. She never missed being on the Honor Roll, a fact that made both her mother and grandparents proud.

***

Continual Honor Roll achievement and high grades resulted in Lee being awarded a full scholarship to study Biology. She eventually chose to specialize in Marine Biology. A dedicated student who excelled in the college environment, she was well liked by her professors for her intellect and hard work. Although somewhat quiet and reserved by nature, her easy going manner, sense of humor, and kindness to her fellow students earned her several close and supportive friendships. There were times she did participate in some group activities with her friends, still most of her extracurricular life revolved around her relationship with a fellow student, Brian White. By the time she was a college junior they were sharing an apartment.

Lee met Brian at the door a month before she graduated from her Masters program. "Hey, girlfriend. What's up?" He gave her a quick hug before he got them each a beer from the fridge.

"I got a job offer today. I'm going to be working in the Maryland research facility."

Brian led her into the apartment, his arm casually around her waist. "Thank God! At least one of us will be gainfully employed."

"Oh stop. You'll find something soon." Lee was prophetic. Brian not only found a job, he fell madly in love and moved in with his new boyfriend less than six months later.

Lee enjoyed the work at the lab and excelled at writing up the reports. Her boss, Angus McGrath, complimented her abilities frequently. "Lee, you possess unique skills and gifts. I wish I had your capability to describe all these very complex concepts in such plain English that even an untrained reader can understand them clearly. Additionally, your ability to include illustrations is singular in this field. So many scientists can't get it right, always presenting things too technically. You have a real gift there, Lee."

Dr. Angus McGrath relocated from Maryland to Connecticut in 1998, taking a job at a research center near Groton. He recruited Lee to make the move with him and to join him as his research partner. "I need you there with me, Lee. You know I can't put any of this research I'm doing into plain English. I need you with me to complete my team."

Flattered, Lee joined Angus without a backward glance. As part of their job, they conducted several studies, reaffirming their effectiveness as a team. His skill at compiling and digesting the information was enhanced by Lee's ability to convert the data into easily consumable text.

Lee stopped in to visit Fiona, Angus' wife. It seemed as if Fiona and Angus had been married forever. Fiona was tall, blonde, and slender like her husband, with a warm smile identical to her husband's ready grin. "Hey girlfriend," Fiona said giving Lee a warm hug and kiss. "You moving back in?"

"You wish." Lee hugged her back, holding on and enjoying the extra squeeze Fiona gave her. Lee felt that knowing Fiona enriched her life. Until Lee located and purchased her house, she'd stayed with Angus and Fiona, cementing an already close friendship. They often found themselves spending evenings together after work. Angus and Fiona also owned a small residence near Key Largo, in Florida. Fiona, who was also an avid diver, often accompanied Lee and Angus on their dives. "By the way, I got the last six rolls of pictures back from the photo lab today from our dives along the coral barrier reef. Want to see them? I haven't even shown them to Angus yet. This batch of photos can be used in our next book."

The three friends had spent several vacations in Florida working and diving along the reefs to photograph the marine life found there. Lee and Angus had compiled their notes into a book on native undersea wildlife, which Lee illustrated with her photographs and artwork. "Fiona, look at the clarity of this shot. Just amazing. It might make a nice cover photo."

Two weeks later, Lee was visiting Fiona one evening while Angus was at a meeting. After dinner they were chatting over tea. "Why aren't you dating anyone, Lee? I mean you're attractive, smart, successful in your vocation, and yet your personal life seems to remain in limbo."

"Come on, Fiona. We've discussed this before. I have a close group of friends from college and good, nurturing relationships here with my coworkers at the center. I'm very close with you and Angus." She laughed. "At least for now." Lee paused for effect, raising one eyebrow. "On the other hand, things could change if you don't get off my case."

Obviously undaunted, Fiona pushed again. "You know I just want to see you as happy as Angus and I are."

"I'm not sure that's ever going to happen." Lee shrugged. "Anyway, I am happy. You know that."

Lee never dated. Her life always seemed too full of other things. Initially, in college, she'd been too busy. When she began working, she was focused on her career. Writing and illustrating the book she'd written with Angus consumed two full years of her life, and the travel associated with gathering the photos and drawing the illustrations occupied all of her spare hours.

The conversation with Fiona did resonate though. It wasn't long after their conversation that Lee's best friend, Maggie, called. She waited until the end of their phone call to deliver the message that was the real reason for her call. "I know you hate it when I try to fix you up. You've turned me down every time in the past. This time it's different. Luke is my husband's best buddy at work. He's already a friend, not some stranger."

Lee's first response was the usual, "I don't think so. I'm nearly thirty-six years old and too set in my ways to get involved with anyone new."

Over the next week Maggie and Fiona teamed up, each taking turns. Individually, they wheedled and coaxed Lee to accept the date.

"Come on Lee. It's just a party at Luke's house. You don't even have to be alone with him. It'll be a group of us." Maggie's final effort reaped results.

Exhausted by the struggle, Lee finally gave in. "Okay, I'll go. I don't promise anything more, so don't get your hopes up."

On the evening of the party, the large gathering of people at Luke's house was a mixture of Luke's work and social friends. Because Luke was the host he actually had little time to spend with Lee, and she found herself alone for most of the evening. Bored with the chatter around her, Lee withdrew to the peace of the patio.

Lee rounded the doorway and was nearly knocked over by a tall, muscular woman. "Hey, whoa there. Where are you running to so quickly?" The voice was deep for a woman's, and it wrapped around Lee like a soft silk scarf.

Wanting to hear more of that voice, Lee waited for the woman to speak again. Eventually Lee realized that she wasn't going to say any more until Lee responded. Lee finally answered, her speech hesitant. "Uh...nowhere. Well, just outside to get some air."

The woman's full lips curved into a dazzling smile. "Since I interrupted your trip to nowhere, I think you should let me make up for nearly knocking you over by allowing me to get you a drink. I'll be right back, okay?"

Lee nodded, not quite trusting her voice.

"I'm Kendra, by the way. Kendra Harris."

"Uh, Lee. Lee Foster."

"Okay, Lee. Wait right here. I'll be right back."

Unable to think of anything to say, Lee simply nodded. *What's the matter with me?*

True to her word, it only took a few minutes for Kendra to return with two drinks in hand. As Kendra handed Lee her drink she raised her own glass as a toast. "To chance encounters."

Their glasses clinked leaving a melodic note ringing in the air. "So tell me everything I should know about you, Lee Foster."

"I don't really know where to begin." Lee took a sip of her drink, hoping it would calm her beating heart.

"How about at the beginning?" Kendra smiled broadly. "I've found that's always a good place."

"No. No, that's pretty old news. How about I tell you about my trip to the Keys that I have planned for this summer?"

"Are you taking a tour?" Kendra arched her eyebrows.

"No, I'm going as part of a marine expedition with my boss and his wife to do some research for my next book, which is probably a number of years away from being written." She laughed. "Honestly, I've learned that researching is actually easier than writing."

"I'm impressed by your accomplishments." Kendra leaned in closer. She held Lee's eyes with her own.

Lee breathed in the crisp, clean scent of the intense woman's perfume. *Her eyes are the exact shade of the water around some of the islands where I've dived, a clear blue, nearly turquoise color.* "Your eyes are beautiful," Lee said, blushing at the brashness of the compliment given to a complete stranger. "I'm sorry, I'm not very good at small talk." She pulled her eyes away.

"Are you shy?" Kendra asked.

Lee smiled self-consciously, not really used to someone so direct and self-assured. "Not really shy," she replied, reticent to admit that Kendra unnerved her for some reason. "Mostly I'm just quiet."

"Tell me about your trip. There's always time for personal history later. I'd love to hear about your plans." Kendra casually linked her arm through Lee's leading her away from the distracting din of the party inside to a more secluded corner of the patio.

Lee began to relax as she related the details of her upcoming trip, explained her purpose for traveling, and her plans for her next book with Angus. It didn't take too long before she and Kendra were laughing and joking like old friends.

"I've been talking nonstop and you haven't told me one thing about yourself."

"No, and I'm not going to because I have to leave. I'm late already. I'd love to see you again and pick up our conversation where we left off. Is that possible, Lee Foster, with the chocolate brown eyes, captivating smile, and exquisite dimple?" Kendra lightly touched Lee's dimple with her index finger tracing her finger along Lee's cheek. Her touch was as gentle as a butterfly's kiss.

How does Kendra's feather light touch create such a parade of goose bumps up the back of my neck and clear into my hairline? A nervous response caused Lee to run her fingers through her short, nearly black hair.

Kendra reached into her pocket to withdraw a business card. "Call me." As if it were the most natural thing to do in the world, Kendra leaned forward and lightly pressed her lips to Lee's. It happened so unexpectedly, was over so fast, and was such a light touch that Lee wasn't even sure she hadn't imagined it.

Lee automatically grasped the card that Kendra pushed into her palm before she hurried away. Still wondering if she'd imagined the whole thing Lee stood fixed in place, her fingers pressed to her lips that still tingled even after Kendra's departure.

Seconds later, Lee jumped when Luke said, "There you are. I wondered where you disappeared to for so long. I'm sorry. I got tied up in my hosting duties. I've been a terrible date."

"No. It's okay. The evening was so lovely I decided to come out for some fresh air. I ended up talking to...um, one of the other guests out here for a while." For some unknown reason, Lee was reluctant to share information about the time she'd spent with Kendra. The back of her mind buzzed with thoughts of the fascinating woman. Alarm bells sounded as well. *Why did she kiss me? That was a strange thing to do. She must have meant to kiss my cheek. I probably turned unexpectedly.* In her mind she tried to explain what had happened, to justify or excuse Kendra's forward behavior. Exercising the self-discipline she was known for, she pushed the incident with Kendra out of her mind for later evaluation and turned her focus to Luke instead.

Later that night Lee's mind raced, although not about possibilities with Luke, despite the fact that he was nice enough. Unlike the thoughts she had of Kendra, thinking of Luke did nothing for Lee's libido. A consummate scientist, she set about analyzing her feelings. She had never found herself attracted to a woman before. If she were honest, she'd have to admit that she'd never been attracted to anyone before, either male or female. Two voices held a dialogue in her head.

"Maybe there's just something wrong with me. Most other people have either been married or have had several lovers by the time they are my age."

"That's true. You've been busy. You've worked hard, put yourself through school, worked overtime..."

"Yeah. On the other hand, I'll soon be thirty-seven and have never

had a serious romantic relationship—never wanted to have one, even. I don't think that's normal."

"You know what they say, there's a lid for every pot. Maybe your lid just hasn't shown up yet."

"Yeah. Maybe."

As Lee mulled her feelings about Luke and Kendra she had one final thought. *"Maybe my lid is a woman."*

"And how does that make you feel?"

Lee shook her head and whispered. "I'm not sure."

CHAPTER 7

LEE FOSTER - 2000

LEE DEBATED ABOUT WHETHER or not she should call Kendra, unsure if she was open to being involved with a woman. It was not a topic that she'd ever considered about herself before, nor one she'd ever discussed with any of her friends. She called her friend Maggie two days after the party. "Hey Mags. It's me, Lee."

"Hi babe. How'd it go with Luke after the party?"

"Okay. Listen, I wonder if you'd like to meet me for lunch tomorrow."

"Hold on a minute. I'll check." Maggie flipped through her calendar. "Sure. How about the pub? I'm in the mood for a good burger." They arranged the details, agreeing to meet at one.

***

In the corner of the bar where Maggie and Lee were eating, the television newscaster was relating the headlines for the day's news. Over the shoulder of the announcer the screen announced that Vermont had legalized Civil Unions for gay and lesbian couples. Lee glanced up, uttering a silent prayer of thanks for the opening she'd been waiting for to broach the subject with Maggie that was weighing heavily on her mind. "Hey, look at that. They just signed Civil Unions into law in Vermont. How do you feel about that?"

"I'm not sure. Haven't really given it much thought." Maggie shrugged. "It doesn't impact me in any way. I don't think I even know anyone who is gay or lesbian. It shouldn't matter though. If they love each other, why shouldn't they be able to have their relationships recognized? Why not? Where's the harm? How do you feel about it?"

"Let's make it more personal Maggie. What if I were a lesbian? Would you think I should have equal rights?"

"Don't be silly, Lee. You're not gay, so it doesn't matter, does it?"

"How do you know I'm not a lesbian? You seem so sure about that."

Maggie stopped eating, placing her fork on her plate and studying Lee's face. "What are you talking about? Of course, I'm sure. I mean you went out with Luke last week. He tells me he wants to see you again. He just hasn't had time to call. Of course you're not a lesbian."

"Listen, I need to tell you." Lee hesitated. "Something happened that night at Luke's party that makes me wonder. It...uh...makes me have doubts."

"About your sexuality?"

Lee nodded. Her face felt hot.

"What in the world would make you think you're a lesbian? Didn't you tell me you used to live with a guy in college?"

Lee didn't want to go into details about her relationship with Brian because she didn't feel it was her right to confide his secret, even to a close friend. It was not for her to reveal. "Yes, I did. We ended up just being friends. That was all there was to it."

"But you did live with him?"

"Yes. Regardless of appearances, our relationship wasn't what everyone thought. I mean, look, just forget that. It's just not relevant to this discussion. Trust me when I say that I've never had a serious romantic relationship. At my age, that's not normal, is it?"

"You've been focused on other things. You've done more in thirty-six years than most people do in a lifetime."

"I've told myself the same thing. Still, I harbor the concern that I've never really been sexually attracted to anyone, at least not until last week. I met someone at Luke's party—a woman." Lee checked for Maggie's reaction expecting shock.

Maggie's face remained unchanged, showing no shock, just interest and concern. "And?"

"And," Lee paused formulating a response. "Well, she was different."

Lee wasn't sure how much of what happened she wanted to reveal. "We talked. Just before she left, she...she touched my face. It gave me chills, raised goose bumps. After that she kissed me, pressed her card into my hand, and told me to call her."

"What happened next?"

"Nothing. She left."

"Oh, wow! I can't believe she kissed you. So, did you call her?"

Lee shook her head and exhaled a long sigh. "No, not yet. I'm not sure I want to. I mean, I want to...I'm just not sure I want to want to. Know what I mean?"

"I think so. You find yourself romantically or sexually attracted to someone for the first time in your life. That someone is another woman. And you're feeling, I'd guess, confused or maybe even excited." Maggie's eyebrows arched as she tilted her head sideways, her palms turning up indicating she was seeking confirmation of what she had surmised.

"Maybe a little of both." Lee's smile and look of interest indicated that Maggie should continue.

"So you're excited that you're finally attracted to someone?"

A tilt of her head, and a shrug was all Lee could muster in response.

"At the same time, I assume you're reluctant to pursue this attraction because if your response that night to this mystery woman was not some sort of a fluke, it could mean you're a lesbian. Does that sum it up correctly?"

"Yeah, I guess so. Are you shocked?"

"No. Maybe just a little worried about you. Not because you might be interested in a woman, just because you seem so upset by it. Believe me, though, I'm not shocked."

"I am. I may have discovered something about myself that I'd assume most people figure out when they're in their teens or early twenties."

"So, are you going to call her?"

"Will you still be my friend if I do?" Lee could feel herself blushing although she maintained eye contact with her friend, hoping Maggie would not turn away.

Maggie reached across the table to give Lee's hand a quick squeeze. "You idiot. Of course, I'll still be your friend. Why wouldn't I be?" Maggie picked up her fork. "Now finish your lunch before your salad wilts from all that heat coming off of your face."

CHAPTER 8

LEE AND KENDRA

IT WAS THE FOLLOWING Thursday evening, nearly a week after Lee's lunch with Maggie. Kendra's card sat on the table in front of Lee. She'd picked up the phone at least four times already, even started to dial twice before her courage evaporated. *Okay, I'm going to do it this time.* She reached for the phone and punched in the numbers as quickly as she could. After three rings she was ready to hang up.

"Kendra Harris."

"Uh...uh...I'm sorry. I think I've made a mistake."

"Lee?"

"Yes. Look, Kendra, I'm not even sure why I'm supposed to be calling you. When you left that night you said to call you. So, here I am. Calling. You."

"And you really aren't sure why you're calling? Really?"

Regaining some of her composure, Lee took the offensive. "Well, that's true. After all, it was you who told me to call. Why did you do that?"

Kendra chuckled. "Nicely done. You put the ball firmly back in my court. Okay, I'll go first. I told you to call me because I wanted to spend another evening with you, so I could get to know you a bit better without so many people around. Will you have dinner with me?"

49

So, there it was. Dinner. That's all, just dinner. Lee could feel her pulse pounding in her temples. "Yes, I think I can manage dinner. When?"

"Um, let me see...are you busy tomorrow evening?"

Lee thought a moment. "Uh, no, not really. Where shall I meet you?"

"Give me your address. I'll pick you up. Do you like Italian food?"

"Absolutely. It's a favorite." *It's only dinner.* Lee relaxed a little.

"Please wear something red so I won't get your white shirt dirty if I twirl my pasta and splash."

Joining in the light banter, Lee joked, "What if I don't have a red blouse?"

"There are other options. I guess you'll have to sit next to me, in that case."

After a few more minutes of teasing, they hung up after Lee gave Kendra her address and directions to her house.

***

The pile of blouses that Lee selected, rejected, and then discarded onto the bed taunted her. She wanted to look nice for her what...was it a *date? No, she'd prefer to think of it as just dinner plans.* She settled on tan pants and a dark blue blouse. Sandals, silver earrings, and a necklace that peeked out from the opening created by the top two buttons that remained unfastened after being buttoned and unbuttoned twice. One was too few because the necklace didn't show. Was two too many? No. It was okay she decided.

Lee applied a light coat of mascara and gave her hair a final brushing and light touch of spray. Satisfied after one last check in the mirror, Lee tidied the clothes she'd piled on the bed and straightened the spread.

Now that everything in the house was in order Lee had another fifteen minutes to wait for Kendra to arrive. She paced back and forth in front of the window several times until she forced herself to go to the kitchen to get a glass of water. Even though she was expecting her, Lee still jumped when Kendra rang the bell.

Kendra was facing away from her admiring the view as Lee opened the front door. "Hello, Kendra. Won't you come in while I get my jacket and purse?"

"Thank you." Kendra gave Lee an appreciative once over. "You look nice." At five-five, Lee was a couple of inches shorter than Kendra. She had a gorgeous tan, beautiful, expressive dark eyes and hair, sporty good looks, and a firm, athletic body. Dragging her eyes away from Lee, Kendra glanced around the neat living room at the comfortable looking contemporary furniture. Off to the right was a counter that separated the kitchen from the living room. Beyond that was a small eating area, too small to be called a dining room. The table centered in front of a window that offered another great view of the water. "I assume the short hallway leads to the bedroom and bath?"

"Yes."

"You have a great view here, and your place is really nice. It's small but cute. I like it."

"Thank you. It's all I need even though there's not much to it." Lee could feel her accelerated breathing and was aware of her sweaty palms that she ran across her jeans in an attempt to dry them. Needing to engage in some sort of activity, Lee rubbed her palms together. "Shall we go?"

I'm hungry enough to eat."

Lee locked up and they walked side by side to the curb. Kendra opened the door to her sports car for Lee. Once they were buckled in, she began the drive to the restaurant. "I'm glad you called, even happier that you agreed to have dinner with me."

Unsure of how to respond to Kendra's statement, Lee changed the subject. "So, tell me a little about yourself."

Kendra's expression showed her amusement. "Okay, I'm thirty five. I'm a project manager by title for a mid-sized company. That basically means I organize, coordinate, and keep everybody on task, collect data, report progress, and do all the odd jobs that others can't or won't do to ensure things are completed on time. I'm kind of the oil that keeps all the cogs turning smoothly. Certainly nothing as glamorous as what you do."

"Trust me when I say that the majority of my job is far from glamorous. We probably both spend a large portion of our work day doing the same thing, writing reports." Lee was pleased when Kendra smiled.

"You're too kind."

Lee looked at Kendra's strong hands gripping the steering wheel, and imagined what it would be like to take one of them in her own. "What do you enjoy doing when you're not lubricating things at work?"

"Ha! That certainly puts my vocation in perspective. President Reagan was the great communicator and I'm the great lubricator."

Their shared laughter helped ease Lee's nerves. Based upon the level of comfort they had achieved the night they had first met, her nervousness was unexpected. She was relieved that they were once again able to laugh together. For the moment Lee's question went unanswered as Kendra turned into the parking lot of the restaurant.

Once seated, with menu in hand, Lee commented on how quaint the restaurant decor was. "I think *Lady and the Tramp* could have been filmed here. I love this place."

"Wait till you taste the food." As if on cue, the server came over to take their order. Kendra said, "I'll have the spaghetti with meatballs."

"That sounds good. Me, too."

The server wrote the order on her pad. "Want some wine?"

Lee nodded as the server opened the wine list. "May I suggest this one? It's the house red and it's excellent. We always get positive comments about it."

Lee and Kendra made eye contact, nodded and Kendra said, "That'll be fine. Thank you for the suggestion. I think I had that the last time and you're right, it was very good."

A few seconds later, a different server delivered a basket of fresh baked rolls. Unable to resist the yeasty aroma, they dug into the bread, ripping off pieces and dipping them into the garlic and roasted red pepper flavored oil that was delivered with it.

Afraid that her question would remain unanswered, Lee refocused Kendra. "You were going to tell me what you like to do when you're not working."

"Hmm, what do I like to do beside take a beautiful woman to dinner, you mean?"

Lee blushed. "Is that something you do often?"

"Often? Probably less often than I'd like." Kendra smiled. "I guess I date often enough. What about you? Do you date often?"

"No, I rarely date. That party, meeting Luke, was the first time I've had a date in, I'm ashamed to say, since I've been here. Before that, there was school. Despite having a scholarship I still had to work hard to pay most of the expenses that weren't covered."

"Your parents didn't help you?" Kendra asked.

And there it was—the question about the subject she generally tried to avoid, her parents. "No. My father is dead and my mom wasn't in a position that paid enough money to spare any for me. My grandparents helped all they could." She always felt a bit dishonest when she hid her colorful family history with partial facts and half-truths. After so many years, she was used to the dance and quickly changed the subject. "So what about you? Seriously, when you're not working or dining, what do you like to do for fun?"

"Well, the most fun I've had recently was meeting a beautiful biologist at a party. I found her fascinating."

Lee felt her face turning red.

Thankfully, the server arrived with their salads. "Can I get you anything else," she asked. "More bread?"

Both women shook their heads and smiled in response, and conversation turned to a discussion about the food. "Their dressing here is wonderful," Kendra said between bites. "They have the best quality virgin olive oil I've ever tasted. And wait till you taste the spaghetti. I eat here at least once a week. Do you cook for yourself or eat out?"

"A combination. I don't like to eat in restaurants alone, so I usually cook at home or get take out if I don't have plans with friends."

They compared favorite restaurants and take out joints until the server delivered their meals. "Here we go, spaghetti and meatballs all around. More wine?"

"I think we're good, thank you." Kendra said with a wink for the hard working server as she hurried away. Kendra lifted her glass and waited for Lee to tap hers against it. "Cheers. I hope you enjoy your meal."

Once they'd finished dinner, they lingered over coffee and tea, and took a short walk through town. The rest of the evening passed pleasantly as the couple window shopped and commented about things they saw in the store windows. Returning to the car, they made the trip back to Lee's house. Kendra pulled to a stop in front of Lee's place and parked.

Lee debated about inviting Kendra inside. "Dinner was really delicious, thank you. You certainly didn't exaggerate about the food."

"You'll learn, I hope, that I never exaggerate."

"Tell me more about you...what you're like."

"Okay." Kendra picked at a thread on the steering wheel, her expression serious.

Lee waited, giving Kendra the time she needed to organize her thoughts.

"I tend to be very honest, many times direct. I think honesty is important, a critical personality trait. I don't like to beat around the bush. Diplomatic is most likely not a term ever used to describe me. Head games, and those who play them, piss me off. I guess most people would say I'm reasonably intelligent, hard working, and kind to animals. Sad movies make me cry. I hate fish, especially those hairy little jobs they sometimes put in Caesar salad. Patience is not one of my strong points, and I don't suffer liars, bigots, and narrow minded people well." Almost as an afterthought she added, "I guess that comes along with the fact that I'm a lesbian and not ashamed of it." Kendra put her hand on the door handle. "Come on, I'll walk you to the door."

As Lee gathered her belongings, Kendra got out of the car, came around, and opened the passenger door. They walked up the path to the front door. Kendra stopped and turned to face Lee. "What about you?"

"I'm not sure."

Kendra's eyebrows furrowed. "You're unsure about how to describe your own personality traits, likes and dislikes?" Suddenly she laughed. "Oh, I misunderstood. You mean you aren't sure whether you're a lesbian?"

"Yes. I can't recall having ever been attracted to a woman before."

"Before me, you mean?"

Lee looked down at the keys in her hands.

"Look at me."

With reluctance, Lee raised her eyes to meet Kendra's.

"And you think you're attracted to me, although you're not sure."

Lee's answer was very nearly a whisper. "Yes."

"Okay, then let's answer that question for you, shall we?" Kendra moved forward, pressing Lee's back to the door. Gently, she leaned in to place a soft kiss on Lee's cheek. She pulled back to see if Lee would protest and when she didn't she kissed her again, trailing little kisses down Lee's jawline, finally claiming her lips with a gentle brush of her own. When Lee started to kiss her back Kendra leaned in, kissing Lee in earnest. Lee opened as Kendra sought to explore Lee's mouth with her tongue. They were both breathless when Kendra pulled away.

Kendra smiled when Lee opened her eyes. "Well, I guess that answers that question, doesn't it?" Kendra pulled away. "Maybe you need to let this sink in a bit. As much as I'd love to make love to you, I'm not sure you're ready for that yet. I had a wonderful time tonight, Lee." Kendra leaned in and kissed Lee again. She pulled away, her reluctance evident when she exhaled a long sigh. "Call me when you're ready to talk." Kendra quickly turned and walked to her car. When she glanced back at Lee's front door, Lee was already inside.

Lee didn't waste any time seeking the comfort of her home. She closed the door behind her, her heart still pounding. Unable to stand on her shaky legs unaided, she leaned against the door for support. She could feel her pulse pounding as her blood still raced through her veins. *How could it be possible for me to have lived this long and not known such a significant detail about my own nature?*

Strange as it seemed, she felt somehow reassured that she had finally found the missing piece, the piece that made her like everyone else—someone with normal desires and physical needs. *It's ironic that discovering my attraction to women, or more specifically to Kendra, would make me feel normal when the unnamed, 'they,' always pointed a finger at gays and lesbians as being abnormal.* She took a moment to enjoy the new and exciting emotions and sensations she was feeling. Her nipples were erect and she felt unfamiliar moisture pooling between her legs making her panties wet. As she ran her hand over her breasts she felt her core contract in pleasure. Not that she hadn't felt the need for physical release before, though this was the first time a physical desire within her had been incited by another person, not by her own hand. Lee took in a deep breath exhaling slowly, hoping to quiet her pounding heart.

Once composed, Lee straightened up and went to the kitchen to make a cup of tea. Feeling physically depleted, she added two teaspoons of sugar instead of her customary one. Her mind raced as she sipped her tea. *What would my mother think, my grandparents, my friends? Why now...and why Kendra? Am I only attracted to Kendra or could there be others I would want as much? Why haven't I ever felt this way about any of my other friends?* Switching gears, she tried to analyze her motives. *I like men. Some of my closest friends are men. I've had crushes on a couple of my female teachers but I was attracted to their minds, wasn't I?* She recalled her teacher Mrs. Niederman, her biology teacher in high school, whom she'd adored. *I loved her. She made me think. That was why, wasn't it?*

Her answering voice responded. 'Yeah, that's true. Also, you were eighteen and she was probably nearly fifty when she taught you. Explain Miss Oldies. Everyday in class you thought about how wonderful it would be to bury your nose in her neck and inhale that wonderful aroma she exuded.'

Voice one responded. 'True, but I still liked her mind.'

Answering voice countered. 'I'm sure that's true. You also couldn't keep your eyes off her breasts. And what about your best friend in high school? Remember how you felt when she started to date Tommy and became less available to you?'

'Oh, shut up!' Inner voice shouted.

Answering voice reasoned. *'Come on. It was true. How could you have been in denial all these years?'*

'So what now?' Lee reached for the phone. *"Let's find out shall we?"*

Kendra answered the call and Lee blurted, "I'm ready now. To talk, I mean. You told me to give you a call when I was ready to talk. So, I am. Ready. To talk."

"This isn't going to be easy, is it? Kendra laughed quietly. "It could be fun though. You know, to uh, talk."

"Yes."

Kendra kicked off her shoes and settled onto her sofa. "Okay, go ahead. I just walked in the door and made myself some tea, so I'm ready to listen."

"You want me to start?"

"Well, it would seem obvious. You did call me and said you wanted to talk. So, I'm listening." When Lee gave no response, Kendra said, "All right. Let's try this. Are you okay?"

"I think so. I can't do this on the phone, though."

"Okay. Breakfast tomorrow?"

"Okay. That's good. I'll meet you at Seaside Restaurant at 9."

***

They met for breakfast at nine, as agreed at a small restaurant with a beautiful view of the water. After the initial greetings, they ordered and made some small talk before Lee screwed up her courage. "I have a couple of things I need to say." Now that Lee had started, it became easier. "Last night you said that honesty is important to you, and you hate people who lie. So I need to tell you something right out. I have a huge secret that I keep because I've learned that when people know my secret, I feel it, um...changes how they perceive me. It may or may not be true. It's just that's how I perceive it. So before we talk about anything else I need to tell you my secret. I don't want you to think I lied to you by omission. I want you to respect me."

"Lee, you don't have to do this. That stuff I said, it was about how I live my life. They are my shoulds. That doesn't mean they have to be yours. Don't tell me anything that you'll feel so uncomfortable about that you won't be able to look me in the eyes again."

"No, I think you're right. Regardless, it's better you know before...uh...before we decide what happens next, rather than after."

"What do you want to happen next?"

56

"No." Lee shook her head. "There'll be time enough to talk about that later. Right now, first things first. I'm glad you're sitting down."

"Geez, Lee, you're starting to frighten me. You're not an escaped convict, or a drug pusher, or anything like that, are you? Maybe it's better I not know."

"No, not quite. Remember I told you that my father was dead?"

"Yes."

"He was murdered."

"I'm so sorry Lee. Recently?"

"No, and please don't be sorry for him. He more than had it coming to him. He was cruel. He belittled my mother and me. I was close to my mom. She tried hard to keep him away from me. Nevertheless she couldn't always protect me from his abusive ways. It was no wonder that I always felt anxious whenever he was due home."

"Please tell me you're not in the witness protection program, and if you tell me any more I'll have to relocate somewhere if I ever want to see you again."

Lee could tell by Kendra's tone that she was trying to lighten the conversation. She did see the humor and gave a quick giggle. "No, nothing like that. He was just a bully and an abuser. I can't tell you how many times he beat my mother or how cruel he was to her and to me." Lee paused and her voice became quiet. "My father terrified me. I had a little white kitten when I was um, about five." Lee motioned with her hand to indicate the age was approximate. "She was my first pet and I cherished her. I named her Puff because she was so soft and sweet. She loved everyone, but was special to me. One day my father got really mad at me and picked Puff up and tossed her against the wall. When she didn't move at first, I thought she was dead. Luckily she was just stunned. She survived. My mom gave her away to a friend the next day, but I had nightmares about it for months. Still do, sometimes. My mom protected me as best she could. As I started to get older..." Lee exhaled a long breath before she continued. "Well, she began to have other fears. She'd never leave me alone with my father and often took the brunt of his anger to spare me his punishment."

Kendra's voice was soft as she replied. "He sounds like he deserved to be murdered."

"Yes. When I got older and talked with my mother about what happened the day my father was killed, she told me that while he slept, she toyed with the idea of taking her own life. Then, as she recalled all the horror he'd inflicted on both of us, she realized she couldn't leave

me behind to cope with him by myself and decided not to do herself in."
Lee met Kendra's eyes. "Funny you say he deserved his fate. That's
exactly what my mother concluded before she dispatched him with the
butcher knife."

"Wow!" Kendra's eyes widened. "I wasn't sure what to expect. I
surely wasn't expecting that."

Lee remained silent allowing Kendra time to process the information
and to reply. "Good. He deserved it. I'm glad your mom made the
decision she did and that she protected you. From the sounds of your
father, there's no telling what he was capable of. Based on what you
told me, your Mom's worry was clearly justified, as were her actions. I
hope they gave your mother a medal."

"No, they didn't. Unfortunately, my mother went to prison."

"Oh, no. I can't imagine why they'd do that. Lee, I'm so sorry. Your
mother wasn't treated fairly, for sure." Kendra shook her head. "I don't
understand, though. It puzzles me why you'd think that people would
think less of you if they knew. After all, it wasn't your crime, and from
what I've heard your mother was certainly justified to do what she did. I
can understand that you wouldn't want to drop your story in casual
conversation, but I hope your friends know. It's a heavy secret to carry,
I'd assume."

"Yes, it is. I'm separated from it now by time and distance to a point
that most people don't know. High school, except for a few close friends
who stood by me, was pretty much hell. You know, sometimes, high
school boys can be evil and cruel. Some of the girls were no better. It
was a relief to get away from town and start fresh at college where no
one knew me. Here, only Fiona, Angus, and Maggie know. And now you,
of course."

"Well, I'm glad you told me because it's always good to divest
yourself of secrets. It's like breathing in fresh air and nourishing to the
soul, in my humble opinion. I will promise you that I'll keep your
confidence. What you just shared with me is not my secret to tell. What
your mother did should not be a cause of shame for you or for your
mother for that matter. Your father had it coming, and if our laws
protected abused and battered women and children better, maybe
she'd have felt she had other options." Kendra touched Lee's hand.

Lee studied their linked fingers. "Thank you. Now I have another
secret, don't I?"

"You mean your attraction to me? That depends on several things, I
think."

Lee squeezed Kendra's hand before releasing it and raised her head to face Kendra. "Yes, I guess so. I wonder if you're busy tomorrow?"

Kendra leaned in closer to Lee. "To do what?"

Lee glanced away to search the horizon and the view of the ocean. "I thought we might do some snorkeling, or if you're not up for that, maybe some kayaking. I need to be near the water, it calms me."

"Will you teach me how?"

"Yes, I will. If you'll teach me how to make love to you."

"Wow...right to the point."

"Yes."

"Well, let me put your mind at ease, Lee. I won't make love to you tomorrow. I think you need to take this slowly and, for my sake, so do I. You're very different from the women I usually...uh, for want of a better term, date. I want to be sure we're looking for the same thing. A quick tumble I can take care of easily. If you want more...we'll have to be careful. I don't want to see you hurt. I live my life openly and I'm not sure you can or will do that." Kendra hesitated for a few seconds. "You've been honest with me, and I need to warn you of something. I've never been very good at long-term relationships, but like I said you're different. So we need to be sure that this is something both of us want if there's to be more than a quick tussle in the sheets. Is that what you want, to just know what it's like to be with a woman, or do you have hopes for something more meaningful?"

"I would hope for the latter, wouldn't you? Now that you've kissed me, I'd probably come to you either way. You made me experience something I've never felt before."

"Really, what's that?"

"Desire." Lee explained about how kissing Kendra had made her feel normal for the first time.

"Geez, you're going to give me performance anxiety."

They both laughed.

"Thank you, Kendra, for being understanding. I agree with you, though. Easy does it. We'll both know, if and when the time comes. It'll feel right for us to take things to a different level. So, we'll just be friends for now. Right?"

Kendra considered her response carefully. "Do you kiss your friends?"

"Only special ones, I think."

"Think we can be special friends?" Kendra's look was hopeful.

Lee laughed. "Definitely. Definitely, special friends."

"Okay, you offered me a snorkeling or kayaking adventure. I pick kayaking. What time are we getting started?"

"How about we meet at my house at five-thirty? I love to watch the sunrise."

"You mean in the middle of the night?" Kendra's groan set Lee into fits of laughter.

"Here's our first hurdle. I'm always up with the chickens."

"Ha. I'm always up with whatever barnyard animal it is that sleeps the latest." Kendra sighed. "All right. I often see the sunrise, but it's normally on my way home." She shook her head in resignation. "I'll be there at five-thirty. I'm warning you right now that I'll need a nap in the afternoon."

"Hmm. That sounds promising." Lee raised a suggestive eyebrow. "Do you snore?"

"Like a locomotive."

Lee rolled her eyes towards the sky overhead. "Can this relationship be saved?"

"We'll see. I'll see you in the morning. We can chat more about ground rules."

"I understand." Lee insisted on paying the check and when done, they both made their way to their cars parked in the lot.

Lee turned to face Kendra. "See you tomorrow morning. Have a good rest of the day. I'm sorry I have to stop by the lab and finish up a few things."

Kendra said, "Yes, too bad. I'd suggest dinner, but I have plans with an old acquaintance tonight. Tomorrow then?"

Lee leaned in for a quick hug. "Tomorrow."

CHAPTER 9

LEE WAS CHECKING THAT her two-man kayak was secured to her roof rack when Kendra pulled up to the curb. Lee's heart doubled its rhythm when she saw Kendra emerge from her vehicle.

Kendra stepped from her car with containers and a bag. She flashed a beaming smile at Lee. "I know you drink tea, so I got you a tea and for me a coffee and some donuts. Hope that's okay."

"Perfect," Lee said, giving Kendra a quick hug and a peck on the cheek. She linked her arm through Kendra's to lead her up the steps and into the kitchen.

"I know you can do better than that for a greeting." Kendra sat the cups on the counter and placed the bag there as well.

Lee came around the counter and slid her arms around Kendra's waist. The kiss started slow and built rapidly into something neither had expected.

Kendra was the first to pull back. "Wow! Let's have some hot tea and coffee to cool down. For someone who claims to be so inexperienced, you sure know how to kiss."

"So do you." Lee turned away, placing the counter between Kendra and herself. "So what are these ground rules of yours?"

"I don't have a set of them printed up or anything. I just think we should agree to a few basics. First, I need to tell you that I won't go back into the closet for you or sneak around so no one knows or suspects. Not if we agree to pursue a relationship. I've never brought anyone out before. Usually, when I date, I date other lesbians who know exactly what they want from me."

"And what is that?

"Honestly?" Kendra looked away. She shrugged. "Sex mostly. They don't confuse need with the love kind of sex."

"Is that what you want from me, sex?"

Kendra met Lee's eyes. "Initially, yes. I found you to be attractive and thought it would be fun to take a tumble with you. That was when I thought...well you know."

"That I was a lesbian."

"Yes." Kendra reached for Lee's hand. "The more time we spend together, the more I learn about you, the more I think there might just be potential for more than just sex. You're different." Kendra looked away. "I have a number of women friends, Lee. And most of them..." Her voice trailed off. "Look, I'm not proud of the fact that I've slept with most of them. It's not a big lesbian community here. How will you feel about that?"

Lee shrugged. "I have no claim on you right now, so why should I have one that extends back to before I met you. I will tell you that I won't tolerate being with anyone who cheats on me. My father was a cheat and a liar, and I saw what it did to my mother. I won't accept anyone who treats me with anything less than complete respect. Understand that. It's non-negotiable. In return, I offer the same."

"Fair enough." Kendra nodded. "I've been warned, and understand that."

Lee gestured to the door. "So ready to get your feet wet?"

They barely made it onto the water before the sun peeked above the horizon. "I can't remember the last time I got up to see the sunrise," Kendra admitted. "This is nice."

They paddled till they were both tired, then drifted peacefully. They talked, sharing tales, funny stories, and observations. Kendra got tears in her eyes when Lee told some of the situations and events of growing up with her abusive father.

"Your mom must be an incredible woman to have raised you to be the woman you are—smart, caring, funny, gentle. She should be proud of the way you turned out. How will she feel about this, about us? That is assuming we decide there is an us?"

Lee pursed her lips as she considered the question. "I've no idea. Really. I suspect if she knows I'm happy, she'll be okay about it. My grandparents, probably not so much."

"Well, we can cross that bridge..."

"Agreed."

Kendra stifled a yawn. "How about that nap?"

"Not yet. Lunch first, followed by the nap."

Kendra smiled. "You're already too bossy for my own good."

Following lunch they stopped by Maggie's house where Lee stored her two-man kayak behind Maggie's garage giving her friend a chance to meet Kendra. By the time the three women had chatted for nearly an hour an idle observer might have thought that Kendra and Maggie had known each other for years rather than minutes. It didn't take them long to gang up on Lee and tease her mercilessly. Lee suffered the ribbing with equanimity. Finally taking pity, Kendra reached for Lee's hand. Lee stiffened just for a second, quickly glancing at Maggie for her reaction to the natural display of affection. Maggie smiled and Lee relaxed.

Kendra asked to use the restroom. "Okay, you two don't talk about me while I'm gone." She chuckled and added, "But when you do, be kind." She went down the hallway that Maggie directed her to and stopped a few feet down just for a couple of minutes to hear what would be said.

"Is all this really all right with you, Maggie? It is so new, so strange for me. Your opinion means a lot to me. I couldn't bear to lose your friendship over this."

"Gosh, Lee. It's a good thing you saw her first," Maggie said. "She's very nice, and no one can deny she's hot."

Kendra withdrew to the john, allowing them privacy to talk. Lee had come out to her closest friend and had been told it was okay.

In the car, on the way to Lee's, they discussed their time with Maggie agreeing that the time they'd shared had been fun. As the topic was exhausted, Kendra asked, "So, is it nap time?"

"Yes, my dear, you've earned a nap."

Once inside the front door, Kendra pulled Lee into an embrace. "I think I've earned something else too." Their kiss was gentler and sweeter than the one they had shared that morning. "Come nap with me."

"Nap?"

"Yes, just a nap." Kendra said, "I told you nothing more until we're sure.

"Oh. I know." Lee rested her head on Kendra's shoulder.

"Disappointed?"

"Maybe just a little," Lee said, pulling back to display a mischievous grin. "I'd like to get closer to you. Maybe I can change your mind."

"Nope. I'll need my strength for our first time together, because it'll take hours for me to make love to you the way I want to. So, there's no chance today. I'm too tired."

"You're one hundred percent sure."

"One hundred and one percent," Kendra emphasized her resolve with a stern expression as she nodded.

"All right. Come this way." Lee led Kendra to the bedroom. At the doorway, they shared a lingering kiss as they maneuvered their way to the edge of the bed. Kendra pulled away and kicked off her shoes, as did Lee.

"Clothes?" Kendra questioned.

Lee turned away and went to her dresser. "Why don't you take off your shirt and jeans? I'll give you an oversized T-shirt."

"You too?"

"Sure, why not. You're one hundred and one percent sure, still?"

"Lee, does this frighten you? The fact that we may be intimate at some point."

"Not exactly, at least, not in the way you might think." Lee brushed her hair back and exhaled.

"I promise you're safe. I made the decision today. After today, it'll be you who decides if and when anything more happens between us."

Lee quickly stripped off her clothes, everything except her panties. She removed two big shirts from the bureau and turned around to find Kendra standing by the bed in just her panties, watching. Lee blushed but could not look away. As though drawn by a magnet she slowly made her way towards Kendra. "You're beautiful," Lee murmured as she approached. She reached her hand out to touch Kendra.

Kendra took the shirts and tossed them on the bed. She grasped both of Lee's hands and tugged her closer. "You may look. You can't touch."

"May I kiss you?"

Still grasping Kendra's hands with her own, Lee leaned in to trail kisses down Kendra's neck. Reaching the soft roundness at the top of her breast, Kendra resisted by stepping closer to Lee, wrapping her in her arms. "Remember the look but don't touch directive? I'm not sure I'm as strong as I thought I'd be, so just cool your jets for a couple of minutes until I argue all the outposts into compliance with command central's wishes."

Lee chuckled as she brushed her breasts lightly against Kendra's.

"Your breasts against mine, umm...they feel so good."

"I know. Let me put my shirt on before we get beyond the point of no return here."

"You told me I could decide when."

"You can, just not today. You're not ready yet. You need more time. At least, I want you to take more time. You need to be sure you can really do this, and I need to be sure I'm able to offer all you need." Kendra rubbed her breasts against Lee's causing her to gasp in pleasure. "Not this. This part is easy. The rest of it is more difficult."

"For example?"

"Being a minority, for starters—to live with not being a part of the majority."

Lee smiled ruefully. "You don't think that I learned how to do that when my mother killed my father?"

"Yes, I'm sure you did. It's a shame you still carry that burden of shame with you. I don't want you to feel ashamed of this, of us. If you can't be proud of us, this part won't go any further. Understand?"

Lee nodded. In an unexpected move, she rotated Kendra so the back of her legs were against the edge of the bed and gave a push. Kendra reflexively held onto Lee dragging her onto the bed with her. They landed in a pile, Lee on top, with them straddling each other's legs, just separated by the thin material of their panties.

Kendra exclaimed, "Wow! You're strong.

Lee pinned Kendra to the bed and kissed her thoroughly. They were both gasping for air when Lee released Kendra's mouth. She began her journey down Kendra's neck, following the same path she had followed before, destined for Kendra's breast. She didn't want to force Kendra, but she had such a need to taste her. "Please, I swear I'll stop when you ask me to. I just need to...to put my mouth on you, to kiss your breast. Please?"

Lee felt more comfortable being in control. Knowing she would have to allow Kendra to reciprocate later worried her a bit. Lee wondered about her own willingness to touch, also about her reluctance to be touched. It had always been an issue for her. In high school, in an effort to fit in, she had done things with a couple of the boys she'd dated. Yet she had never allowed them to touch her. No one had ever touched her. Teenage boys being teenage boys, no one had ever complained or questioned her refusal. That part of sex was where she had always drawn the line. Lee had always been afraid to let herself be vulnerable, to show a need. With Kendra, it was different. She'd never felt like this before.

"Are you ready for me to do the same to you? This can't be one sided."

"I know." Lee released Kendra's hands. "If I tell you something about myself, will you accept it if I say I'll try?"

"Yes. Now kiss me first. After that, tell me your secret."

Lee kissed Kendra, softly and gently, the urgency cooled by what she was about to reveal. Her eyes filled with tears as she confessed to the woman beneath her who was patiently waiting.

Kendra listened, intensely focused, and when Lee finished, she wrapped Lee in her arms cradling her. She slid her hands up her back and slowly began to scratch her back, the purpose to soothe and comfort more than to arouse.

As they began to kiss, the desire to possess Kendra's breast with her mouth returned to Lee. Her lips found their target and she gently sucked the erect nipple in. They both groaned at the pleasure they shared. Tentatively at first, Lee touched Kendra's breast with her palm watching in fascination as the nipple again hardened. Her confidence growing, in a hushed tone Lee observed, "It's like having a magical power, isn't it? I still don't understand how touching you can make me feel this way."

"That's just how it is. Now would you deny me the same pleasure? You might find that you'll enjoy that part too."

Finally understanding, Lee nodded. She rolled onto her back offering herself to Kendra's exploration.

"Are you sure it's okay?"

"I'm sure. I trust you." Lee tucked her hand under her head, exposing herself first to Kendra's gaze, then her gentle touch. Closing her eyes, she tried to relax.

"Lee, look at me." Kendra kissed her softly. "Just look at me. I want you to know it's me touching you."

Lee opened her eyes locking them with Kendra's.

"Just stay with me." Kendra kissed her way down Lee's neck, always stopping to return to Lee's lips and reestablish eye contact, until she sensed Lee beginning to relax. Kendra slid lower to use her tongue on Lee's stomach, thinking maybe doing what she wanted to do with her breasts might be too much too soon. When she felt Lee relax more, she slid her hand up to caress Lee's breast using the lightest touch she could manage. Lee arched towards her hand as Kendra kissed the other nipple.

"Oh God," Lee gasped.

Kendra switched her lips to the other breast, continuing to stimulate the wet nipple with her fingers while she used her tongue on the other. Soon Lee was begging, pulling Kendra's mouth to her.

"Lee. We have to stop."

"I don't want to. I want you, Kendra."

"That's good. If you want me now you'll most likely want me more sometime in the future. Now, come here. You promised me a nap and I promised I wouldn't make love to you today. We're both going to keep our promises because I don't want to screw this up."

Two hours later they awoke wrapped around each other.

Kendra kissed Lee. "Want something to eat?"

"Sure. Sandwich, omelet, or salad?"

"Surprise me."

Over dinner they made plans to get together again later in the week for dinner and a movie.

By Tuesday, Lee couldn't wait two more days to see Kendra. Giving in to her need to talk to her, Lee called. When Kendra answered, Lee wasted no time. "I've given a lot of thought to you in the past couple of days."

"Good thoughts or otherwise?"

"Mostly good...some dirty."

Kendra laughed. "Hmm. That sounds promising."

"I hope so. You make me feel things I've never felt before and want things I've never wanted before. I want you in my life, and I'm willing to do whatever it takes to make that happen. How do you feel?"

"A little like I'm sawing off the limb I'm standing on. Fair warning coming here Lee—I'm not a very good risk. I'm not good at commitment. I've never had a relationship last more than a couple of years. Truth be told, most don't last more than a couple of hours."

"What happens?"

"I'm ashamed to admit what usually happens. However, I've already begun to care about you. Maybe with you it can be different. By now, normally, I'd have already slept with a new woman in my life, and most likely we'd both be ready to move on. Lee, you need to know the ugly truth. Usually my relationships end because of me. I become bored and before you know it, I do something stupid."

"What happened to honesty? You mean you cheat?"

"Sometimes. I'm honest until it arrives at a point where it's just no longer worth it, after which I sometimes just become too obnoxious to be around. Sometimes I drink too much. You should know that I'm capable of using alcohol as a crutch. And if that's not enough, I can be jealous, bitchy, and sometimes I tend to do childish stuff. Eventually, I push the woman I'm with to the point that they get sick of me, and they toss me out. It's always easier for me if they end it. I want out, and they feel justified to end a relationship with such a selfish bitch."

Lee looked down and studied her fingers as she processed the information Kendra shared. Raising her eyes she asked softly, "Is that what will happen to us, too?"

Kendra shrugged. "I don't know. I hope not. Still, you need to know it's my pattern. It's not one to be proud of."

After a long pause, Lee asked. "Do you want to break that pattern, or are you comfortable repeating it over and over?"

"Being with someone is always a dream, isn't it? Unfortunately it's not one I've ever been able to realize for any length of time. I do have to say that I feel different about you than I normally do about," Kendra paused and shrugged, "...well, all the others. Yes, I'd definitely like to change, and I swear I'll really try."

"I won't tolerate a cheat, Kendra. I can't take that. You'll have to promise me fidelity or we won't stand any kind of a chance at all."

"Don't you think this relationship is doomed if we're already talking about how it will end before we've even really begun?"

"I don't know. As a scientist, I like to have a working hypothesis for any research I undertake. I guess I tend to extend that to my life as well. So let's say our working hypothesis is that..."

"Oh, Doc, you're getting a little deep here." Kendra smiled to soften the criticism.

"I'm sorry, it's just the way my mind works. Let's just start with what each of us thinks would be required for us to make a partnership successful. If we can define what our expectations are, and if each of us works to meet or exceed those expectations, we should be successful as a couple."

Kendra laughed. "You really are a scientist aren't you? Okay, tell me what you want me to do."

Lee set up the guidelines. "All right. Make your list. I'll see you here tomorrow at six for dinner."

"I can't believe you're serious about this...even more, I can't believe I'm going to do it."

***

Dinner was fun. After dessert, they cleared the dishes and sat opposite each other at the table. Lee had showed up with a neatly computer generated list of things she would need in a relationship. Kendra had six scraps of paper with barely decipherable symbols haphazardly scrawled in several directions. Even she had difficulty reading them.

"Okay, you first, Lee. This was your idea."

Lee picked up her list. "All right. My core requirements include fidelity, respect, and no physical violence. What are yours?"

Kendra shuffled the papers. Her face very serious, she replied, "First is no talking about anything serious before I have my coffee in the morning."

Lee's face registered her surprise. "Seriously? That's your most important criteria to satisfy your needs in a relationship?"

"No. Probably the first is not to criticize my criteria."

Lee laughed before responding with a smirk. "You're right. I apologize. Please continue."

"Okay. My biggest problem in any of my previous relationships was being bored. I get bored intellectually and physically. So how do I word that...don't bore me?"

Having learned from the first item on Kendra's list Lee replied. "How about we just leave it as you wrote it. It works. What else?"

"I need to feel like decisions are my own. Not that I always need to have my own way, it's just that I need to feel if I don't get my way I've elected to make the choice. It can't be forced down my throat."

Lee propped her chin on her hand and studied Kendra's face. "Are you open to negotiations when differences of opinions occur?"

Kendra pursed her lips and tilted her head first to the left and then to the right. "Theoretically, yes. However, I think you need to realize that I, like you, have been solely responsible for my own decisions for thirty some odd years. Making joint decisions will be a true learning process for me. Change is difficult."

"Yes. I'll probably have difficulties with that, too." Lee checked her list. "Now is probably a good time to add one of mine. I can't tolerate arguments. No raised voices or defamatory epithets during discussions even when we disagree. I realize there'll be differences of opinion. To resolve the issue, there needs to be reasoned and rational discussion working towards a shared solution instead of screaming, swearing, and verbal stamping of feet."

Kendra shrugged. "My traditional approach to dealing with issues is that I tend to ignore rather than confront a problem."

"Haven't you proven that tactic doesn't work? If you're not willing to talk about things where do you think we'll end up?"

Kendra stuck the fingers of both hands into her hair brushing it back before admitting, "That will be tough for me."

"If you won't tell me what's wrong, how can we fix it?"

"Theoretically, I know that's true. I'm just saying that historically I'm not good at it."

They were both silent as they considered the impasse. Lee was first to offer a solution. "Will you agree to talk to a counselor to help us if we get into problems we can't solve?"

"I don't know, Lee. Even this conversation is so foreign to me. I can't imagine sitting down with a stranger to share my feelings when I have such a long history of being successful in avoiding them."

"Successful?" Lee chided. "Would you classify your past relationship history as successful? Really?"

Kendra grinned. "Point taken." After a brief lull she countered with, "I want...no, need romance. I think one of the most exciting parts of any relationship is this early dance. How do we keep that spice, that spark? How do we keep it new?"

"I'm not sure. I'll think about it. I can be a pretty creative problem solver. I'll get back to you on that one."

They worked through the rest of their lists. Some of the items were humorous, others extremely serious.

For the most part Kendra's concerns dealt with her tendency to avoid issues and to bore easily. "Obviously what I did in the past was destructive."

"So what are your options now if we want this to work?" Lee asked.

"I have to tell you honestly that I have genuine issues and a poor track record. Maybe, if we can work on it together..." She paused before she shook her head. "Still, if history means anything, you'll be taking a risk with me, Lee."

"I'm thinking we're both making a leap of faith." Lee reached for Kendra's hand. "You have no way of knowing I'll hold up living as part of a lesbian couple and I have to worry you'll tire of me. At least we can talk. If we can keep up this kind of dialogue that's a good start, don't you think?"

Kendra brought Lee's hand to her lips and gently kissed the tender skin at the inside of her wrist. "Yes. That and the fact that you're incredibly hot and kiss like a thousand dollar a night hooker."

"How do you know how well a thousand dollar a night hooker kisses?"

Kendra shook her head. "Remember all those things like independence and trust and whatever else is on that damned list? Now is a good time to start trusting me by not asking too many questions."

CHAPTER 10

LEE'S FIRST HURDLE WAS to tell Fiona and Angus about Kendra. She was nervous when she showed up at their house.

Lee sat at the table while Fiona made tea for them. "Angus is off at the gym teaching his scuba class. He should be home soon. I'm glad you stopped by. Haven't seen too much of you this last couple of weeks. What's keeping you so busy?" Fiona placed the teacups on the table in front of them and settled opposite Lee at the kitchen table.

Lee stirred her tea to give her something to do with her hands. "I've been dating."

"Good. It's about time. You know what they say about all work and dullness."

"Yes, I do, and I hope you'll still think it's good and will still love me after I tell you." Lee could feel her pulse pounding in her temple and she wondered if the sweat on her brow was visible.

"Nothing would make me not love you. And if you don't know that by now you're hopeless. Give it up."

Lee exhaled a long calming breath and said, "I'm dating...uh...I'm dating a woman."

Fiona's expression remained unchanged. "Okay. I'm not sure what you expect from me. I feel like I'm supposed to be offended, shocked, or angry at this news. What you need to know is that I don't care who you date, as long as he or she makes you happy. Oh yeah, and that we like him or her. That last is really, really important." Fiona stood and came around the table to encircle Lee in her arms and pull Lee into an embrace. "I hope you haven't been stewing over this for too long. Oh, by the way Angus won't care either. Want me to tell him for you?"

"Tell me what?" Angus asked rounding the corner into the kitchen. "Got any more of that tea, Hon?"

Lee blushed furiously, as she told her friend about the new woman in her life. He and Fiona asked her a couple of questions about Kendra's background. After telling Lee to bring Kendra over for dinner, much to Lee's relief, the subject soon changed to more general topics of interest to all of them. Before Lee left, they arranged for Lee to bring Kendra over for dinner the next evening.

***

Despite Lee's worry about the evening, dinner at Angus and Fiona's house proved to be a fun event. When Kendra admitted she didn't snorkel or dive, Angus told her they'd be willing to teach her. The evening was a success, which made Lee feel like she and Kendra had passed a huge hurdle in their fledgling relationship.

It had been a little over two weeks since their afternoon they'd spent in bed kissing and touching. Although their parting kisses were becoming more intense and separating at the end of each evening was more and more difficult since the nap event, there had been no more intimate physical contact. Sexual tension was at an eleven on a ten-point scale.

Kendra courted Lee. Flowers, romantic candle-lit dinners, walks along the water at sunset, all ending with a light make out session at the door when she dropped Lee off. Lee invited Kendra to a picnic on the beach, left little love notes tucked in surprising places in her apartment, and left suggestive messages on her answering machine. However, although they were affectionate and loving, Lee still hadn't made a move to deepen their relationship to include sex. Kendra kept her word that Lee would have to make the first move.

While strolling through town one Saturday morning after breakfast, Lee and Kendra bumped into one of Lee's coworkers, Carol. Carol introduced her husband, Craig.

"Nice to meet you Craig." Lee grasped Kendra's hand. "This is my girlfriend, Kendra."

The couple showed little if any reaction other than their pleasure to meet Kendra.

Kendra turned to Lee, her grin expressing her acknowledgement of Lee's gesture. It felt like a turning point in their relationship.

CHAPTER 11

THE FOLLOWING FRIDAY, ON her lunch break, Lee called Kendra and asked her to meet for drinks at their favorite pub. "I'll be waiting for you at the bar. Get there as soon as you can after work."

Kendra hurried through the door of the pub anxious to see Lee. A quick glance around the place initially failed to locate her. As her eyes adjusted to the dim light, Kendra's focus settled on the redhead in the low cut top sitting at the bar. "My God! That's Lee," she whispered. Kendra approached and slid onto the stool next to Lee.

Kendra didn't spoil the fun by saying anything directly to her, just smiled in her direction and ordered a drink. Lee placed her hand on Kendra's thigh, and leaned into her, pressing her breast against Kendra's arm. "Hi beautiful. I hear you're a girl who likes a little excitement. Want to buy me a drink?"

"You know, I have a couple of options for a response in a situation like this. You see, my girlfriend and I have this list of relationship criteria. Number one on her list is fidelity." Firmly and gently, Kendra peeled Lee's hand off of her leg and placed it gently on the bar. "Thanks, but no thanks, Honey. I have a girlfriend waiting for me back at her house. I just stopped in here for a quick drink. I can't wait to get home to her. I'm pretty sure she'll be there waiting for me when I go to see her. So I need to leave because I want to stop at the liquor store for some champagne on the way to her home. I think it's possible that we might be celebrating tonight."

A broad grin spread slowly across Lee's face. "That's a great idea. You must be a wonderful girlfriend. And I suspect you're right. I think you have something special to look forward to and celebrate tonight." Lee slid from the stool and sauntered away, exaggerating the sway of her hips. The cheap five-inch spiked heels she'd found on the close out rack at the bargain shoe store pinched her toes. The fact that she could feel Kendra's eyes on her all the way to the exit made the temporary discomfort worthwhile. Lee paused at the doorway, glanced back over her shoulder and wiggled her fingers in Kendra's direction in a parting wave.

***

Kendra smiled. She was very pleased with herself. Her immediate thought was that this relationship was going to last, especially since Lee had demonstrated her willingness to experiment with role-playing. She silently vowed to herself that she was seriously going to try to avoid her prior ingrained habits and make this relationship work. She was happier than she'd ever been before and wanted that feeling to continue. She was sure she had finally found 'the one,' and knew she'd fallen in love.

When Kendra arrived at Lee's house she didn't even need to ring the bell. The door flew open as she approached. Lee wrapped her arms around Kendra's neck before greeting her with a welcoming kiss.

"You know, I could have had an assignation tonight with a very hot redhead. You'll be happy to know that I turned her down because I wanted to come home and make love to you," Kendra whispered as she nuzzled Lee's ear.

"Now there's a coincidence, because I'd like to make love to you. How convenient that we both want the same thing, don't you think?" Lee took Kendra's hand and led her down the hall to her bedroom.

Lee kissed Kendra softly and traced her hands from Kendra's neck down to the front of her blouse. She slowly unbuttoned it. When the front hung open, she slipped it from her shoulders then quickly unhooked Kendra's bra, freeing her to kiss each breast in turn. "You're so beautiful. I'm in love with you, you know."

Kendra hadn't verbalized her feelings before. When Lee bravely confessed her feelings, Kendra acknowledged them. "I'm glad, because I feel the same way about you." Unable to be patient any longer, she quickly slipped out of the rest of her clothes and stripped Lee to her underwear. They clung to each other kissing and caressing freely.

"Make love to me, Kendra. I want you to touch me. I need you to touch me. No one else ever has."

Kendra was surprised by the emotion that she felt in response to Lee's confession. "I wish I could say the same thing to you, Lee. I hope it will be enough if I say this is the first time I've made love to someone I'm in love with."

Passion exploded between them as they kissed their way to Lee's bed. Once they were there, their few remaining articles of clothing were shed without formality.

As they settled into the bed Kendra kissed Lee, leaving them both breathless. "I wanted this first time to be slow and easy, however I don't think I can wait to do that. I need you now."

"I don't want slow and easy." Lee reached for Kendra's breast, rolling her nipple with her palm. Kendra moaned. She flipped Lee onto her back and began to make love to her.

Kendra's hands, lips, and tongue were everywhere at once. Just when she thought one caress was too intense to stand, another part of her body was stimulated. Sensations danced from one location to another. The aroma of her arousal mixed with Kendra's. When she felt Kendra's fingers stroking through the curls at the apex of her thighs, she arched into her touch.

Kendra's hand stilled. "I love you, Lee."

"I love you too. Please, I want you so much. Touch me."

Kendra began to stroke Lee, each stroke becoming a little more intimate, traveling gradually closer to her core. Before she entered Lee, she paused again rising up on one elbow so she could see Lee's response. "I want to come inside you, okay?"

Lee nodded. Kendra watched Lee's hips rise up to meet her as she slid one finger deep inside eliciting a moan of pleasure. Kendra took her time, despite the fact that every nerve ending in her own body wanted her to move more quickly. Lee began to move her hips in rhythm with her lover's thrusts as Kendra added a second finger creating even stronger responses from Lee. She knew that Lee was close. She lowered her head and with her mouth on Lee's clit she tipped Lee over the edge. A long loud moan of pleasure accompanied Lee's orgasm.

Kendra was ready to explode. She needed Lee's touch, but she was prepared to wait for Lee to recover. She was surprised when Lee pulled her up and kissed her thoroughly. "I can taste myself on your lips. I want to do that to you now."

Lee didn't wait for a response. As if she had been taking notes while Kendra made love to her, she followed the pattern that Kendra had used. Her hands were everywhere. She tasted Kendra's lips, her neck, and her breasts before she settled between Kendra's legs to explore. She tried several different approaches, licking, nipping, and sucking at Kendra's swollen center. She paid attention to which stimulation garnered the most response. As she took Kendra into her mouth, using her tongue, Kendra whispered between gasps for air, "Just a little harder." Lee complied and Kendra called Lee's name as she came.

Once they'd satisfied their initial hunger for each other they made love more slowly the second time. They touched all the places they'd been dreaming of over the past several weeks of their courtship.

"I'm amazed at how much I want you and how comfortable I feel when you touch me. I was afraid I'd have trouble accepting you touching me, being intimate like this."

Kendra was surprised how competent a lover Lee was for someone inexperienced in the art of lovemaking. Together they learned the secret places and the proper touches that elicited the highest degree of pleasure. They made love again and Lee cried out in release as Kendra fastened her mouth against her.

"This time I want to come inside you. Teach me," Lee asked.

"There is no wrong way," Kendra encouraged. "Mmm. Yes. That's it. A little faster. Oh, yessss."

Exhausted after several rounds of making love, they rested. When their strength returned they again took turns touching and learning each other's bodies.

"So," Kendra wondered. "Was that everything you'd hoped for?"

"Yes, all that and more. Kendra, did we put regular lovemaking on our list? Lots of it."

"I don't recall. I guess we can always add it on, can't we? It can be codicil number one."

Lee and Kendra began their relationship optimistically believing, as all new lovers do, that they would be successful as a couple. They had many positives to build on—they truly loved each other, were physically well suited, and genuinely liked each other. Regardless of that fact, when obstacles presented themselves they struggled. To their credit, despite the difficulties, after four years they were still together. During their third year as a couple, Lee had begun research on an exciting new project at work where she met and became friendly with several staff members. They all worked well as a group and often socialized outside of the work environment. Kendra was jealous of Lee's success both professionally and personally. She had not progressed in her career, so she began to feel stagnant at work and at home.

Lee suggested, "Why don't we enroll in a couple of graduate classes." They did, and while Lee flourished in the academic environment, Kendra struggled, hating the discipline the advanced classes required. When Lee told Kendra she wanted to get her doctorate Kendra protested the investment of time.

After repeated requests from Lee, Kendra finally agreed to attend couples counseling. They showed up at the counselor's office where Dr. Pat Bond welcomed them into the office. "Please sit down and be comfortable. May I call you Kendra and Lee?" When they each nodded, the counselor introduced herself, told them about her background, asked them to call her Pat, and explained a bit about how she ran her sessions. After the initial session where they revealed why they were there, they scheduled a second visit. During the second visit, Pat asked Lee to talk about growing up. The story was nothing new to Kendra, but it was during that session that Lee learned something about her partner she'd never shared before.

All Kendra had ever revealed about her family to Lee was that her father was dead and she and her mother hadn't had any sort of a relationship after she'd revealed the fact that she was a lesbian. Lee was shocked to learn during that session that Kendra was a twin.

Seeing the surprise register on Lee's face, Dr. Bond focused on Kendra. "Obviously, that fact is a surprise to Lee. Why haven't you revealed this information before?"

Kendra shrugged. "I don't like to talk about it."

Lee opened her mouth to ask a question, Dr. Bond stayed her with a look. "Why is that Kendra?"

Again Kendra shrugged as she folded her fingers together and studied her hands. With a sigh she said, "When we were sixteen years old, both of us were injured in a school bus accident. My twin, Kayla, didn't survive."

With careful questioning by Dr. Bond, Kendra elaborated on her family life. "While my sister and I were growing up, our parents always favored my sister, and I was always jealous of Kayla. One night I overheard my parents arguing about us, about the accident. My father said to my mother that the wrong twin died." Tears filled Kendra's eyes. "I was heartsick. I loved my parents. Still, hearing that changed how I felt."

Kendra's father had died long before she began her relationship with Lee and way before she had been able to tell her father how painful his words had been. If competing against her sister for the affection of her parents had been difficult before he died, it was impossible to measure up after his death.

"When I came out to my mother, although she never uttered the phrase specifically, the impression I was left with was that she was sure her other daughter wouldn't have disappointed her in that way."

"How did you deal with that? Dr. Brown asked.

Kendra made eye contact with the doctor. "Simple avoidance worked best for both of us. When my mom died I went home to arrange her burial and to clean out her apartment. It was during that trip that I found and read my mother's journal where she detailed her feelings about us, about Kayla and me, I mean."

The counselor asked the question Lee wanted to know the answer to, as well. "What did you learn from reading that?"

"I'd be lying if I said that reading about my parents' pain over the loss of my sister, their favorite child, while I survived, and that my mother's disapproval of my own existence as a lesbian wasn't hurtful to read. After all, it was something I already knew. Still, I have to admit, seeing it in black and white somehow hurt more and it really stuck with me."

The counselor responded, "I'm sure it did."

"I don't know why all this is so important to you. I don't understand why any of that makes me feel like I do, or react like I do to things. Why it has anything to do with me being hurtful, or pushing people away." She glanced quickly at Lee who had been listening quietly.

"Why do you think that happens?" Pat asked.

"If I knew, I wouldn't be here paying you a lot of money to give me the answers, would I?" Kendra stood up and strode quickly to the door. "I'm done here," Kendra announced before she left the office. It was a surprise to both the counselor and Lee that she didn't slam the door.

"Give her time," Dr. Bond advised. "She needs to realize that this deep-seated hurt needs to be dealt with. I think Kendra needs individual counseling Lee. This is a long-term, deeply ingrained pattern she's developed and it probably needs to be dealt with before you and she will resolve your difficulties as a couple."

Lee left the session and went home. Kendra wasn't there and didn't return before Lee had to leave for her evening class. Lee left her a note telling her dinner was in the fridge and found it untouched when she returned at ten-thirty.

Kendra was drunk when she arrived home much later that night and crawled into bed. Lee feigned sleep. The next morning, Lee was up early, as usual. Kendra could sleep in for another forty-five minutes. The room smelled of alcohol. Lee figured Kendra could use the rest, so she didn't wake her. Instead she opted to leave a note saying she hoped Kendra would be ready to talk when they got home. She signed it with 'I love you' and her name.

Dinner was a relatively quiet affair. After they ate, Lee said, "Want to talk while we have some tea?"

"I don't know how much talking I'm going to do. I don't have much to say."

"Kendra, I know you're not happy, and because you aren't happy, we're not happy. Is it me, you know, something I'm doing or not doing?"

"No, it's not you. It's me. You know I told you in the beginning I was a bad risk and that I never last in a relationship."

"Honey, I love you. You know that. It doesn't have to be this way." Lee related the information from Dr. Bond and passed her business card across the table towards Kendra. "Won't you even try?"

"I have tried, Lee. If only you knew how hard." Kendra leaned back in her chair and massaged her temples. "I do love you. It's what's keeping me here." She picked up the card, read it, and slipped it into her pocket. "I'll call."

After three months, Kendra couldn't shake the melancholy she felt despite repeated visits to the psychiatrist recommended by Dr. Bond. She'd begun to drink more frequently in the evenings, spending more and more time at the pub.

That next semester Kendra declared she didn't want to take a class. "I need a break. I need some fun."

As Lee worked on her doctorate, Kendra began to party, often coming home after being at the bar with one or two 'friends' to hang out with at the house. The noise they generated made it difficult for Lee to study.

Lee eventually broached the subject with Kendra.

"So what do you want me to do, just shrivel up and waste away while you study? You're an academic, Lee. I'm not. I need...more."

"More what? Kendra, this won't last forever. I have one more year and my classwork is done."

"Yeah, your classwork. After all that comes the dissertation. How many years will that take?"

"Come on, Kendra. You can't say I've neglected you. Yes, it's true that I have classes a couple of nights a week, and I do admit that I have homework. Despite all that, we spend at least Saturday and most Sundays together. I try not to let my studies interfere with our life more than absolutely necessary."

Kendra sighed. "I'm sorry. I'm just feeling out of sorts, I guess."

"Please don't pull away, Kendra. Maybe we need a vacation to help us reconnect. Want to go to the Keys with Angus and Fiona at the end of the semester?"

When Kendra didn't answer, Lee asked, "Would you rather we go somewhere else alone?"

A shrug was Kendra's only response.

Lee's waning patience caused her to stand up and sharply snap out, "Why are you being so difficult?"

Again, Kendra gave no answer.

"You know, in the beginning, you described to me behavior you resorted to when you were done with a relationship. You told me you behaved this way or cheated. Are you at that point? Do you want out?"

Tears flooded Kendra's eyes, and for the first time she gave Lee her full attention. "I don't know. What's the matter with me, Lee? The only reason I'm still here is because I do love you. Unfortunately that doesn't change the fact that I'm just not happy. Worse yet, I don't know what would make me happy. I hate my job. I hate supervision. I hate the people there at work. In contrast, you love your job, and you love the people you work with. You actually have fun doing your job. I envy you, Lee. You have it all. I only have you."

"I'm sorry you feel that way. It makes me sad that you feel so unhappy and unfulfilled in your life and in our relationship, and that I, and all that we have, are not enough for you."

Kendra repeated, "It's not you, it's me. I feel so trapped. Not trapped in our relationship, just like my life is a dead end."

"Would you be happier without me?"

"No." Kendra stood, went around the table, and pulled Lee into her arms. "The truth of the matter is I probably won't be happy anywhere. If my depression is making us both miserable, maybe I should leave. You might be happier without me."

"Kendra, I love you. I don't want to lose you. Yet I know that if we can't get through this soon, we won't make it. You know it and so do I." She rested her head on Kendra's shoulder. "How can two people who profess to love each other be so miserable together?"

They walked hand in hand down the hall to the bedroom where they made tender love. When they were finished, they continued their conversation.

"What if you left your job and found something you enjoyed doing. Do you think it would help?"

"I don't have any training to do anything else. There are rumors the place where I work might sell. As much as I hate what I'm doing, what the hell would I do if I lost my job?"

"I earn enough money to support us. What if you were to quit, study something else, start over."

"I've thought about it. I literally have no idea what I'd like to do. It's not like I don't have a degree. There's unfortunately no job requiring my skills and qualifications that is close to here for me. I promise I'll look into it though."

"We'll figure it out."

"Lee, what if I find a really great job somewhere else?"

"We'll cross that bridge when we come to it."

CHAPTER 12

KENDRA AND LEE'S NEXT next six months were a little better. Kendra brightened a bit as she became involved in looking for a different job. She came home one evening and slid a letter across the table toward Lee.

"What's this?"

"I found a job."

"Really, that's great." Lee's enthusiasm was sincere and genuine.

"Well, I have to interview for it. Things look promising, I think. I've had two interviews already. The first was a screening on the phone with the immediate supervisor, and the next one with the full interview committee on the computer. Now they want to meet me."

Lee wondered why Kendra hadn't met with them in person. "Kendra, where is this company located."

"Well, that's the problem. The job sounds perfect. Unfortunately, it's in Chicago."

Lee frowned. "Chicago?"

"I know. I really, really want this job, Lee. Because of us, and my commitment to you, I know I can't accept it. Maybe it'll be enough if they just offer it to me. I'll feel better just knowing they chose me."

"So, you're going to interview for it? When do you leave?"

"Yes. They want me on Monday."

Lee's anger crept into her voice. "I can't get off at such short notice. And I have my classes."

"I know. That's okay. I figured you couldn't come so I just booked a flight for myself. It's not critical you come at this point."

Lee blinked back her tears. "You're going to get this job and you're going to accept it, aren't you?"

Kendra's measured response was, "Let's worry about that if and when we have to."

***

Lee picked up Kendra at the airport upon her return. She was already a bit annoyed that Kendra hadn't called her after the interview. As Kendra buckled her seat belt, Lee pulled into traffic and headed for home. She didn't say anything to her partner as she navigated the exit from the airport.

"You're pissed I didn't call. Right?"

Lee signaled and changed lanes, but didn't say anything in response to Kendra's question.

"I know you're angry, and you have a right to be." Kendra sighed. "Look, after I finished the interview, I had to race to make the plane. I'm sorry."

"You and I both know that's a crock. So are you going to tell me?"

"Yes." Kendra paused before finally blurting out, "Lee, I accepted the job they offered me right at the interview. I leave in two weeks. Now what?"

Through gritted teeth, Lee said, "Let's discuss this when we get home. I can't even talk to you right now."

The conversation at home was unpleasant, filled with accusations by Lee that Kendra didn't love her or respect her. Kendra countered that Lee was being selfish. In the end, they agreed that Kendra would take the position and they would address their relationship when Lee finished her degree. Until then, they would remain faithful to their relationship with the hope that Kendra would find happiness in her new job. Lee found it annoying that Kendra hadn't even discussed taking the position with her or the ramifications of that decision on their relationship, before making the commitment. Two weeks later, Kendra left for Chicago.

Lee filled the void Kendra's absence left in her life with her studies and with friendship, spending time with Angus, Fiona, and Maggie. She spoke frequently with her old college roommate, Brian. She had the support of friends and family, something not available to Kendra who was alone in a strange city.

They tried to maintain a long distance relationship initially, flying back and forth for long weekends whenever they could manage it. Between Kendra's new work demands and the rigors of Lee holding a full time job while writing her thesis, their relationship faltered. They hung on for the first six months. In the end, they finally agreed that maintaining a monogamous long distance relationship was not working, especially for Kendra, who asked to be released to have sexual relations outside their relationship.

"I swore to you I would never cheat on you and I haven't yet. The longer we live apart the more likely it becomes that eventually I will. Honestly, it's getting harder to behave and keep my promises. Neither of us should have to live like a nun, Lee."

"Can't you just hang on for a little longer? I'll be finished soon and maybe I can find something in Chicago. If not field work, maybe I could teach." Lee implored Kendra to wait a few more months.

"I'll try. Let's talk during your next visit."

Lee flew out the following weekend. Both admitted they still cared, as they discussed their future. "That's why this is so hard, Lee. I still love you and I know you feel the same. However, I have a future here, and your goal is to eventually move to the Keys so you and Angus can live and work there. You know that's not for me. I can't stand that incessant heat and there's no work for me there."

Tears brimmed in Lee's eyes. "I know. True, it's a dream, just one that I don't have to realize right away. It can wait."

"Perhaps. But why should it?" Kendra released Lee's hand and wiped an escaped tear from her cheek. "Why shouldn't we each have what we really want? All of what we want, not just the bits and pieces left to us from our partner realizing her dreams."

Lee slid into Kendra's arms. "I don't want to give you up, to give us up."

Kendra cuddled Lee against her. "If you let me go as a partner now, there's a good chance we'll always care for each other for the rest of our lives. If we keep on like this, I'll eventually break your heart by cheating on you and you'll come to hate me."

Kendra tightened her arms around her lover. They held each other for a long time before they agreed that ending their relationship was the right thing to do for each of them. Lee was five months away from finishing her dissertation when they finally called it quits after almost seven years.

By the time Lee was awarded her doctorate, in moments when honesty took precedence over feeling sorry for herself over the end of her relationship with Kendra, she had to admit that she was a much happier person without having to live with her partner's daily struggle with depression and jealousy.

For Kendra, although she told Lee that she still did truly love her, returning to her old commitment-free ways seemed to make her life much less complicated and demanding. She reported she was happier in her job and, as a result, happier in her life in general.

By the time they finally parted, they both agreed it was hard to end a relationship while still caring for each other. Each also admitted that, at the end, they were happier apart than they had been together.

Section 3 - Kate and Lee

CHAPTER 13

KATE – AFTER MAX

KATE MUMBLED HER DISPLEASURE at the beam of light coming through the window that woke her before she was ready. She slowly rolled off the bed and stripped off her T-shirt on the way to the bathroom. Finished with her shower, she walked nude into her bedroom to dress. The fifties style mirrored doors on the closet were a sure indicator that the bedroom had not yet been renovated. In fact, the bedroom was the only room that remained untouched in the cottage she had bought for herself just before she met Maxine Montebank.

Just as it did every day, Dr. Kate Martin's reflection stared back at her in the mirror. Her hair was prematurely greying. An abundance of silver strands mixed into her medium ash brown hair, giving the impression it was frosted. Short, wavy hair framed her face perfectly, emphasizing her high cheekbones, striking green eyes, and full lips. She risked a second look at the mirror, critically reviewing what she saw there and taking inventory of her nearly forty-two year old body that she was not as religious about maintaining as she used to be. She was five-eight and muscular for a woman, due in part to the physicality of her profession, as well as to her attempt at working out with weights two or three times a week whenever she had time. She ran her hands over her still flat stomach and up her body to cup her breasts, noting they were not as perky as they used to be. All things considered, she concluded, she was aging relatively gracefully.

The deep sigh she exhaled was indicative of how tired she felt. The years since Max left had been a harrowing period. When she and Max split, it meant she'd lost her lover, her friend, and her business partner simultaneously. Her mind traveled back over the now all too familiar memories.

Max had returned from the conference she'd attended, with a distant and remote demeanor. In the break room at the office, Kate pulled Max aside and tried to encourage conversation. "How were the classes at the seminar? Did you learn any new or cutting edge practices we need to know about?"

Max resisted Kate's question. "We need to talk." She hesitated, "Just not here." Max stared at Kate with no expression on her face, as if debating whether she should say more. Seconds later, she turned away and retreated. Pausing at the door she turned, narrowing her gaze. "I guess I'll see you later at home. We can talk there."

The conversation that took place at the kitchen island later that evening, as they sipped hot chocolate, proved to be a difficult one. Without any preamble Max announced, "I'm not sure how to break this news to you gently so I'm going to just say it. I need a change. This isn't working for me anymore. I met someone at the conference. His name is John." Max sought Kate's eyes, her gaze steady. "I can't do this anymore, Kate."

Kate stunned, mumbled. "Met someone?" she echoed, feeling stupid and as stunned as if she'd been hit hard in the stomach. It took her a moment to process the information Max had just divulged. Seconds passed. She closed her eyes and covered her ears with her hands against the words, but she was too late. She couldn't prevent the words from seeping into her brain. She sat up and placed her hand over her heart to prevent it from beating out of her chest.

Max stared back silently watching as the tears coursed down Kate's cheeks. She closed her eyes and shook her head. "I'm sorry." She turned away and left Kate to grieve alone. That evening, Max moved into the other bedroom.

Over the next few weeks they argued, they made up, and they argued again. Kate begged Max to reconsider what she was doing, to no avail.

Two months after returning from the conference Max announced, "I'm moving to Arizona to be with my lover, John. Either figure out how to buy me out or put the practice up for sale."

Kate was stunned into silence. She knew that Max was unhappy in their relationship, but never expected this result. "That's it? Are you really going to give up all we've built here together for someone you met at a convention less than two months ago? My God! You had one lust filled week during the convention and you're ready to chuck it all and move to Arizona? Do you even have a clue how hot it is in Arizona?"

Months later, as she reviewed their conversation in her mind, Kate couldn't resist the chuckle that came as she recalled her reply to Max's announcement. It was the only moment of levity in an unimaginably painful period of Kate's life. *What an inane statement to make. The woman had just declared an end to my life as I've known it, and my response had been to comment about the weather.* Max had told her as much.

"You're an idiot," Max snapped back. "I tell you I'm leaving you for a man, and your primary concern is to be worried about the temperature where I'm going?"

It took them several intense conversations spread over the next few days to begin to get to the root of Max's issues. Eventually, she summed up her feelings concisely. "If it were just me and you we could probably be happy forever. Unfortunately you won't or can't be satisfied being as you put it 'isolated here with just me,' and I can't go openly hand-in-hand with you into a world that still disapproves so vehemently of relationships like ours."

Kate implored. "Look at how happy Kyle and Mike are living openly. They have a rich social life, gay as well as approving straight friends, and supportive family members, all of which nourish their relationship. You refuse to let us have that kind of support and it's destroying us. Won't you at least try being more open? You can't love this guy, not like you've loved me. Please don't do this, Max."

"Kate, stop! Don't beg." Max snapped.

They stared at each other. Max was the first to look away. "I'm truly sorry, Kate. Believe me, if I could, I would." Her expression conveyed the anguish she was feeling. Her eyes met Kate's. "I know this is hurtful for you. I know you feel that everyone who has ever loved you has left you, and that makes it even harder for me to do this." Max took a deep calming breath and lowered her voice to a gentle tone. "I do love you, although I know it's hard for you to believe it right now." Max shook her head in denial. "I just can't give you what you want, what you need. I don't know why they call it gay, there's nothing happy about living a life everyone despises."

"Max. That's just not true. Look at Kyle and Mike…"

"No. I can't be like them. I just can't. I can't give you what you want. I'm truly sorry. I just can't do this anymore. You deserve more and I can't give it to you."

Despite all of Kate's protests and pleading, Max steadfastly resisted. Their final conversation on the topic ended with, Max saying, "I want a normal relationship I can be proud of and that society can sanction. I want to be married Kate. I want kids."

No matter what Kate said or the amount of tears she shed, Max remained unmoved.

When they'd split, Kate struggled to buy out Max's share of their business. Taking on the responsibility of the entire practice was a daunting task. She went to Kevin and told him what was happening. He wrapped her in his arms and held her as she cried.

"I'm sorry you're hurting, Kate. I knew there was something happening between the two of you, but I never expected Max to just up and quit. We'll get through this. I promise I'll do all I can. Just tell me how I can help."

***

Kate and Kevin barely survived the first four months after Max left. They notified their patients of Max's departure and announced that until further notice they would open the practice on Sunday until they could find a replacement. They each worked their normal day off to absorb Max's patients into their schedule until Kate was finally able to recruit a recent veterinary grad to come work with them. The new doctor fit into the practice well and life at the office returned to normal.

Kate immersed herself in work. It was her salvation. Kyle and Mike supported and loved her as she adjusted to Max's absence in her life. Kate, Beth and Kevin developed a strong partnership that included a firm basis in friendship. Dr. Beth Barlow, a short, dark haired, compact woman twelve years Kate's junior, learned quickly. Her kind and gentle manner, bubbly personality, and unfailing good humor helped to endear her to the clients and to Kate and Kevin as well.

CHAPTER 14

KATE STRUCK HER HEAD Into Kevin's office. "Staff meeting at six when we close?"

"Sure. Not a long one, I hope."

Kate smiled. "Should be short. Just want to recap the week and talk about any concerns. It was a good week as far as I know, so maybe fifteen minutes tops."

Kate, Kevin, and Beth had quickly become good friends. They shared a common desire to care for their paying clients as well as for those less fortunate creatures who had no permanent home or loving family looking out for their welfare. Kevin and Beth each donated time at the local shelter, spaying or neutering strays that the agency put up for adoption. Kate, now that she had partners and a bit more free time, went back to volunteering her services at the wildlife sanctuary. There she often treated owls and hawks with broken wings, orphaned baby animals who'd lost their parents for one reason or another, and helped with other wild, large and small animals who were in need of her help. Many of these animals had experienced unfortunate encounters with cars and any number of other situations. She loved the time she spent at the sanctuary, especially when she got to work with the larger wild animals. It allowed her to use her specialized training and reminded her of her early years when the clinic's practice was comprised of mostly large animals.

The small group gathered as soon as Kate locked the front door. "I'm so glad you guys agreed to buy in as my partners. I no longer have to carry full responsibility for the practice, which means we get to take turns seeing Wicky's Way." Kate's partners groaned in unison.

"I saw her last time." Kevin pretended to wipe his brow. "That means I'm off the hook this time. That cat is evil personified, and her owner is impossible."

"You are such a drama queen, Kevin!" Kate turned to Beth with an evil grin. "And I did it the time before that. So it's your turn, Beth. They have an appointment with you tomorrow. Don't forget to bring the heavy gloves. That old cat can move like lightening if he thinks he can grab a finger." Beth groaned and the other two laughed as she dropped her head onto her folded arms in front of her.

Beth raised her head, moaned and cast her eyes upward. "You guys suck! You know that cat hates me most of the three of us. Won't either of you take pity?"

Kate and Kevin shook their heads in unison.

Kate grinned, enjoying the camaraderie she shared with her partners. That past summer Kate offered, and both Kevin and Beth accepted a partnership in the business. Kate retained a fifty-one percent share of the practice for herself. Each doctor received a salary based on the number of hours they put in each week. A percentage of the profits went into escrow to support the cost of running and maintaining the facility. At the end of each year, the remaining profits not earmarked for improvements and new equipment were shared by percentage of the practice owned. The money she received from the sale allowed her to pay off the huge loan she had to take out to buy Max's share of their business with a small amount of cash left over to add into her retirement account. Before they finalized their agreement, Kate came out to both Kevin and Beth. "I'm tired of living with secrets. No more secrets, and no more lies for me," she vowed.

Kate dragged her attention back to the meeting. "Okay, that's settled. Beth gets to do the honors. Mrs. Brikley made an appointment for tomorrow at ten.

"I'll give you fifty dollars to do it." Beth looked in the direction of her partners. "Kate? Kevin?" When met by shaking heads, Beth blew out an exasperated breath. "You guys are the worst. If I'd known being a partner meant seeing that evil cat a third of the time, I might never have taken the offer."

Kevin put his hand on her shoulder. "Think of it this way. If you hadn't become a partner, you'd get her every time."

"Oh. Didn't think of that." Everyone joined the laughter as she reached up to give his hand an affectionate squeeze.

"Part of the reason I wanted to get together tonight is that I need to take some time off. I need a vacation. I'd like to take off a couple of weeks after the holidays. It's only six weeks from now so I thought we should talk about how we'll cover my hours." Kate felt worn to a nub and knew she needed a vacation. Not that she didn't enjoy being a vet, she did. When working with people's pets, it was sometimes more challenging dealing with the owners than it was ministering to the animals. Most of the time she could credit her sense of disquiet to being tired, as she was now.

"We'll manage." Kevin said with confidence. "Beth and I and the new vet tech should be able to hold the fort for two weeks."

Beth nodded. "Yes, I think so, too. I'm glad we hired her. We can use the extra help, and she's very capable."

They agreed to Kate taking two weeks off after the first of the year. Kate offered to work extra hours during the holidays to give her partners some extra time with their families in exchange. With business settled, they wished each other a good night and headed in their separate directions.

Kate stopped and picked up a calzone. Her dog, Cody, greeted her as she unlocked the door, excited that she'd be taking him out. After their walk, she returned to the kitchen, heated the calzone, and took it into her office. She picked at it as she searched the Internet. Online, Kate located a cabin a few hours drive from where she lived. It was her first experience using the Internet to find a rental. She searched the listings for some place different from her previous trips, yet still within a day's drive, finally settling on one ad that caught her interest...*1 BR, WATER VIEW. Hiking, skiing, bird watching, museums and history. We have it all.*

She read the ad aloud to Cody. "What do you think fella? Sounds good to me. Shall I call tomorrow and see if they'll have us?"

Cody answered with a bark that Kate assumed meant, "It sounds good to me, too."

CHAPTER 15

"I'M SORRY I HAVE to leave you alone," Mary Blackwell told Missy Green. They shared a small workspace in the real estate office that in addition to selling properties managed a large number of cabin rentals in the Berkshires. "I'll just be gone the last half hour of the afternoon to meet with my daughter's teacher," Mary said. "You know what to do, right?"

Missy, a new employee, was still feeling her way through the booking process. "I think so." She steeled her resolve and with more confidence said, "I'm sure I'll be okay." She sneezed three times in quick succession. "Sorry. This cold is getting worse. Hope it's not the flu."

Hurrying now, so as not to be late, the older woman shrugged into her coat. "You'll be fine. Just record everything on the tablet like I showed you. It's faster that way. When you're done with the caller, don't forget to enter the confirmed booking into the database."

Fifteen minutes before closing, the raucous sound of the phone ringing dashed Missy's hopes that no one would call while she was alone in the office without Mary's support.

"Hello. My name is Dr. Kate Martin. I'm calling about the cabin you have advertised."

"Hi. I'm Missy Green. Please tell me which property are you referring to?"

"The advertisement reads: Berkshire Mountain Retreat, Log Cabin,

1BR, Water View, Pet Friendly, Reasonable. It's on your website."

"Oh yes, I know that property. It's lovely—small, though. How many of you are there?"

"I can do small. It'll only be my dog and me. The ad said pet friendly. I hope he won't be a problem. He's two years old and very well behaved."

"Let me check the pet policy." The congested agent sniffed repeatedly as she shuffled through a stack of papers. "Oh, here it is. Small dogs allowed."

Between bouts of sniffling, sneezing, and near deafening fits of coughing, Missy asked, "Is your dog under fourteen inches tall?"

"Yes."

"And he weighs less than twenty pounds?"

"He does."

"Tell me the dates you are interested in renting, please." Missy put the woman with the soothing voice on hold while she checked to see if the cabin was available for the January dates the woman had specified. "You're in luck, it's available. I'll need your credit card number and your name and address."

Kate answered each question the tentative agent asked and waited patiently as Missy recorded all the required information.

"The combination for the lockbox on the door is 2236. Open the box using that combination and you'll find a key inside that will open the cabin door. I'll send you explicit directions, rules, and any other information you'll need for your stay in an e-mail."

A few minutes later, Missy sent the promised e-mail confirming the booking, popped a cold pill, and locked up the office before leaving for home.

A little more than halfway home, when Missy braked to a halt at the intersection, she realized her oversight. "Agh, crap!" She pounded the steering wheel with her fist. Returning to the office to fix her error would be the proper thing to do. Unfortunately, she just felt too lousy. Realizing she just wasn't going to be able to muster the energy to drive back to the office, she heaved a long sigh. A shiver swept through her body. *Great. Now I'm probably getting a fever.* She wrapped her scarf tighter around her neck before reaching over to punch the fan for the car heater into a higher speed. *I'll go in early tomorrow and correct my oversight first thing in the morning. No one will even know.* The promise appeased her.

The next morning, Mary Blackwell checked her messages as soon as she arrived at her office. Missy's gravel-voiced message made her sound weak and nearly delirious. "I'm too sick to come in. Don't expect to see me for at least today and probably tomorrow." The message, punctuated by two loud sneezes, ended abruptly.

Mary exhaled a long breath blowing her bangs up off her forehead. Punching delete, she mumbled under her breath, "Geez Missy, could you pick a busier time to be out and leave me alone here in the office for the whole day, during the height of ski season bookings, the busiest time of year? I guess I'm better off without you sharing your germs." The minute she sagged into her chair and slid it up to her desk her phone rang. "Hello. My name is Lee Foster. I'm calling to inquire about renting a small cabin in January just for myself. I saw an ad featured on your website on the Internet, '1BR, water view'.

"Yes, I know that place, Shaw Creek. Hang on a minute and I'll get the detailed description for you." Lee could hear pages flipping and shuffling. "There's a loft with a queen sized bed. The main floor is a great room that consists of a kitchen, a dining table with two chairs, and a couple of leather chairs flanking the fireplace. There is also a bath with a shower off the great room on the first floor."

"I saw the pictures on the website. It looks lovely and should be perfect for just me."

"Don't let the description fool you. The place is quite small. In the interest of fair play, I think there's a bit of liberty being taken calling the first floor area a 'great room.' I don't think there's even room for a sofa in there. Also, the ad says water view. If I remember correctly, it's a distance away from the water. It's pretty remote, too. I'm sure I could find you a larger cabin closer to town for not too much more money."

"Thanks for the heads up. It's okay, though, I don't mind remote, and I'm sure the size will be more than sufficient for just me."

"Right. It wouldn't do for more than one or two people but it does have the plus of allowing you to bring your dog."

"I'm sure that's an added benefit. That's not a consideration for me, because I don't have one. I'm interested in area because I like visiting the Shaker Village. On the map, it looks like it's near there. Correct?"

"Yes, it's just a short drive away. I'm not sure the buildings are open to visitors this time of year although sometimes there are special group tours off season."

"That's okay. The grounds are lovely. I've been there before and liked the area. I'm sure there are many other sights to see in the vicinity."

"I'll check to be sure it's available." She pulled up the cabin in the database. "Right, we do have that lovely little cabin on Shaw Creek available for rent on the dates you've requested. It should fit your needs very well. I'll reserve the cabin as soon as I get some information from you." The agent finished recording the required data. "Okay, all appears in order. Give me a minute while I enter your reservation into the database."

Lee impatiently listened to the recording of distorted jazz music while she waited for Mary to return to the line.

"Okay Ms. Foster, I've recorded your reservation. I'll send you a confirmation in a few minutes. Are you familiar with how to use a lock box?" Once she ascertained the woman from Connecticut understood what to do, she hung up and sent an e-mail confirming the reservation and providing the access code for the box.

It was a full four days later that Missy returned to a desk piled high with tasks left unfinished in her absence, her promise to record the booking into the database for Dr. Martin long forgotten, thus creating the most life-altering booking error ever made in their office.

***

Kate hung up and wondered idly who made up the rules for renting. She had to restrain herself from asking more about the weight limitation for the dog specified in the contract, curious as to whether someone was going to show up at some point in her vacation with a scale to measure the weight of her dog.

Kate wasn't worried about the size limitation. She had no doubt Cody, her compact little dog would fit whatever requirement there was. Penny, her previous dog would have never fit the requirement. However, Cody, her little mutt who weighed only fifteen pounds and looked like someone had shrunk a sled dog into a diminutive version, would have no problem.

At the conclusion of the thorough grilling about Cody's attributes, Kate mused that she had been required to provide more information about Cody's suitability to stay at the cabin than she had about her own. After a few tenuous moments with the reservation assistant concerning the dates, she was reasonably assured all the details had been worked through despite the young woman's initial confusion. Kate's measured repetition of the information in the professional voice she used to calm and soothe her nervous clients and patients seemed to work equally well on the harried agent on the phone. The agent had responded well to the tactic, slowed down and begun using a calmer tone as she proceeded with the booking.

When Kate received the e-mail confirmation from Missy Green, minutes after she'd hung up, Kate began to relax and allowed herself to anticipate her time away after the holidays.

CHAPTER 16

LEE - DECEMBER 2008

"HAPPY NEW YEAR!" LEE and Brian always talked to each other on New Year's Eve. This year she'd called him. After a brief exchange of greetings, they began catching up and sharing the latest news.

"So nothing is new, huh? What you need is a vacation, something different," Brian advised.

"I take a vacation every year. I go to the Keys with Fiona and Angus."

"Yes, and what do you do there? Work, work, and more work."

"It's not work when one would do it for no pay," Lee countered.

"Have you heard from she who shall remain nameless?"

Lee laughed. "Yes, we speak every so often, at least once a month. I won't go so far as to say Kendra's happy. Still, she's definitely more upbeat and she's enjoying her job. We don't discuss her love life."

"So, there's no chance the two of you would..."

Even before Brian had finished his thought, Lee responded, "Nope, not a chance."

"For someone so adamant, why haven't you dated anyone in, what's it been now, about a year?"

"Yes, just over. Honest, I'm over her. I just haven't met anyone I'm remotely interested in dating. Work is crazy busy." Lee switched the receiver to her other ear. "Angus and I are under deadline for the book.

I have to select the pictures for the examples he's cited, simplify some of the text or, as he describes it, translate it into an acceptable readability quotient. Oh, yeah, and in my spare time there are several sketches I need to make."

"Lee, take off a couple weeks, go someplace different, and finish up what you have to do. Work will survive without you for a couple of weeks. I promise you."

"It may surprise you who thinks he knows everything there is to know, but I've actually looked into it."

"Really?" Lee enjoyed Brian's low chuckle after which he asked, "Which island this time?"

"Ha! Just to show you that you don't know everything, Brian, surprise again. I'm thinking of going to the mountains a couple of weeks from now."

"The mountains? You? In January? Talk about a fish out of water. Good for you. Where?"

"Western Mass. The Berkshires."

"Interesting...Why there?"

"Well, it's close, less than three hours by car. There's a Shaker Village nearby. I went there for a weekend once with Kendra." Striking a preemptive blow, Lee added, "...and no comments about my interest in the Shakers and my lack of a sex life."

Brian laughed. "I guess you beat me to the punch line there. When are you doing this?"

"I leave in two weeks."

"Oh, that's too soon I think." Brian flipped through his calendar. "I thought I might be able to sneak away for a long weekend to join you, but it's too soon for me. Maybe we can meet somewhere half way later in the spring? I miss you."

"Yes, that sounds good. Let's plan on it. I'll call you when I get back. Until then, hugs to you and a happy New Year!"

"And to you, Lee."

CHAPTER 17

ON VACATION - DAY 1

ANGUS CAME AROUND THE corner past Lee's office on the way to his own. He expressed his surprise to find Lee still sitting at her desk. "Hey! What are you doing here? Aren't you supposed to be on your way to Massachusetts? Did you decide to wait till after the storm?"

It was already eleven thirty. Her original plan included leaving two hours earlier for the less than three hour trip to the cabin but, at the last minute, she concluded that a couple of hours to finish the report she was working on would give her a clearer conscience about taking a two week vacation. *Funny thing about vacation...the two weeks before you leave and after you return are always spent doing the work you would have done while on vacation. No escaping the responsibilities of the job.* "No. I'm just about to head out. I just wanted to finish this report for you. I was so close. Now you can make any edits you need to and won't have to wait to submit it. We'll be done ahead of schedule."

"Thanks, Lee. You didn't have to do that. We have plenty of time to finish it when you return. Though I won't deny that it will be a relief to submit the report and get started on that new project without the old one still hanging over our heads. Now, get out of here. Have a safe trip and call Fiona or me when you get there so we don't worry about you." Angus hugged Lee goodbye. "Drive carefully but don't dally. You need to beat the snow. They're predicting a bad storm coming to that area. Be sure to bring enough food with you to the cabin just in case you can't get out for a couple of days. This storm could be bad depending on how it tracks. They're still not sure of the path the last I heard."

Lee returned home, gathered her suitcases, the supplies she had purchased the day before, and packed up her car. It was already raining at twelve-thirty when she left. If all went well she anticipated she'd be there by three-thirty or, at the latest, four o'clock.

Lee crossed the harbor on the Gold Star Memorial Bridge and headed out of the city. She reached Hartford and headed north on ninety-one where the rain had already changed to sleet and snow. Roads were slick and the progress slow. It was already after four when she navigated through Springfield and by the time she arrived in Westfield, the snow was howling with strong wind gusts blowing the snow sideways. Accumulation was at least four inches. The roads were snow covered. Luckily traffic was sparse as she turned north on MA-8 for the last leg of her journey. Visibility was poor as she followed the directions of her GPS to turn right onto a nearly invisible road. Having difficulty determining where the margins of the road were, she straddled the crown in the middle and followed the lone set of nearly filled in tracks up the mountain. The defroster worked overtime as it unsuccessfully tried to clear the windshield and the wipers caked with snow that had melted into ice. The wind gusted and the snow swirled in front of her headlights.

Lee had a death grip on the steering wheel while navigating the narrow road as it climbed upward. She approached one mailbox but was unable to read the number due to the five-inch high pile of snow covering the number. The GPS announced that she was at her destination. Relieved, she exhaled a long sigh and pulled into the driveway so she could get out to check the number on the mailbox. She pulled the confirmation e-mail from her pack to be sure. "Okay, I need number seventy-five," she said aloud as she flipped the button on the armrest releasing the lock. The storm ripped the car door from her hand as she stepped into the howling wind and blowing snow to make her way back to the end of the driveway. After brushing the snow from the mailbox, disappointment washed over her when she saw the number twenty-seven on the box. Not the one she was seeking. Wind whipped snow stung her face as she struggled toward her vehicle. Back in the car, she rubbed her frigid hands together and blew air into them to warm them. Engine running and heat blowing full blast, she paused a few minutes to warm up. The radio announcer she'd been listening to for the past hour again upped the snow totals.

"Okay, almost there. Off we go. When did I start talking to myself?" Lee glanced out the window. "Since you made the stupid decision to drive into the middle of a frigging blizzard all alone, idiot." Slipping the gearshift into reverse, she made an effort to turn the car around. "Oh no." As the tires spun she said a silent prayer. *Please, don't let me be stuck. Ah crap! Well, at least I'm almost here. Worst case, I can walk up the road to number seventy-five.*

Lee rocked the car forward and backward, trying to free herself from the grip of the heavy, sticky snow. After a few minutes the realization hit that she wasn't getting anywhere, and she gave up. *I'd better let Angus and Fiona know I'm here, so they don't worry.* She made a quick call to her friends, got their machine and left a message. Phone service was terrible so she kept it brief, simply saying she was almost to her destination, the weather was horrible, and she'd call them back when the storm ended and cell service was better.

Once she finished with that chore, she gathered the bag of food she'd brought and her backpack. The backpack had her essentials in it—a pair of warm-ups and a sweatshirt, a change of underwear and socks, toiletries, her tablet, and her computer. She crammed her folder containing all the work she'd brought with her into a plastic bag then into one of the pockets of the pack, put on her gloves and pulled up her hood before braving the weather.

Trudging through the half a foot of snow was no easy task on the road that climbed steadily. The gusts were coming fast and furious and the wind driven snow and ice particles stung her face. Lee kept her head down and pushed on. The next house she came to was at least a quarter of a mile up the road and the number was only number thirty-three. Lee was concerned that there seemed to be so much ground to cover between numbers. Returning to her car didn't seem to be a viable option so she kept hiking since there appeared to be no choice at this point but to keep going.

It was at least ten minutes later that she heard the sound of an engine churning its way toward her. Turning, she looked back at the ground she'd covered and watched the slow progress of the lights on the vehicle as it climbed towards her. She waved her arms when it came into proximity. The window slid down as the SUV pulled abreast of her. "Get in out of that weather," the voice commanded. "Cody, get in the back."

Lee was relieved that it was a woman driving. *At least I don't have that to worry about that.* "Thanks for the lift. My name is Lee, by the way. Lee Foster."

"Kate Martin. That's my dog Cody in the back seat."

Lee glanced at the cute little dog in the back seat. "Hi Cody." Turning back to Kate she said, "He's cute." Lee got in, put her bag on the floor, her pack in her lap and buckled the seat belt.

"Thanks, and don't think for a minute he doesn't know that he's cute. So, how did you end up on foot in this weather?"

"I got stuck when I stopped to look at the number on the mailbox about three quarters of a mile back."

"Oh yeah, I saw the car in the drive. You must be chilled clear through. I'm just about a mile up the road. What number are you looking for?" Kate put her four-wheel drive vehicle into gear and started back up the road.

"Yes, my feet are frozen." Lee slipped off her glove and brushed the snow from her face and eyelashes. "I've rented number seventy-five."

Kate's brow furrowed. "Number seventy-five?"

"Yes. Is that near your place?"

"Yes. Yes it is. I think there must be some sort of mistake. I've rented number seventy-five." Kate glanced over to see Lee's puzzled expression.

"What? How can that be?"

"I don't know." Kate's medical training took precedence over her concern about the rental mix-up. "We can figure it out later. Let's get you inside and out of those wet clothes and warmed up. Once you're warm and more comfortable we'll tackle the rental issue. Agreed?"

"Warmth sounds good. Thanks."

CHAPTER 18

KATE CAREFULLY NAVIGATED HER way up the mountain to the driveway of the cabin. "Let me get the food I just bought out of the back. Do you need help with your bags?"

"No, I'll be okay. I brought food we can share, too."

Kate handed the cabin keys to Lee. "If you can take care of bringing in my food along with your stuff, I'll put some additional wood on the porch in case this gets much worse. I can also bring in a couple of extra loads to dry out overnight for our use tomorrow. I moved some inside this morning. However, I should probably bring in some more. I used a good bit of what I brought in earlier to heat up the cabin today."

Lee carried in the food while Kate worked on stacking up the wood. Less than fifteen minutes later, Kate came inside stamping her feet to get the snow off. She found that Lee had already changed into sweats. Kate's eyes swept over Lee's tight, athletic body. Grabbing a towel out of the bag next to the door she called, "Cody, come over here and let me dry you off." Task finished, she opened some food for her pet and changed his water.

"I put the kettle on. I hope that's okay, Kate." *Well, if I have to be trapped in a cabin with someone, at least it's a woman, and a very attractive woman at that.* Lee allowed herself the luxury of observing Kate as she stripped off her wet coat and hat and tended to her dog. *Umm, definitely nice-looking.* She glanced around the tiny cabin noting how compact it was. *It's definitely cozy, so the fact that she's nice is a plus, too.*

"That's great. A nice warm cup of tea would hit the spot. Thanks." Kate untied her boots, stepped out of them, and slipped on the moccasins she'd left by the door when she went to town for supplies earlier. "Did you check your face and feet?"

"Yes, I seem to be okay. I'm cold, for sure, although not yet frozen solid thanks to you. I'm surely grateful that you came by when you did. I was debating what to do, whether to go back to the car, or to just break into the next cabin I came to."

Kate surveyed the pile of food on the counter. "Between us we have quite the larder. At least we won't starve to death. I think another inch of snow was added just since we got here."

"So, you think we're stuck here?"

"I think so. I made it up in the car this last time. Even with the four-wheel drive it was already touch and go in a couple of spots. Until the road is plowed I suspect we're not going anywhere. I moved my car to the end of the driveway. We'll definitely have some shoveling to do. At least we won't have to shovel the whole drive to get the car out."

"Very smart. Thanks."

Kate added a couple of logs to the fireplace while Lee poured the water into the cups over the bags. "Sugar?"

"No, I like honey. I'll get it."

While the tea brewed, Lee glanced around the small cabin. It was definitely cute despite its diminutive size. The kitchen was tucked in one corner. Two stools rested under the overhang of the counter that separated the kitchen from what the agent had described as the 'great room.' *Definitely a generous term for the tiny area*, she thought. Next to the kitchen was an incredibly tiny bathroom containing a toilet, a sink, and the smallest shower she'd ever seen. The remainder of the first floor contained a small parson's bench against the wall that provided seating for one side of small rectangular shaped table. Two chairs provided seating on the other side of the table. Lee wondered idly why there were four seats. *Where would four people sleep in the tiny cabin?* There was a large window behind the parson's bench to the left of the door leading to the porch, and two good-sized windows on either side of the stove. The wood stove took up the majority of the remaining wall space between the windows. Flanking the stove were two swivel recliners covered in dark green leather. Although the small space was utilized efficiently, there was no room for even one more item of furniture despite the cabin being sparsely appointed.

Lee watched Kate add the wood and poke at the logs in the wood stove until the blaze was perfect. A serious amount of heat began to radiate from the carefully tended fire. Kate was apparently skilled at fire management. "Girl scout?"

Kate laughed. "No. I have a fireplace at home. A wood stove is a little different for me. I've been here since a little before lunchtime and think I've got a handle on it now. Considering the weather I'm glad I am an early riser and got started before I originally planned to leave this morning. I was fortunate to arrive here before the snow got serious which allowed me to get things set up, the wood moved, and the cabin heated before the snow really got underway." Kate stirred a spoonful of honey into her tea. Holding up the container, she offered some to Lee who declined. Tea in hand, they settled on the two recliners. "Umm. That really hits the spot. Thanks for making it."

Lee nodded and reached into her backpack to produce the confirmation she'd received from Mary Blackwell. "Here's my confirmation on the cabin rental," she said handing the paper over to Kate. "How can it be possible that we've both rented the same place?"

"I don't know. Let me get my e-mail." Kate fished her confirmation out of her jacket pocket and returned to her seat next to Lee. She compared the two papers. "Mine was sent by someone named Missy Green, yours by a different agent named Mary Blackwell." Kate pointed to the two names. "Obviously, we've both rented the cabin for the same dates. I suspect that the problem stems from the fact that we have confirmations from two different agents. Clearly, they made the mistake somehow."

A loud crashing sound from outside just before the lights went out interrupted their conversation. Cody sprang to his feet and raced toward the window. After jumping up on the bench, he put his front feet on the windowsill. The fire in the stove provided sufficient light for the two women to make it to the window to peer into the darkness. "What do you see, Cody?" Lee asked the purely rhetorical question of the dog. She turned to Kate. "I guess Cody isn't talking tonight. What about you, can you see anything?"

Kate smiled. "He's the strong silent type. I can't see anything. You?"

"No. Probably a tree fell and it took out an electrical wire as it went down. What about you, Cody? See anything?"

Kate smiled at Lee. "I'm glad to see I'm not the only one who talks to the dog like I expect an answer." She glanced back outside. "Think anybody is at the realtor's office? I think there was an emergency number to call. I doubt we'll get anybody there tonight. Let me get my cell and we'll give them a try." Kate turned her cell on. "I don't have any bars. You?"

"I had really sketchy service down by my car. We're higher here though so it won't hurt to check." Lee got her phone. "Nope. Nothing on mine, either."

Kate shrugged. "I guess we're stuck with each other, at least until tomorrow when we can get hold of someone."

Lee nodded. "It could be lots worse. You could be a hairy guy with a penchant for burping, passing gas, and picking lint from his navel."

A laugh burst from Kate in response to Lee's unexpected comment. "Well, there's no argument from me on that point."

"Let's see if we can find some candles, a flashlight, or maybe a lantern," Lee suggested.

"At least we have the wood stove. With the electric off we've no heat other than that. Our next problem is water for flushing the john. There's a water storage tank in the bathroom, so we will probably be okay for a day or so."

"Aren't there any emergency instructions anywhere?"

They began a search of the cabin, each collecting supplies that might be helpful. They found a stock of candles and matches, a battery-powered lantern, and under the sink, several gallons of water in plastic bottles.

"Hey, here's a note on how to use the generator." Kate carried the instructions to the table.

"What generator?"

Kate pointed to the note in her hand. "It says there's a generator located under the deck that will supply power to run the well pump, the fridge and a light or two. If it's okay with you, I'd suggest we deal with that tomorrow. We should be okay for now if we're careful with the water."

Lee summarized. "So, we're stuck here, no capability to contact the realtors, limited water till tomorrow, no heat other than from the wood stove, and no chance to get out of here until the road is plowed."

Kate nodded.

"All in all, it could be much worse," she said flashing a bright smile. "We're warm, we're dry, we have sufficient food, and pleasant company."

"A positive attitude. I like that." A broad grin spread across Kate's face. "I'd have to agree with your assessment. It could be worse indeed, a lot worse."

"Let's see what we can come up with for dinner. I'm hungry. You?"

They agreed to not open the fridge until they had to. After they ate salsa and taco chips, they each made a peanut butter and jelly sandwich. "Well, not necessarily the most healthy, still it was a fun meal. I will admit that I enjoyed it."

Kate took exception. "Now wait just a minute. We had whole grain with the bread and chips," she pointed to the taco chips, "...vegetables in the form of tomatoes, peppers, onions, and cilantro. The jelly is our fruit, and protein was provided by the peanut butter. I mean, technically, tomatoes are a fruit...I just can't bring myself to call them that."

"I thought I was the queen of rationalization. Here, I surrender my crown. You definitely deserve it." Lee laughed as she mimed removing a crown from her head and pretended to hand it to Kate.

"So, tell me about yourself, Lee, where you are from, what do you do...hobbies, whatever."

"I live in Connecticut, in Groton. I'm a Marine Biologist." Lee smiled. "As for whatever, I enjoy anything done around water. Kayaking, canoeing, snorkeling, diving, you get the drift."

"Pardon the bad humor, but aren't you a bit of a fish out of water here?"

"I was looking for a change." Lee arched her brows and glanced towards the windows. "I'm not sure I was looking for quite this much change. We could conclude that this precipitation is just a frozen form of water. That means I'm sticking within my element."

Kate smiled and Lee grinned back. "Usually, I vacation with my boss, Angus, and his wife, Fiona. They have a home in the Florida Keys. So we go there whenever we can to do research for our next book."

"Next book?"

"Yeah, we finished one and are working on the next one now. I slowed us down by taking off a few years to get my doctorate. I haven't had a vacation that didn't involve work in..." Lee stopped to consider how long it had really been. "Well, I guess in forever."

"So, you decided to vacation here to this specific area. Why?"

"There's a Shaker village near here that I visited once before when I attended a seminar. Unfortunately, it's closed this time of year or I'd go back. When I was here last time I spent so much time in the village while I wasn't attending meetings, that I didn't have time to see anything else around here. I decided that I liked the area and that if I had another opportunity, I'd come back to see what I missed before. That and the fact that the cabin was inexpensive."

"Even more so now that they have to return at least some of our money."

Lee nodded. "Right. I didn't think of that."

"So, it's Doctor Foster then. Why Shakers?"

All too aware of the conversation she had with her friend Brian before she left, about the Shakers and sexual frustration, Lee replied, "I guess, at first, I became curious about their furniture. I wanted to know who created such beautiful things, so I started to read about it and became interested in them as a society. There are several villages located in New England—in New Hampshire, Maine, and here in Massachusetts. I started to learn about the society's beliefs and found them extremely interesting. For their time, they were considered a progressive society because they believed in the women and men being equal. They also believed in separation of the sexes. Each sex was housed in separate areas although they ate, worshiped, and worked together. The village in Canterbury, New Hampshire is probably one of the most peaceful places I've ever been."

"More peaceful than here in the dark, in the snow?" Kate chuckled. "Hard to believe."

"Well, we'll see. It looks like we're stuck with each other for a day or two, at least, so I can let you know how this compares."

"Actually, I don't mind the company. It's been pleasant enough so far." Kate shifted in her chair. "You know, if anyone ever asked, I'd say I don't mind living alone. Being on vacation by myself though is um, I don't know, it's somehow different. Do you agree?" Kate paused, raising her shoulders in a gesture of resignation. "I guess it's nice to have someone to share thoughts with, and a definite step up from talking to myself."

"Thank you, I definitely agree."

"Although having Cody is companionship, life on one's own can sometimes get lonely." Kate stood up to tend the fire again, giving it a few pokes and stimulating the blaze brighter before placing another log on the coals.

Lee watched Kate as she fussed with the fire thinking how open Kate was, how easily she divulged information about herself. *So different from Kendra,* she thought.

Finished with the fire, Kate retrieved her cup. "More tea?"

"Yes, that would be nice."

***

Kate reheated the kettle, thankful for the gas stove. She leaned against the kitchen cabinets as she waited for the water to boil, admiring the view of Lee in front of the fire. Lee was busy rummaging through her backpack, which gave Kate an opportunity to study her unobserved. She had to admit Lee was an attractive woman, very attractive. Not only was the physical package appealing, with her trim athletic looking body, but she also had a quick wit and warm way about her. Kate wanted to know more about the woman. The kettle whistled and Kate made their tea.

Kate carried the tea in and handed a cup to Lee. "Tell me more about the Shakers. What you told me so far is interesting. Where did you learn about them?"

"Well, first from visiting the villages, of course, where I learned a lot first hand via the tours." Eyes twinkling, she added, "Afterwards I used the source from which all modern day knowledge flows, the Internet."

Kate rewarded the charming woman's humor with a hearty laugh.

"Later, as my interest grew, I read a few books on the subject. The Shakers were credited with many inventions. I'd imagine you've seen their ladder-back chairs. During my tours I learned that they are credited with inventing clothespins, steam driven washing machines, several different farming machines, oh, and the regular flat broom we use today. They're also quite famous for their basketry. When I visited the villages, I saw examples of their work. There were many other inventions, very few of which they ever patented. Their furniture designs are simple and functional, while at the same time being very beautiful. The buildings are wonderful. I especially like the round barns."

"Interesting." Kate finished the final sip of her tea. "Why did they call them Shakers?"

"They were supposedly given the name Shakers because many of them trembled during worship services. The lecturer on one of my tours told us that the shaking was the result of their religious zeal. Some people in our group joked it was from the fact that the women and men slept in dormitories that kept the sexes separate and ensured their celibacy."

"Celibacy, really? How did they continue to flourish if there was no sex? No sex must have meant a real shortage of little Shakers, right?"

"That's a great question, Kate. There were obviously converts to the community. Some of them joined and brought their children with them. Interestingly, they provided homes to many orphans. The community assumed the responsibility for raising each orphan they adopted. This included teaching them several trades. When they reached adulthood, they were given a choice. They could remain or opt to leave to make their way in the world outside of the community."

Kate collected their empty cups, carried them into the kitchen, and placed them into the sink. "Well, the community certainly prepared them to survive if they were trained to have several trades. I've never heard any of this before. I assume that it was hard to recruit people to such a strict community committed to that sort of deprivation." While she was up, she tossed another couple of logs on the fire and poked at them until they lit.

"Yes, that was part of it. The changes that occurred to the adoption laws that prohibited adoption by religious organizations had an even bigger impact. I don't remember what year that was but, as a result of the changes in the law, they could no longer offer to provide homes to the orphans. Little by little their numbers declined. Two very elderly sisters, the last two members of their community, lived in Canterbury for many years. They are both long gone now." Lee sighed. "It's too bad the place here is closed now. I'd love to go back."

"Now that you've told me about the Shakers, you've piqued my interest, Lee. I'm disappointed that the village is closed this time of year, too. It sounds like something I'd enjoy visiting."

"You can always come back when they're open."

"True, but getting away isn't always easy for me." Kate stood. "I'm going to take Cody out, check on the weather, and bring in some more wood for tomorrow. We should have enough dry wood for tonight."

"I'll help."

The weather was horrible. Snow was accumulating very quickly and the wind was still howling. They finished bringing in the wood from the porch. Lee said, "I'm glad you stacked this here this afternoon. I'd hate to have to go all the way to the woodpile to drag wood in here in this weather."

Lee shrugged out of her jacket. Kate reached out her hand for Lee's coat and hung it on the back of the door. She shook the snow off herself, hung her jacket next to Lee's, and dried off Cody who, now used to the routine, sat patiently waiting for his mistress.

"Kate, teach me how to do the fire. It's not fair that you have to do it all the time."

"It could cost you later if I have to share my fire making skills." Her eyes twinkled and a smile played on her lips as she glanced over at Lee.

"Cost me? How so? I'm already indebted to you for rescuing me. And I'm going to impose again to get you to take me to my car when we dig ourselves out of here tomorrow." Suddenly a smile spread across Lee's face. "Okay, I've saved my best for last. I have chocolate..."

"Hmm. Now you're talking. There's almost nothing I won't do for chocolate." Kate paused and carefully considered her previous sentence. "Is that proper grammar? What I mean is that I'd do almost anything for chocolate."

"I got it. So, will you teach me about the fire in exchange for some chocolate?"

Pausing, Kate considered the offer. "How much chocolate?"

"Half of what I have." Lee reached for her pack.

"Let's get more specific. Are we talking half of a pound, a bar, or a piece?"

Lee sighed and Kate stopped teasing, tentatively resting her hand on Lee's shoulder. "Yes, I'd be happy to teach you. You don't even have to bribe me. If you'd like to share I'd be appreciative." She flashed the most sincere smile she could muster in Lee's direction.

Lee just shook her head. "I never know when to take you seriously." From her pack, she produced a bag full of assorted individually wrapped chocolates, which she dangled enticingly in front of Kate.

"I think I'm in love with you."

Lee's eyes met Kate's briefly. Lee gestured towards the fire with her head. "Prove it."

Kate spent the next few minutes instructing Lee on the finer points of managing the fire, after which they each picked a piece of chocolate from the bag.

"So, Kate. Tell me your story. So far, you know all about me, and I know nothing about you. What do you do for a living?"

"I'm a veterinarian." Kate leaned back in the recliner. "I live in Farmington, Pennsylvania. A little while ago I sold part of my practice to the other two vets that have been working with me. It's why I'm able to get away on this trip. I can't tell you the last time I had two weeks in a row off—probably never, now that I think about it."

"Anyone special in your life?"

Kate's eyes snapped up. "Yes, Cody."

"You?"

"No, not any more. I don't even have a dog."

"Well, Cody doesn't think he's a dog." Hearing his name, Cody jumped up onto Kate's lap, turned around three times before he settling into a round ball. He heaved a big sigh that caused them both to laugh.

"Would that we all could be so easily satisfied."

"How true," Kate replied.

"So why did you choose this area?"

"I did a web search on mountain cabins for rent, and this one popped up first on the list. I had to look up on a map where it was. After I started to research things to do in this area it seemed a good place to visit. My needs are simple. I can be happy almost anywhere, as long as I have some time to just relax. I've had a...well let's just say I needed a change of pace. I'm tired. It's been a relief to sell some of my practice and not to have to pull the load entirely by myself. It's too late for me to do something different in my life even though, sometimes, I wish I could call a 'do over' and have a second shot at things. Don't get me wrong. I love being a vet. I used to love my job when I first started practicing. We had a primarily large animal practice. It was very different then. I love working with the animals. A small animal practice is different. It's the people who can sometimes be difficult. All the responsibilities of owning the practice can be daunting, too. It was much simpler when I was just an employee and not the owner." Kate shrugged. "And if I were to be totally honest, I guess I'd wish other, personal aspects of my life could be different."

"Don't we all. It's never too late to make a change, Kate."

"Maybe. It's no good to simply run away though. I think you need to run toward something new, not away from what is. Know what I mean?"

Lee nodded. "Yes, I do."

They spent the next several minutes staring into the flames of the fire. "Before we go to sleep," Kate said, "I'll show you how to bank the fire so it'll last longer."

It suddenly dawned on both of them that there was only one bedroom. Sensing Lee's reaction to her statement, Kate offered, "There's only one bed upstairs. I can sleep down here on the recliner."

"Don't be silly, I'll stay down here. You take the bed."

"Maybe we're both being silly. As the fire dies down, it'll get cold in here without the electric heat. Both of us will be warmer and more comfortable if we share. It's a good sized bed."

"I agree. We can manage. It's just one night."

They spent the next couple of hours in idle conversation, talking about their jobs and the towns in which they lived. Their shared time passed enjoyably, with animated conversation interspersed with laughter.

Lee began to yawn. "Sorry, it's been a long day. Maybe you can show me what to do with the fire before I go upstairs?"

Kate taught Lee how to bank the fire in the stove. They took turns using the bathroom before heading upstairs to get into bed.

Neither woman was able to stand up fully in the loft. "Geez, this place is really compact. I think I'd have to go downstairs to change my mind. It doesn't matter though, since the only clothes other than the wet ones that I have hanging up down there are the sweats I'm wearing."

Kate tossed an oversized T-shirt in Lee's direction. "Here, I have an extra with me." Kate sat on the edge of the bed to pull off her jeans.

Lee turned her back to give Kate some privacy as she quickly changed into the borrowed nightwear and slid into bed. She felt the bed shake as Kate slipped into the bed next to her.

"Will Cody be okay down there by himself?"

"I guess. I didn't think you'd appreciate having to sleep with my dog. It's bad enough you're stuck sleeping with me."

"No more stuck than you are."

"Well you have a point there." Kate chuckled. "I'll admit that sleeping with a dog can be an acquired taste."

"Is he warm?"

"Like a little hot water bottle."

"In that case, by all means let's get him in here with us. I'm freezing! Will he come if we call him, Kate?"

"Yes."

They both called his name at the same time. The small ball of energy came bounding up the stairs and with a daring leap he landed squarely in the middle of the bed. After giving each of them joyful kisses he settled on the bed between them.

"Why do I think we'll be the ones keeping him warm?"

Kate smiled. "Give him a minute, you'll see."

During the night, as the fire waned, Cody's position between them was infringed upon as Kate and Lee, completely unaware in sleep, moved towards each other seeking warmth. Cody ended up sleeping at their feet.

CHAPTER 19

DAY TWO – SATURDAY

NORMALLY AN EARLY RISER, Kate woke up at her regular time. It took her a brief moment to realize where she was. It was freezing cold. She and Lee were pressed together, back to back. Deep, even breathing indicated that Lee was still asleep. *She's a quiet sleeper. None of that racket Max used to make.* She hadn't thought about Max for...how long? Well, a long time. She'd been gone five years—only about three years less then they'd been together.

It felt strange being in bed with another woman, a darned attractive woman at that. She wondered what Lee's reaction would be if she knew that she'd spent the night in bed with a lesbian. Since Max's departure, Kate had made it a point to never hide or deny her sexual identity although she still didn't advertise it either. The only subtle public acknowledgement of her sexuality came in the form of the necklace she wore that Kyle had given her for her birthday the year he opened his own practice. It was a small gold pendant with her initials on one side and the number '1138' engraved on the other side. When she questioned the significance of the number he explained, "It's purported to be the number of rights the federal government denies us by prohibiting same sex marriage. It is something we all need to remember and fight to overcome."

Kate glanced at the clock on the dresser. Ten past five. Setting an alarm was something Kate rarely had to do. She seemed to naturally wake up between five and five-thirty every morning. *I'd better get up and check the fire. Hopefully there are enough coals left I won't have to start another one from scratch.* Kate exhaled a long sigh.

"You awake?" Lee whispered in a hushed tone.

The question startled Kate. She moved away and turned onto her back. Lee did the same.

"Yes, sorry." Kate said referring to the close and intimate position they were in when they had awakened. "I guess we were both cold."

"Yes. And Cody abandoned us."

"I think we probably edged him out." Kate raised her head. "He's at the bottom of the bed."

Hearing his name mentioned was enough to cause Cody to jump up. He walked across each of them seeking attention and affection.

"Ooooh, Cody. How many times have I, your special person, tried to teach you to not step on my bladder in the morning?"

Lee laughed. "Man, it's cold in here."

"I've been debating about getting up to put some wood on the fire but didn't want to wake you. It's probably tropical up here, compared to downstairs. Heat rises."

"The wind is still blowing." Lee looked towards the window. "Wonder how much snow we got. There was at least a foot last night when we went out to get the wood. It's still too dark to see."

"I'll check it when I let Cody out and let you know." Kate shivered as she tossed the blankets back. "Brr! Well, shall we brave the elements and go down to get a fire started, or do you want to sleep some more? I can handle the fire."

"No, I'll come with you. I'm normally up around this time. I love the mornings. I like to go in to work early to beat the others there. That first hour and a half at my desk, you know, the time before everyone else arrives, is the most productive part of my day."

"Yes, I know exactly what you mean. Okay, let's do it." Kate groaned as her feet hit the cold floor.

Each woman shuddered as they got up and faced the cold air. They would have laughed had they known that identical thoughts drifted through each of their heads, Lee's of Kendra and Kate's of Max. Neither of their previous partners had been an early riser.

Quickly dressing in yesterday's clothes, Kate used a flashlight to light the way and the two women headed downstairs. They lit the candles and lantern. Kate went immediately to the stove while Lee put water on to boil for their tea. "We're lucky the stove is gas. At least we can cook."

"Yes, true." Kate grinned when she found enough coals remaining to start the fire roaring with little effort. "I'm glad we stocked up the wood box. Everything dried out overnight."

With the fire roaring in the stove, Kate gave it a final poke before she stood to take Cody out. It was only a matter of minutes until she returned to make quick work of drying him off before she settled in front of the fire next to Lee. Her tea, prepared exactly the way she liked it, was waiting for her when she sat in the recliner. Cody jumped into Lee's lap, turned around three times, and settled down. Lee pulled the comforter from the back of her chair and covered the two of them, careful to leave Cody's head out from under the blanket. She glanced up to find Kate's eyes on her, a smile on her lips.

"What?"

"Nothing. He likes you."

"Good. I like him. He's warmer than you are." Lee blushed at the spontaneous comment that had just popped out.

"Really? It wasn't him you were cuddled up to this morning." It was Kate's turn to blush.

"Well, in survival training, don't they teach you to share body heat?"

Several responses came to Kate's mind including how she could think of several ways to generate more body heat in bed with the lovely woman sitting next to her. This time, instead of blurting out the first thought in her head, she controlled herself. "I'm sure they do," she replied casually.

"Would you mind handing me my tablet from my bag?" Lee pointed to her knapsack. "I don't want to disturb Cody."

"Sure. God forbid we disturb the dog." Kate shook her head.

"Is that wrong?"

Kate smiled. "No, not at all. I can't tell you how many times I've done something or avoided doing something just so he wouldn't be inconvenienced. I like that you like and are kind to him. Obviously, he appreciates it, too."

After adding another couple of logs on top of the fire, Kate poked them into the exact position she wanted them. With Lee's tablet in one hand and hers in the other, Kate returned to her seat next to Lee in front of the fire. They sat near the stove enjoying the heat in companionable silence, sipping their tea, and reading on their tablets.

A short time later, Kate got up and took their cups to the kitchen where she reheated the kettle of water. "I'm going to wash up. There should be enough water here for both of us. Once the sun comes up, we can tackle the generator and run the well pump and maybe the heat so we can warm up the place."

"That sounds good. I'll wash up and brush my teeth as soon as you finish."

Finished in the bathroom, Kate grabbed a throw and settled in what had become her recliner while Lee took her turn washing up. Joining Kate in front of the fire Lee teased. "I see Cody already abandoned me."

"He's very loyal. I don't mean to me particularly, just to his personal needs."

"I can see that." She directed her gaze at Cody. "Hey Mister Any Port In A Storm, my fair weather friend." She ruffled his head as she passed by on her way to her recliner.

A couple of hours passed. When Cody stirred and glanced towards the window Kate said, "Hey, listen. Is that a chainsaw I hear?"

"Yes, I think so. Let's go check it out."

Kate folded the comforter down and Cody jumped to the floor.

Despite a few sporadic flurries that appeared for a few minutes at a time, it appeared that the worst of the snow was over. "Wow!" Kate surveyed the drifted snow trying to figure out how much they'd received. "The snow is really deep. Must be about sixteen or eighteen inches."

Cody was having a ball running and jumping in the snow. "Look at him," Lee said. "He seems to love this weather. If he were two feet taller he'd look like a husky."

"Shhh...he's sensitive about his height."

They were still laughing when they reached the end of the driveway. The road had already been plowed, and the road crew was working on the tree that had taken out their electricity. Using the shovel she'd brought with her from the porch, Kate started by cleaning off her car adding to the snow on the ground. With the car clear of the accumulation of snow, she shoveled around the perimeter of the vehicle while Lee went to talk to the guys working on the tree.

Lee returned to share the information she'd learned. "It seems that there are a number of wires and trees down in the area. The mayor of the town lives at the end of this road, which is probably why we got plowed right away. They hope to have power restored later today or tomorrow at the latest."

Gesturing towards the car, Kate asked, "Want to help finish digging out the car? If we can dig mine out, maybe we can go down and get yours out, too. At the very least you can get the rest of your clothes and belongings out of the car."

"That would be great. Maybe when we finish with that chore, we can call the realtor's office about the mix up with the rentals."

Kate nodded her agreement, handed Lee the shovel she was using, and got her own out of the trunk. After they dug out the car, they tackled the area of the driveway between the car and the road. They still had to deal with the huge pile of snow the plow left at the end of the driveway. Staring at the pile blocking the access to the street Kate said, "This is almost four feet deep."

"I don't think we'll be able to get through this with just shovels." Lee returned to the guys who were just finishing up the tree. She returned with a huge smile on her face. "They're going to move the worst of this for us with their plow. Then they'll help us get my car out."

"Sweet! I don't know how you feel, but I'm tired of shoveling already." Kate glanced around. "This is a hell of a lot of snow."

They dug out Lee's car after they cleared the drive. By the time they cleared a path wide enough to allow Lee to get her vehicle back onto the main road, it was nearly eleven. The two guys who helped them, Jimmy and Joe, refused Lee's offer of money. "Buy us a beer next time you see us in town." They waved cheerfully as they drove off.

Kate and Lee drove back to the cabin. Working in unison, they cleared a spot for Lee's car next to Kate's and shoveled a path from the cars to the house. "At least we don't need to wade thigh deep through this stuff to get to our cars now."

They warmed up, had something to eat, and tried to contact the realtor's office. Kate had no service at all, and Lee's phone showed only one bar that flickered off and on. Kate suggested, "Why don't we just drive down to town and see if we can find the place."

"Let's take your car. It's four-wheel drive, right? My front wheel drive isn't bad in the snow, but I'm willing to bet that yours is probably better."

Kate stopped at the gas station to fill up the gas tank and ask directions. They did as instructed and found the realtor's office without incident. They had to park on the street in front of the office because the lot was still snow covered and there appeared to be no life inside the building.

Lee, who was able to get a better signal on her phone, tried calling the agent. "There's a message," she told Kate as she listened to the tape.

Kate waited patiently while Lee listened.

"Can you believe this? The office is closed until Monday morning. Wait, here comes the beep." Lee left a message explaining the mix-up with the booking. She left her cell number, asking for a return call as soon as possible. "Well, I guess that's all we can do for now."

Kate looked the area over. "Want to have some lunch here and walk around town a bit? Maybe they'll check messages at lunch time and call you back."

They found a little family style restaurant on the main street that was crowded with people. Apparently the snowstorm had brought a number of people to the area, all of them eager to avail themselves of the winter activities provided by the freshly fallen powder.

While waiting for their lunch, Kate commented about how quickly the town was clearing the snow from streets and sidewalks. "Back home, a storm of this magnitude would cripple us for the weekend, at least."

"Tell me more about where you live in Pennsylvania."

Taking a couple of extra napkins from the dispenser on the table, Kate handed one to Lee and kept the other for her own use. "I live in a little town a little less than two hours northeast of Philadelphia. It's a beautiful location. Before I moved there it was mostly rural, and a large portion of our practice consisted mostly of visits to the local farms in the area. Not too long after I was hired, it had already begun to change. One by one, the smaller farms sold off and were replaced by housing developments. As the nature of the community changed, our practice had to adapt. We began to provide services to more domestic pets than we did to the larger farm animals. I was amazed to learn that Pennsylvania loses something like forty acres of farmland a day. It's had a huge impact on our practice."

The waitress brought their meals, and they began to eat.

Lee sprinkled salt on her potatoes. "So you miss working with the larger animals?"

"I think I mentioned that last night. I guess I do. Not that I don't like the little guys. It's just that my job is very different now than it was when I trained. I focused a large number of my electives in large animal care. I even volunteered at a wild animal sanctuary for a while when I was in school, something I continue to do today. I love it. It's really interesting. Originally, my area of specialization in large animals is what landed me my job. The vet who hired me and I both had to adapt as the community changed."

"Have you ever thought about moving?"

"Sure. At this point in my career it's hard to change. I'm established where I am. I owned the place with my partner, another woman vet. I bought her out when she left for something she felt would better suit her. When it was too much for me to handle on my own, I sold shares to the two other vets I'd been working with. So now, I still own just over a fifty percent share. I'm comfortable with that arrangement."

"Comfortable yes, but are you happy?"

Kate shrugged. "I'm not unhappy." She was quiet for a moment. "I guess that I've settled for being not unhappy for so long that I'm not exactly sure how happy would feel. What about you, are you happy?"

"Hard to say. For the most part, I guess I am. Sometimes, I'm lonely. I like my job, have good friends and, I guess, like you, I'm comfortable."

"I'm sometimes lonely, too." Kate shocked herself at the next admission. "Would you think I'm a total whack job if I admit that I'm not the least bit upset about the mix-up with the bookings? I've been enjoying the time we've spent together. I mean, it's nice to be away from work and all. At home, at least there are friends around for my off time. When one travels alone, the fact that it's a paired world is even more evident than when on familiar, home turf."

"No, I don't think you're a whack job, as you put it. I actually agree with you. I mean, think about it this way—if we took a cruise or a tour, don't they often pair you up with a stranger if you want to avoid the single supplement?"

"Good point." Kate took a sip of water and wiped her mouth with the napkin.

"I mean, we just had that done to us without our knowledge or agreement."

Kate ate the last bite of her sandwich. "One minor problem, we each paid full fare for this trip. I wonder what the story is with the error and how long it'll take them to figure out what happened."

Lee pulled her cell from her pocket. "Before we head back to the cabin, I'll check to see if the realtor returned the call."

While Lee made the call, Kate paged through the local paper that she'd picked up on her way out of the restaurant. There had been no call back from the realtor, so they headed back to the cabin. Once there they spent some time playing with Cody who seemed quite annoyed at being left in the cabin alone. His disposition brightened after he had some attention. Kate confessed, "He's very spoiled because he gets to be with me most days. He doesn't like it when I leave him alone."

"I bet. He's lucky he's able to be with you all the time. Uh, I mean, lucky being with his person." Lee turned towards the cabin. "Are there any chores we need to do right now?"

Quickly reviewing possible tasks, Kate shook her head. "Other than tackling the generator, none I can think of. The guys told us the power should be back on later this afternoon, so maybe we should let that wait until later in hopes we won't have to deal with it. If the power doesn't come on, we need to fire it up to fill the water tank so we can take a shower. Other than that nothing to do that I can think of. Why do you ask?"

"I just wondered if there's nothing that needs doing, would you mind if I do some work? I have a pile of pictures to sort through. I need to pick out the ones I want to use for this chapter of the book my boss and I are working on."

"No, I don't mind at all. Can I help you?"

"Umm, I'm not sure, but that's sweet of you to offer, Kate. I have a ton of photos I've collected over time that I just threw in a box. I haven't taken the time to organize them. If they were organized, it might make selection easier."

"If you show me what you want, maybe I could organize them for you while you work."

Later, settled in front of the stove, Lee demonstrated how she wanted the pictures arranged. Kate looked through some of the photos and began sorting them into categories Lee had requested. "I'm appreciative that you're willing to do a job I hate doing," Lee said. As Kate set to work on the photos, Lee got out the printed proof copy of the book and began to read, adjust, and simplify the text. "I'm looking for a picture of a coral formation I took last year. It's memorable because I stupidly got a picture of my own foot in the photo. I can crop that out though, I think."

"I remember that photo. I put it in this pile here." In just a few seconds, Kate located the picture and handed it over. "Okay, what's next?"

Lee smiled. "I love your enthusiasm about this job I hate. I need a picture of a snook."

"Okay. I would gladly produce that for you if I knew what it looked like. Can you describe it?"

"Sorry. A snook is a fish. A dark stripe down the length of its side is a distinguishing mark, plus its lower jaw protrudes forward." Lee demonstrated.

"This one?"

"Yes, that's it. Next up is a George Creavalle. It has kind of a big, rounded forehead. The picture I have has a description of that one as a fish looking like he's having a bad day. He looks cranky."

Kate laughed. "I never thought of fish having a bad day before, or of having expression. I have a friend at home who is a semi-vegetarian."

"What's that?"

"She only eats veggies and living things that don't have expression. She includes fowl and fish. I'm going to have to tell her about this fish."

"Ha. I'll even give you a copy of the photo to prove your point."

The two women worked for over an hour sorting and locating photos as Lee needed them. As they collaborated on the task, Lee told Kate stories of the research she and Angus had conducted.

"What's this picture here, Lee?"

"Which one?" Lee checked the photo Kate held up.

"Is this deer really this small, or is it just perspective?"

"Oh, that's a Key deer. They are really quite tiny, like a good-sized dog, maybe two or so feet tall at the shoulder. They were very endangered although through conservation efforts in the Keys, their numbers have rebounded. There's a refuge for them not far from where Angus and his wife, Fiona, have their place."

"Interesting. I've never heard of them." Realizing the ambiguity of her statement, Kate clarified her meaning, "Key deer, I mean."

"I know. Say, I'm at a good stopping point now. Want some dinner?"

Just at that moment, the lights all came on and the well pump hummed, a welcome sound.

"Hey! Perfect timing." Lee stood up and began searching through the kitchen pantry. They agreed on pasta and a salad for dinner and worked as a team to prepare the meal.

"At least we won't freeze to death tonight" Lee smiled as she made her comment.

"Oh, come on, it wasn't that bad, was it."

"No, not at all. I'm still glad there were three of us to help keep warm."

After they ate, they each got out their tablets to do some reading. "Lee? Do you like to play Scrabble?"

"Sure."

"Want to play?"

"Yes, that would be fun. No Internet here though, so we'll have to pass back and forth. Yours, or mine?"

Lee said, "We can use mine. I already have the app open."

They began to play, chatting as they made their moves, passing the tablet back and forth. Kate handed the tablet to Lee. "Do you ski?"

"Me? Of course, I water ski all the time when we're at the Keys. Why?"

"No, not water ski—snow ski."

"Oh, duh! No, I never tried it. Why? Do you?"

"I enjoy it," Kate said. "Would you like to try it tomorrow? There's a ski area in Hancock. It should be less than half an hour from here."

"Yes. Hancock is where the Shaker Village is. Too bad it's not open. I'd love to share it with you." Lee returned to the topic. "Sure, I'm game to give skiing a try. Will you teach me?" Lee returned the game after she made her move.

"Yes, I'd love to. That would be fun."

"Darn," Kate exclaimed. "You just beat me. I think all this chatter was to distract me so you could win our game of Scrabble."

"So, you figured out my methods. I guess you won't fall for that next time."

"Not a chance." Lee laughed then checked her watch. "Should we have an early night tonight so we can get an early start tomorrow?"

"Cody will be mad at us again tomorrow for leaving him."

"Will he be okay here alone?" Lee asked.

Kate appreciated Lee's concern for her pet. "Yes. We can make it a short day. He can easily go for eight hours without going out, although I try not to make him wait that long on the rare occasions when he's not with me."

***

Lee showered first. Kate had to look away when she came out of the shower fearing that Lee would see the look on her face that Kate was sure would express the desire she was feeling. There were several times during that day that Kate had to remind herself that Lee, who was probably straight, wouldn't welcome any physical contact. *How would Lee react if she learned that she was sleeping with a lesbian?*

Now finished with her shower, Lee sat at the table working on her book while Kate read on her tablet in front of the fire. Every now and again, Kate glanced over at Lee as she worked. Lee had an adorable habit of pursing her lips and tapping them with her pen as she thought about what she wanted to write. Kate added that mannerism to a mental list of the others that she'd noticed during their day together and while she worked. When frustrated, Lee would run the fingers of both hands through her hair and exhale a long sigh. Then there was that thing she did with her tongue as she licked her lips. No, she really didn't lick her lips. That was what other people did. Lee moistened hers with just the tip of her tongue. The gesture made Kate's insides melt each time she did it.

Before they went up to bed, Kate took her shower. It was warmer in the bedroom now that the heat was on, and they spent an uneventful night. Neither woman sensed that the other was equally disappointed by the space between them in the bed.

CHAPTER 20

DAY THREE - SUNDAY

THE NEW DAY DAWNED bringing sunshine and crisp weather. A bonus of the better weather was improved cell service. They checked for voicemail and found that the realtor had returned the call. She apologized profusely for the agency's error, told them she would investigate what had gone wrong, and asked them to meet her Monday morning at the office. Before the end of the message, she apologized again and promised them she would make things right. "I'll try to get hold of Missy and will call you later as soon as I can figure out what happened."

Business out of the way until the next day, Kate said, "It's a great day. Ski conditions should be perfect. Interested in joining me?"

"If you'll give me some instruction. I'm usually trainable."

"Not a problem. It'll be my pleasure."

Lee, naturally athletic and fit, proved to be a quick and able learner on the slopes later that morning. By lunchtime, she admitted to being tired. "I bet I've fallen and clawed myself back to a standing position three hundred times."

"Nah, maybe two hundred."

Lee laughed, rubbing her backside and dusting the snow off her pants. "Regardless, I'm using an entirely different group of muscles than

I'm accustomed to using. Whenever you want to head back to the cabin to let Cody out, I'm ready."

"You're sweet for thinking of him." Kate had enjoyed their day. She felt sorry for Lee every time she fell knowing that she'd be sore later. A purely selfish part of her was glad when Lee fell because it meant she could ski over, help her up, and dust the snow from her. She liked the feel of her hands on Lee's tight body. And she had to admit that she enjoyed the view skiing behind her down the beginner's hill that presented no challenge to her skiing abilities. It left her totally free to enjoy the view of Lee's derriere as she wiggled her way down the hill.

"I bet my backside is the color of a blueberry. The first two hours I spent more time on my ass than I did on the skis. I'd love to do it again though. I love this sport. You've been very kind to babysit me. Why don't I go inside for some hot chocolate and you take a couple of runs on the more challenging slopes."

"Thanks for offering. If you'd like, we can come back later in the week after you've had a chance to recover. It'll be less crowded mid-week and the wait at the lift won't be so long." Once in the car, Kate mentioned that she thought Cody would be happy to see them return early. Back at the cabin they took Cody out and played with him. He frolicked in the snow like a puppy.

"I'm sure you aren't as tired nor near as sore as I am" Lee said, rubbing her behind. "As a skilled skier, you didn't get to do the kind of skiing I'm sure you'd prefer. Thank you. I really appreciate you taking the time to teach me. I'd like to do it again so I can improve on the skills you taught me today."

"I think you certainly did work harder than I did today. I ski often enough at home that I didn't mind taking it easy today. Anyway, it was fun teaching you. If we go again, next time I can take a couple of the more difficult runs now that I know you're capable of making it to the bottom of the beginner's hill without killing yourself. I'm impressed. You have a natural athleticism and you follow instructions very well." Kate allowed her eyes to travel the length of Lee's body. "You're very fit."

"Thank you. I'm glad we'll have time to do it again before our vacation ends." Lee took a deep breath before she asked, "Kate, I've been thinking, um, maybe one day, if you're interested, I'd like to run down to Stockbridge to the Norman Rockwell Museum."

"That sounds like a good destination. I'd enjoy that, too." Kate replied, enthusiasm evident in the tone of her voice. "You know, in organizing my trip here, I planned a day at the museum in Pittsfield. Will you join me there? I think you'd probably enjoy it because they also have an aquarium there that we could visit. And when we were in town yesterday, I read in the local paper about a fundraiser bus trip offered by some local organization, for a group tour of the Storrowton Village. That could be fun. I know you like historic places. The Ventfort Hall tour would be another good place we could go, too. I read somewhere that J. P. Morgan built it for his sister, Sara, in the late eighteen hundreds. I love looking at old places like that."

"Kate, do you realize that without discussing the issue of our living arrangements, we've planned out nearly a week's worth of activities already?"

"I know." Kate watched Cody frolicking in the snow as they talked. "I'm looking forward to spending the week with you. This trip ended up being a lot more fun than I thought it would be. I'm enjoying having the company."

Lee's eyes drifted back towards the cabin. "Are we both just going to continue to stay here?"

Kate's eyes followed Lee's gaze. "It works for me. How about for you?"

Lee turned to meet Kate's eyes, but had to look away to not reveal too much. "Yes, it does."

"Cody and I welcome your company."

They finished playing with Cody and went inside to warm up. Lee made tea and Kate stoked the fire. As she worked, her thoughts wandered. The time she'd been spending with Lee had made Kate wish that there could be more between them, and not just physically. Living together in the small cabin, sleeping in the same bed, naturally incited a desire in Kate for more physical contact with Lee. Although she couldn't deny the physical attraction, there was more to it than just that. They were extremely compatible with each other. She enjoyed Lee's company, perhaps more than she should—it was so easy. Having already discounted the possibility of any kind of ongoing relationship, knowing that they lived too far apart to manage one, Kate pushed those thoughts aside. Even if it were possible, did she want to settle for a brief affair with Lee? Lee had given no indication about her sexuality other than a few off-handed comments about men. Kate knew she was attracted to Lee, but she couldn't come to any conclusion about Lee's sexuality. There were times that she felt there was a chance that Lee could be gay, or maybe bi, or at least open to something physical between them. She seemed comfortable with, almost welcoming of,

Kate's touch today as she brushed the snow off her.

In her own right, Lee was a physically demonstrative person who often reached out to touch Kate's hand or her shoulder as she made a point. Having never seen her interact with anyone else, Kate had no way of knowing if Lee was simply a naturally touchy person with everyone, or just with her. Even after three days alone together, Kate had nothing definitive that would lead her to a conclusion one way or the other. When Kate had looked through the pictures the day she helped sort them for Lee, she'd searched for clues, finding none. The only people in the photos had been of Lee's boss, Angus, and a woman Lee had identified as his wife, Fiona, No other men or women Kate might pair Lee with to give a clue as to her orientation.

Kate was drawn from her thoughts as Lee stood and stretched her arms above her head. Her shirt hiked just enough to allow a peek at Lee's firm stomach. Kate quickly moved her eyes from her breasts to her eyes when Lee said, "I'm going to take my shower, now. Do you need to use the facilities before I tie up the bathroom for a bit?"

"No, I'm good. I'll tidy up here and will take my shower after you finish up."

Lee's cell phone started to ring just as Kate came down the stairs from retrieving clean clothes. Lee called from the bathroom, "Kate, can you get that please. It's probably Mary Blackwell from the real estate office."

"Sure." Kate answered Lee's phone. "Hello, this is Dr. Kate Martin."

"Hello. Was it Kate? This is Kendra Harris. Lee neglected to tell me she was dating anyone. So she finally decided to move on. Good, it's about time. Good for her. How long has she been seeing you?"

Kate was so taken aback by the woman's attitude that she failed to respond with a denial. "Maybe you'd better speak with Lee. She's just finishing up her shower. Do you want to wait, or shall I have her return your call?"

Lee emerged from the bathroom in time to hear Kate's last words. "Here I am Kate. I can take the call. Who is it?"

"It's Kendra Harris for you." Kate handed the phone to Lee, whose hand trembled as she took it from her. Lee's face was flushed and a visible pulse pounded quickly in her neck.

"Thanks, Kate." Lee took the phone and walked toward the kitchen. She turned her back and lowered her voice as she answered.

"I'll give you some privacy." Kate gestured that she'd be upstairs. Going upstairs actually proved to provide Lee less privacy than if Kate had remained downstairs because Kate was now directly overhead and the hushed conversation Lee was having with Kendra was clearly discernible. Kate didn't really want to listen. Being in the confined space of the cabin made it impossible not to hear.

Lee's voice drifted up. "No, Kendra. We're not dating. I told you I just met her." There was a pause while Kendra obviously spoke. Lee responded. "No, that's not true. Anyway, what difference would it make if I were dating. We broke up over a year ago. How many women have you been through in that time? Why shouldn't I find someone new if I want to? You didn't want me."

Again there was a period where apparently Lee was listening to Kendra's response. "Okay, I know. You did want me, and you also wanted any number of other women at the same time. What I offered you simply wasn't enough."

Kate could hear Lee pacing from one end of the small kitchen to the other as she listened to the caller. Lee spoke again. "This is not the time or place to discuss this. In fact, there never will be a good time because you no longer have any claim to me, Kendra. Look, we've remained friends and I don't want that to change. We're done as lovers. You know that. In fact, if you'll recall, it was your idea."

Kate gathered her clothes for her shower a second time and turned toward the stairs. She didn't want to interrupt Lee, but thought maybe being in the shower would let Lee finish up her conversation with Kendra more privately. Kate crept down the stairs and slipped into the bathroom. As she closed the bathroom door she could hear Lee say quietly, "I don't know, the topic hasn't come up. I think she's straight."

Kate turned on the shower and let a long sigh escape as the water sluiced down her body. Well this sure puts a new and different wrinkle on things. *So, she's a lesbian. Moreover, she thinks I'm straight. Where the hell is her gaydar?*

Kate laughed out loud when the answering voice in her head responded, *probably the same place yours was.* Thoughts raced through her mind as she examined the possibilities. She definitely found Lee very attractive even though she'd never seriously considered the possibility Lee was a lesbian. Kate thought through the past several days with the perspective of this new knowledge. They were so compatible. She'd found Lee open, easy to talk to, fun to be with, easy going, intelligent, and companionable. In a way, she was glad they had some time getting to know each other before sexuality became the focus. Now that she knew about Lee, didn't she almost have to come out to her? *If I ever want to continue any kind of friendship with her, I need to let her know who I am. If I don't come out now, it would be awkward to come out at some future time, and it would seem dishonest.*

Kate turned off the shower, dried herself, and slipped into a pair of warm-ups and a sweatshirt. She combed her hair, brushed her teeth, and tidied the bathroom. Once she reached the conclusion that she needed to tell Lee about herself sooner rather than later, she faced her second challenge—how to tell her. Lastly, she needed to be clear about where they would go from here. Would there be expectations that they would both want more once she admitted she was a lesbian. Did she want there to be more? They were incredibly comfortable together. She enjoyed Lee's company and found her attractive. At this point, she wasn't being driven by lust alone. She chuckled. Well, maybe just a little.

Kate closed the lid to the toilet and sat down to consider her position. She had to admit that she'd come to care about Lee and had on more than one occasion wished they lived close enough to each other to continue their friendship. If they got involved, there was no future for them, was there? Kate wasn't able to move nor was Lee. So if anything happened between them it would be a fling with no promise of a tomorrow, much less a forever. It would be another 'love me till it is time to go' situation, much like all her other relationships. Did she want another love 'em and leave 'em relationship? Did she want a simple fling? All her life, all she'd ever wanted was a relationship with someone that would last forever or maybe one day longer than forever. What were her chances of finding someone long term in the small town she lived in? Being objective, pretty limited, she concluded. So, why not have some fun with Lee? After all, this opportunity seemed so coincidental—maybe it was just meant to be.

Kate had been celibate since Max left. At first she was too hurt and too busy. It had just become a habit. Her inner voice challenged...why not? *Why not, indeed? Maybe you can do a long distance thing, take trips with each other a couple times a year, you know, meet half way. At the very least, she and I can be friends—maybe even friends with benefits.*

After several minutes of internal debate, Kate admitted to herself that she wanted more than just two weeks of friendship with Lee. There was still that little voice inside who prodded *be brave...be bold. Be so not like you.* Once she'd decided she was going to say something, Kate wondered how to reveal her own identity to Lee.

Lee was pacing back and forth, and appeared deep in thought when Kate opened the door. As soon as she noticed Kate she approached. "I'm sorry. I know Kendra said something..."

Kate stilled Lee's apology with a gentle touch to her face. She drew her thumb across first her top then her bottom lip. "Shhh, it's okay." Kate stepped closer, put a hand on each of Lee's shoulders, and turned her around before moving her the two steps backward until she pinned Lee against the bathroom door. That's when she leaned into Lee and kissed her.

At first there was no response from Lee. After the initial shock wore off, she began to kiss Kate back. The kiss that had started as a sweet and gentle confession quickly heated into a passionate declaration of what each wanted and was willing to offer. Their tongues sought each other, tasting, testing. By the time they broke the kiss they were both breathing heavily.

Lee's expression showed her puzzlement. "Kate?"

"I figured it was the best way to tell you and to say, 'me too!' Was I wrong?"

"No, not wrong. I think I need you to tell me again." Lee wrapped her arms around Kate and pulled her close. Their bodies melded as they pressed into each other. The kiss they shared seemed so natural. There was none of the tentativeness sometimes so common to first kisses shared by new lovers. They kissed as if they had been doing it forever.

Kate pulled away first. "This is crazy, isn't it? Yet it somehow feels so right."

"Crazy? Maybe. Kate, I'm rarely, if ever, spontaneous. I'm a scientist. I have lists for everything. I would itemize my options if I planned to change my mind. And you...although you were definitely not on my agenda, I want this, Kate. I want you."

Kate let her kiss be her only response, indicating she felt the same. They started to move towards the stairs to the bedroom. Lee took Kate's hand and led the way up. At the edge of the bed, Lee pulled Kate towards her for another kiss as Kate's hands slipped under Lee's shirt seeking to touch her breasts. She'd been longing to feel them ever since she'd watched Lee stretch earlier.

Lee moaned as Kate's fingers found her. Her face showed her desire as she looked deeply into Kate's eyes. She leaned in for the kiss Kate offered. Trailing kisses up Kate's neck, her breath quickened with desire, she breathed into Kate's ear. "We should probably talk about what happens tomorrow."

"I know. Please, I don't want to talk about it. I want to make love to you and let tomorrow worry about itself." What began as a spark of attraction between them, quickly built to a bonfire.

Lee nodded. "It's what I want too, Kate. I need you. Please touch me."

Kate needed no encouragement. In a few brief seconds they had stripped their clothes and were under the covers wrapped together, moving against each other. Kate rolled on top of Lee and began to kiss her way down Lee's body. She used her hands, her teeth, and her tongue as she teased Lee into frenzy. In keeping with her personality, Kate was a generous lover who enjoyed taking her own satisfaction from the pleasure she was giving her partner as much as when her lover focused on her. She wanted to taste Lee, but paused long enough to ask, "What do you like? What pleases you?"

"You please me. Anything you do will please me."

The look of desire in Lee's eyes made Kate's reserve evaporate. Without hesitation, she slipped her fingers into Lee, one at first followed quickly by a second. Lee moaned as Kate started stroking slowly in and out. "Is that okay?"

"Umm. That feels so good. You feel so good. It's been so long." Lee trailed her nails up and down Kate's back as Kate again began to stroke. As Lee's hips rose to meet Kate's thrusts, she set the pace. Their eyes never lost contact. Lee exhaled a long slow breath just before she moaned in release and wrapped Kate tightly in her arms. "Kiss me."

Their kiss ended with Lee turning Kate onto her back. Kate answered, "Anything," when Lee asked what she wanted.

Lee kissed Kate's lips, her eyes, her ears, and neck. "I love the taste of your skin." She explored every sensitive area of Kate's body with her tongue and lips. As she entered Kate with her tongue her hands were busy elsewhere—always moving, stroking or stimulating Kate's breasts, her thighs, her legs. Kate felt that no part of her body had been neglected and she was totally satisfied as it responded, finally finding release in a shuddering orgasm.

They were quiet until their breathing returned to normal. Lee was the first to speak. "Thank you, Missy Green and Mary Blackwell."

The two lovers burst into peals of laughter. "Yes, I'll second that." Kate outlined Lee's lips with her finger. "Do you know that you've been driving me nuts every time you've licked your lips the past two days?"

"Really? I didn't think you'd even looked at me other than when we were having a conversation, and you never gave me any indication that you found me any more appealing than any other piece of scenery."

"I would say that, for a scientist, you're not very observant." Kate teased, a smile playing on her lips. "Brushing snow off of you every time you fell when we were skiing really had me going."

"Oh, this can't be a good sign. You're criticizing me already." Lee pinched Kate's nipple playfully.

"Ouch," Kate said feigning pain, restraining Lee's hand. "No, I'm just kidding. Honest...forgive me?"

"If I forgive your first transgression does that mean we can have make up sex?"

"You mean that wasn't enough? I must be out of practice."

"Oh Kate, we're just getting started. I haven't had sex in roughly well...over a year. I've got a lot of making up to do."

"Your year pales in comparison to my five. So was Kendra your last girlfriend?"

"Yes—first, last, and only. We have a weird relationship. We still loved each other when we broke up. I wasn't in love with her any more although I have to admit, in some ways, I still loved her." Lee, prompted by the look of concern that crossed Kate's face, responded. "Don't worry, she's history in terms of having to be concerned that I'll go back there. She has issues that I'm not sure she'll ever resolve and I can't live with. She'd be happy having a monogamous relationship with me as long as she didn't have to be monogamous. I have to give her credit where credit's due. I don't think she ever cheated on me while we were living together even though I know she struggled with it. She just isn't happy being a one woman kind of gal."

"You don't sound bitter."

"No, I guess I'm not. It hasn't been easy. It took us a while to finally admit it wouldn't work out when Kendra moved to Chicago."

Kate reacted with surprise. "She moved to Chicago and you were in Connecticut?"

"Yeah. I was still working on my doctorate and didn't want to leave school or my job. She hated her job. When she was offered a new position and work she thought she'd like better in Chicago, we agreed to try the long distance thing until I finished up my degree. I asked her to be patient and wait for me to finish. She struggled with monogamy when we were together. Being several states away was torture."

"So the long distance thing obviously didn't work out."

"No."

"I'm sorry it didn't work out. Obviously you cared for her deeply."

Lee smiled. "Thanks. I'm not sure that I am sorry. It wasn't exactly an easy relationship. She had a number of issues that prevented her from being happy. In the end, I'm happier without her than I was when we were together. And I learned a valuable lesson about relationships. I'll never do another long distance thing with anyone. So, what's your story?"

"Max, my partner of about eight years, had a tough time being a lesbian. As long as it was just the two of us she was fine with it. Her problem was that she couldn't own it outside the house. At first that was okay. As time passed and I saw no movement on her part towards any change, it just wasn't enough for me. I watched my friend, Kyle, come out. He and his partner, Mike, have made a life for themselves as a couple living openly. When I pushed for something similar for us, Max resisted. Eventually, she ended up getting involved with a man she met at a seminar."

"Is she happy, now?"

"Would I sound heartless if I say I don't know and I don't care? Her decision to leave me not only broke up our personal relationship, it nearly ruined my practice. I had to buy her out and for several years it was hell. I took in a couple of partners and things are going extremely well now."

"So are you still closeted?"

"No." Kate chuckled. "I don't fly a rainbow flag or anything like that, but at least the people who are important in my life all know. If ever I'm lucky enough to find another relationship, it won't be a secret. You?"

"Obviously, it's not the first thing I announce to people I meet. At work everyone knows. My family and friends know. My grandparents weren't very happy about it though."

Kate shifted her position so she could have a better view of Lee's face. "What about your parents and siblings?"

"I'm an only child. My father...well, he's dead. As for my mother, that's a long story. Can I save it for another time?"

Kate's hand had been idly circling ever more sensitive areas of Lee's body as they talked. As she neared the apex of her thighs Lee had become less interested in conversation and more focused on what Kate was doing.

"Sure. Do you have something more interesting in mind?" Kate cupped her hand between Lee's legs and waited.

"Absolutely. That area you are exploring right now is calling for your undivided attention."

Kate gripped Lee's pubic hair, tugging gently. "You mean here?"
"Perhaps a bit lower down."
"You mean here?"
Lee gasped. "Yes, precisely there."

CHAPTER 21

DAY 4 - MONDAY

LEE OPENED HER EYES to find Kate watching her. "You're beautiful when you sleep."

Lee mustered a sleepy smile, "Only when I'm asleep?"

"No, although you had such a sweet smile on your face just now."

"Umm. Pleasant dreams."

"And what were you dreaming about?"

Lee rolled over, gently touched Kate's face, placing a quick kiss on her lips. "You, of course."

"I'm glad. At least I made you smile."

"It was a nice dream." Lee glanced at the window. " What time is it anyway?"

"It's late. Six-thirty."

"Late?" Lee chuckled. "I thought I was an early riser. You've got me beat."

"Yep, I do. I've already let Cody out, wiped his feet, and fed him. You, my little sleeping beauty, managed to not wake up through the whole thing."

"Ah, the sleep of the innocent."

"Innocent? I don't think, after last night, that innocent is an adjective either of us can lay claim to."

Lee groaned. "Aren't you tired? What time did we finally get to sleep?"

"Around four, I think." Kate winked. "Probably, we'll both need some additional time in bed today."

"You mean napping."

Kate slid her hand up Lee's side enjoying Lee's smooth skin and taut muscles, finally coming to rest on her right breast. "Yes, that too."

Lee slid into Kate's embrace. "Umm, are you always this horny?"

"Complaining?"

"No, hoping."

They made love, took showers, ate breakfast, and were at the realtor's office by their appointed time of nine o'clock to meet with an extremely apologetic Mary Blackwell.

The two women felt so sorry for the agent that they ended up saying, that although it was initially difficult sharing a place with a stranger, they'd already become good friends over the past few days. Lee said, "We've even planned some day trips together for later this week. So we really should be thanking you."

Mary assumed the two vacationers were just being kind, trying to make her feel better. "I hate to be the bearer of more bad news so early in the day. Nevertheless, I'm afraid I have to tell you that I tried this morning to locate another rental that would meet the needs of one of you. With the snow this weekend, I couldn't find any other cabins in the same price range for you. Since you've managed to survive in that little place together, I did find a nice two bedroom cabin right on the lake that I'll rent for you personally. And of course I'll refund the money you each paid for the cabin you're in now. I'll leave it to the two of you to work out how you handle the remaining ten days. Maybe you can each take the larger place for half of the remaining time and swap half way through?"

Kate answered for both of them. "I'm sure we can work things out between us."

Mary showed them the location of the new rental on the map, gave them the key, and informed them that the cleaning woman had been sent in to clean. "Can you give her till eleven to finish up? I guarantee that the wait will be worth it. This cabin is one of the nicest on the lake. If it ever goes for sale, I'd love to own it."

"Sure, we can wait," they replied in unison.

"We're very grateful," Lee added.

Wondering if the realtor had forgotten about her dog, Kate asked,

"And my dog, Cody, won't be a problem?"

"No. I cleared it with the owner. He understood and approved it when I explained my agency had made an error. We rent for him all the time, so he agreed."

Once they'd settled back in the car Kate confessed that she felt just the least bit guilty about taking Mary's offer.

"Let's go take a look at the new place and maybe we can make a counter offer. You and I both know we're not going to use both places, don't we?"

Kate grinned. "Well I sure had my hopes."

* * *

They returned to the cabin to tidy up and pack up their belongings. Lee cleaned the kitchen, packed their supplies, and loaded them into her car while Kate tidied the rest of the place, cleaned the bathroom, and carried their bags out to her car.

Kate loaded Cody into the front seat, clipped his harness to the seat belt and led the way down the hill with Lee following behind in her car. Alone with her thoughts, she marveled at how well she and Lee worked together. Their time in each other's company was so effortless. They had fun with whatever they did—work, play, it didn't matter. When she talked, Lee listened attentively, not like some people who only listened for the other person to stop so they could have a turn talking. Lee listened with her mind, often making the perfect and appropriate to the topic, clever, silly, or intelligent comment. Although they had talked a lot in the past several days, they had enjoyed quiet times, too. The silences were always comfortable, never strained.

Kate glanced in the rear view mirror when she braked at the stop sign to check that Lee was still behind her. She grinned when Lee caught her looking and wiggled her fingers at her. Kate became impatient to get to the new cabin. She was surprised that she wanted Lee again. They had hardly been out of bed for three hours and her desire was already evident. She adjusted her position in the seat while she wished that the seam of her jeans wasn't putting so much pressure on such a sensitive area of her body.

Sex with Lee was the best she had ever had, like every other aspect of their relationship. Kate paused. Relationship? When did the fling they began last night become a relationship? In her heart, she knew she felt that what they were having was already more than a casual tryst. She let her thoughts return to the topic of sex. The sex was also easy. She thought back to the moment before she had kissed Lee for the first time—how nervous she'd been. Once they made it into bed, everything was so intuitive, like they had made love hundreds of times before. She didn't feel shy or worried about her body not being as young as it used to be. Lee had worshiped every inch of her. Neither had been shy in asking for what they needed although, except for an occasional 'faster' or 'harder,' direction had been mostly unnecessary. *I am in deep trouble here. How will I be able to let her go when our time together ends in ten short days?*

***

A few minutes later they pulled side-by-side into the drive of the amazing house that was to be their new home away from home. After carrying in all their belongings, Lee, Kate, and Cody were perched on their seats in the living room. They were enjoying the view of the partially frozen lake below with the snow-covered mountains in the background through the floor to ceiling glass window wall. "Wow! This just keeps getting better and better." Lee reached for Kate's hand. "It's going to be hard leaving here, isn't it?"

"Yes." Kate glanced over at Lee. "Lee, what happens..."

Lee quickly cut Kate off. "Let's not do this now. Can't we just enjoy the time we have and not worry about whatever is next, just for now? Can't we just pretend that this is our life...that we're happy? I could use some happy, couldn't you?"

"Yes, I guess so, if that's what you want." Kate pulled Lee onto her lap and they made love.

They were side by side with half of Lee's body draped over Kate, their hands entwined and spread above Kate's head. Lee rose up enough to allow her to look into her lover's eyes. "I have an admission to make. You are only the second woman I've ever been with like this, so I was nervous the first time we were together." Lee checked Kate's expression. "Does it bother you if I talk about her?"

"No, not at all." She offered a quick, reassuring smile, "Really."

"Your touch is more gentle than Kendra's. I do have a point, it's not just idle comparison."

"Okay."

"Anyway, when we went upstairs at the old cabin, I felt nervous all

150

the way up the stairs. I mean I wanted you even though I was nervous. You know, I'm not twenty any more, nor thirty for that matter. I'm not in awful shape, because I'm so active, still..."

"Believe me when I say I know exactly how you feel." Kate laughed. "I have these tacky closet doors at home, floor to ceiling mirrors that I have a love hate relationship with. Somehow, I never got around to remodeling my bedroom. Max and I redid the whole place, everything except my room. Every morning when I come out of the shower, I'm faced with a good dose of reality when I see myself reflected in those mirrors. They keep me humble." Kate ran her hand appreciatively down Lee's back, cupping her hand around her backside. "You have nothing to worry about anyway. You have a great body. But we digress. You were saying you were nervous at first."

"Yes, I was. I was totally inexperienced until Kendra. Making love with her was amazing. She was very skilled and we had a good sex life. Once you began to kiss me, to touch me that first time, I don't know how to say it other than it felt like coming home. It just felt so right."

"I agree." Kate nuzzled Lee's neck. "Remember when we stopped at the end of the road and I looked back to see if you were there and we waved?"

"Un huh."

"I was having the exact same thought about making love with you, except I think I was thinking that making love with you was easy."

"Hey, who you calling easy?" Lee chuckled at her joke.

Kate flipped Lee over, leaned down, and kissed her on the nose. "Shall we get dressed so we can go talk to Mary and let her off the hook? Maybe she can rent the other cabin out and recoup some of her loss if we tell her we're both willing to stay here."

"I'm feeling just a little guilty that she's paying for this place herself. Why don't we at least offer to pay her for the other cabin? Are you comfortable with that?"

"Why not?" Kate smiled. "We were both willing to pay for it when we thought we were each renting it. It's a win for us to get this place instead."

"Let's stop in to tell her and have an early dinner when we're in town while we're at it."

"Agreed."

They returned to the realty office where they explained to Mary that they were so thrilled with the new, larger place that they would both be willing to stay there. They also told her that they wanted to pay her for the other cabin.

"No, that's not fair. You've both been inconvenienced," Mary insisted.

It was a strange conversation with each of them insisting on paying for the first cabin and Mary insisting they didn't have to. They all ended up laughing about the peculiar business negotiations and finally agreed that Mary would rebate half of the rental fee for the first cabin to each of the two women. They ended up feeling less guilty, and Mary was happy that she had made amends for her agency's error. Everyone felt good about the transaction when Kate and Lee waved goodbye to Mary.

The women stopped in at the local florist where they arranged to have a huge bouquet sent to Mary to thank her for all she'd done to make up for the booking error. Afterwards, they went to the local pub to get some dinner. The weather was crisp and clear as they left the restaurant bound for their new cabin home. Kate took Cody out for his walk while Lee unpacked their clothes and took a shower.

Kate, warm from her own shower, joined Lee in the bed of the larger bedroom. "Wow, look at that," she exclaimed noticing the skylight above the bed. "Look at all those stars."

"I'd rather kiss you, if it's all the same to you."

CHAPTER 22

DAY 5 TO 10 TUESDAY - SUNDAY

Together, they watched the sun rise from their vantage point on the sofa in the living room on their fifth day of vacation. "So, what do you have in mind to do today?" Kate had gotten out of bed earlier than Lee, taken Cody out, and made the tea. "Want to go back and do some more skiing or would you prefer something else?"

"Let's see what the weather has in store." Lee turned on the weather channel. When the forecast ended, Lee said, "Well since the forecast today is nice and they predict rain for tomorrow, maybe we should ski today. If it's going to rain tomorrow, I could do some more work on the book, if you don't mind. Or we can do a couple of the museums and do some shopping to finish out the week."

"Sounds like a good plan to me. Let's go."

By lunchtime Lee, her confidence bolstered, was bored with the beginner's slope and wanted to try something a bit more adventurous. Kate talked with one of the instructors who suggested a slope for them to try. Together they skied it several times until Lee wanted to go inside to warm up.

Since it was mid day, mid week, the bar wasn't crowded. They sat in the middle of the bar situated so that they were facing the ski runs. A short haired woman who looked to be in her thirties sat two seats away on their right and a twenty something couple sat at the far end of the bar.

"Do you mind if I go take a more difficult run?" Kate asked.

"No, I'll sit here in the bar and watch for you to come down. Which slope will you take?"

"Excuse me for eavesdropping," the woman next to them said. "Jackie and I are here skiing, too. She just went up to our room to get something so she should be back in a couple of minutes. Anyway, she's a better skier than I am. I don't like her to take the more advanced runs alone. She thinks I'm silly, but I don't care. It makes me worry for her to go alone. Would you mind taking her with you if you're going to take an advanced run? She's an excellent skier. I'm just overly protective, I guess. I'm Shelly by the way," the friendly woman with the broad smile said extending her hand.

An athletic appearing woman came round the bar in time to hear the tail end of the conversation. "And I'm Jackie."

Kate and Lee introduced themselves.

Turning to Kate, Jackie asked, "Did Shelly just beg you to ski with me? Please don't feel obligated. She does this to me all the time. I think she's afraid I'll break my crown if she's not with me."

"Well, you shouldn't be up there alone anyway, sweetheart," Shelly said.

"It's okay," Kate smiled her understanding. "Honestly, I often do ski alone. Although I have to admit that it's more comfortable to have someone with me, especially on the advanced slopes. I'd like the company. Are you ready to go or..."

"No, I'm ready. Let's do it." Jackie looked toward the slopes. "Do you have a slope picked out?"

"No, this is only our second time here." Gesturing towards Lee, Kate smiled and said, "It's only her second time on snow skis. She's doing great although she's not yet ready for the advanced trails."

"We ski here all the time. My favorite slope is that one." Jackie pointed. "It's perfect too, because you two can watch us come down from here."

"Good," Lee responded. "I'll be glad for the company and even happier Kate's not skiing that trail alone."

Kate squeezed Lee's hand. "See you in a bit." Then more quietly, "Thanks." She winked at her lover and turned to join Jackie.

Lee heard Jackie ask Kate as they walked away, "So where do you usually ski?"

Shelly observed Lee watch as Kate walked away. "So, have you two been a couple a long time?"

Lee laughed. "No, not long at all. Just a few days actually."

"And you're on vacation together already?"

"It's a funny story. You won't believe it, because I don't believe it myself sometimes." Lee searched for Kate's red jacket, finally locating her in the lift line.

"So tell me. We have plenty of time." Shelly signaled the bartender to refill their drinks. "I'll have another beer, and another..."

"Pinot," Lee supplied.

"Another wine for my friend here."

Lee and Shelly spent the next hour getting to know each other. Lee shared the story about how she and Kate had met. Later Shelly told Lee, "We've been together since high school, and we got married in 2004 after gay marriage became legal in Massachusetts."

"You're very lucky." Lee caught sight of Kate and Jackie coming down the slope. "Look, there they are." Lee pointed to the pair about half way down the mountain. They skied in unison, turn for turn as they made their way down the steep incline. "They're so beautiful," Lee whispered. She watched as Kate and Jackie snaked their way down the trail making a sport that Lee knew was difficult look so easy.

From Shelly, Lee learned that the Berkshires, in general, were welcoming of gay and lesbian tourists. Shelly also suggested several museums and restaurants that they should make an effort to visit.

Kate and Jackie returned after their second run down the mountain, cheeks red, and eyes shining. "That was fun." Jackie announced.

The four women agreed to have an early dinner together where they continued to get to know each other. After dinner, Kate said, "I'm sorry, we have to call it a day. I have to go back to our rental cabin to let my dog out. As it is, he'll be really annoyed with me."

"That works for me. I'm tired. That was quite a workout this afternoon." Jackie gave each of them her card. "My cell number is on the back. We'll be here through Saturday. Maybe we can ski together again or do dinner or drinks?"

Kate nodded when Lee glanced her way. "We're planning on staying in tomorrow to do some work because the weather is forecast to be lousy," Lee glanced over at Kate who nodded when she asked the two women, "Would you be interested in coming over for dinner? We're not prepared to make a company quality meal there. Maybe we can order a pizza or something simple."

"Sounds great. Give us a call around lunch time and we'll firm up plans," Shelly suggested.

On their way back to the cabin, Lee and Kate discussed their new friends. "I like them," Kate said." More importantly I'm glad you suggested we have them in for pizza. Socialization was a sore point for Max and me. She didn't want anyone to know about us so we never had friends in, or even went out with other couples for that matter. Sometimes I was more lonely with her than I am now living a single life."

"That's sad." Lee squeezed Kate's hand.

Relaxing in front of the fire, Lee glanced around. "This place is so easy compared to the other one. The gas fire only requires a push of a button unlike the one at our little cabin." The evening passed quickly with them enjoying their time together. They talked about their day, the new friends they'd made, reviewed the restaurant where they'd had dinner, and cuddled on the sofa.

The next day went as they'd planned. They woke up later than usual, made love, and ate breakfast. They took Cody for a short walk during a break in the showers. Kate read some of the medical journals she'd brought with her while Lee worked. That evening their new friends came over. They shared pizza and beer and swapped stories, and agreed to meet again for a dinner in town on Saturday evening.

On Thursday and Friday they went to the museums they'd previously discussed, made love every chance they could, laughed, shared stories about their hometowns, and talked about their lives.

Thursday night, as they lay curled together in bed, Kate said, "You mentioned that there was a story about coming out to your mother. Tell me."

"It's not so much about my coming out to my mother. She accepted it pretty easily. It was about my mom and dad. My mother killed my dad." She told Kate the story and her early years growing up with her father. For some reason, relating the story was so much easier with Kate than it had ever been.

"I'm so sorry to hear that your life was like that, Lee."

"It's fine now. All that is in the past at this point. I used to have a hard time admitting that part of my life to anyone. It's one gift Kendra gave me. The ability to not feel ashamed of what happened. I never blamed my mom, but was always afraid people would view me differently when they found out my mom went to jail for murder. Telling you was not uncomfortable for me."

"I think most people would view your mother's conviction as a miscarriage of justice once they heard the whole story." Kate pulled Lee closer and kissed her temple.

On Saturday, they visited some of the antique stores in the next town where Lee fell in love with a table in one of the shops. "I love this," Lee said. "It's too big for me to take home in my car though. I guess I'll have to pass it by. I asked the salesman. Shipping it would put it out of my price range."

They toured through the rest of the shop and before they left, Lee returned to have one last look at the table.

"If you want it you should buy it. Think of the enjoyment it would give you over time. That'll make it seem more affordable."

"You are able to justify almost anything, aren't you?" Lee smiled. "No. It's a want, not a need."

"Life's short, Lee. If it's worthwhile, you should make every effort possible to get what makes you happy."

"No. It's too expensive. Come on. Let's go home."

They met Shelly and Jackie for dinner on Saturday night and spent another pleasant evening with the couple. There was an awkward moment when they parted, when they invited Lee and Kate to visit them at their home.

Kate spoke up. "We'll let you know. I'm not sure how soon I can get away for a weekend again. I have a few things to work through with my partners after this vacation, so can we give you a call?"

They parted after agreeing to keep in touch.

CHAPTER 23

DAYS 11 TO 14 – MONDAY - THURSDAY

MONDAY MORNING, CURLED TOGETHER in bed, Kate sighed. "I know you wanted to not talk about what happens next. I think we need to. I know that I need to."

Lee turned towards Kate, her head propped on her hand.

"Why don't you want to talk about this, about us, Lee?

"Because there just can't be an us, Kate. How can there be? We live over four hours away from each other. You work most weekends and if you're off, you only have one whole day and a portion of another. How can we make that work? Don't forget I've been through this before. I know that it doesn't work. My experience proves that."

Kate shook her head. "Don't compare me to Kendra. I'm not like her." When Lee didn't respond, Kate pulled her closer. "Lee. Please. Don't give up on us before we've even had a chance to begin."

Lee had tears in her eyes when she looked up. "Just enjoy what we have while we're here, Kate. I can't give you, can't give us, any more than right now. Long distance relationships just don't work. I know this from experience. Please trust me in this."

"I know it's too soon to even think this, let alone say it..."

Lee placed her fingers on Kate's lips. "No. Don't say any more. Please. Just make love to me. Don't ask more of me right now. I'm not

159

able to give it."

"I hear you. No matter what you say, there's no doubt in my mind that I want more than one more week with you." Kate smiled. "Be warned."

"It's not that I don't want more, too. I just don't see a way." Lee kissed Kate. "No more. No more talk. Make love to me while we can. Use every minute we have left to show me how you feel, but I won't talk about a future for us. It's impossible for me to picture one. I'm sorry."

Kate did as Lee asked. She made love to her with every ounce of feeling she had. For the remainder of the day they didn't talk about anything farther in the future than their plans for dinner.

The remainder of the week sped by. Lee did some work while Kate read, catching up on her professional journals and enjoying a lesbian romance novel. They visited the little towns around them, poked through the shops, and returned once again to the antique shop to admire the table that Lee had fallen in love with. Despite the fair offer she made for the table, the shopkeeper held firm on the price. Reluctantly she turned away leaving it behind in the shop. "It's just too much with the cost of shipping. I'll find something closer to home."

On Thursday afternoon, they tidied the house, packing everything except the essentials for that night and the next morning. Without saying it, they knew that the morning would be difficult enough without having to gather their belongings together and put them into their cars.

They went out for a special dinner that evening at a beautiful upscale restaurant. "Dinner by candlelight." Kate smiled at Lee. "This reminds me of our first meal together." When Lee laughed, Kate lifted her glass and they toasted. "To fate."

"Was our meeting fate or a simple accident of time?" Lee took a sip of her wine.

"That depends on how it ends, doesn't it?"

They got home and went straight to bed. Their lovemaking was both passionate and tender. Kate gathered Lee into her arms when they were both satisfied.

"Tell me more about you, Kate."

Kate began to tell Lee the history of her love life before Max. She spoke about her feelings as three woman she'd previously cared about had left her, each pursuing her goals and leaving Kate behind. "I hate to believe that I'm destined to never find someone who loves me enough to make an effort to be with me. I've always been at least second on everyone's list of priorities, never first." She whispered, "Don't do this to us, Lee. Don't go without giving us a chance. Please. Just don't say no. Think about it. We can do it. We can."

Kate felt tears brim over and slide down her cheeks. They cried together when Lee shook her head and denied Kate's request.

***

The next morning, as she prepared to leave, Lee stood just inside the front door. She picked up and held Cody as she whispered in his ear what a pleasure it was to meet him. "Take good care of your mom for me."

Lee turned to Kate. "Well, I guess it's time."

"No change of heart? Lee, you've spent so much time telling me there's no way for us to be together, that we never had a chance to talk about the possibilities. We could have at least one weekend a month together when I come to you. You could come down another when I'm not on call. I can adjust my hours. I'll arrange to have Saturday off on the weekend you come down. We don't even have to drive. I checked— there's a train. We could do vacations a couple of times a year together. There're video cameras over the Internet for during the week. We can do it. I want you as part of my life. Don't give up on us without at least trying. I'm not Kendra. Don't hold that part of your life against me, Lee."

"You make it sound almost conceivable. Having a long distance romance is like having only half of a life. Don't you want a lover with you every night, someone who doesn't sail in once or twice a month and a couple of times a year. I know I do."

"Of course I do. I'm not saying this will be forever. But we need more time to figure out if there's a way for more, if there can be more, or if we even want more with each other. We've had a good start. We just haven't had enough time. Give us that gift, Lee. Give us the gift of time. Give us a chance."

Tears were streaming freely down Lee's face. "I'm sorry. I just can't do this." That was it. She turned and hurried out of the cabin. Kate didn't follow her. She couldn't bear to watch Lee drive away.

Tears dried now, Kate gathered the final few items and clipped Cody's lead to his collar. She made a final check of the cabin. Cody started to bark and Kate looked toward the door as it opened.

Lee stood in the doorframe. "Okay. You win. I can't leave like this." They fell into each other's arms. "Promise me this will end well."

"I can't promise you that. I can only promise you a chance, and that I'll do everything in my power to make things right for both of us. If you're also willing to commit to that, how can it not end well?"

"Call me when you get home?" Lee pressed her card into Kate's palm. "And while you're driving, be working on when we're going to get together again." She kissed Kate goodbye and didn't look back until she got in her car.

Kate watched her drive away. She made one stop before she left town and headed for home.

CHAPTER 24

THE DELIVERY

KATE CALLED LEE AS soon as she arrived home. "I made it home safely. How was your ride?"

"Good. No traffic, thankfully. What's up now?"

"Nothing. Have to take Cody out for a walk. After that, maybe I'll grab a burger and fries for dinner. I don't have anything here to eat."

"I stopped at the food store for a salad. I don't know how you keep in shape with the way you consume fast food."

"Geez, involved less than two weeks and already you're treating me like your girlfriend." Kate chuckled.

"No, that's more motherly, so I'll stop. I promise."

They made small talk for the next few minutes, each promising to call the other during the week.

The next morning Lee called. "I miss waking up with you," she said when an out of breath Kate answered the phone. "What are you doing that you're so out of breath?"

"Exercising," Kate panted. " I usually do it at least three mornings a week when I have the motivation. Helps me keep those breasts you love to torture from wrapping around my navel."

"La la la la. Too much information." Lee laughed. "I'm going to run off to work now to meet up with Angus, but I wanted to wake up with you and this is the best I could do."

"Well, I do appreciate the thought. I'll admit that waking up with you on the other end of the phone pales in comparison to waking up with you in the flesh, so to speak." Kate could hear Lee take a sip of her tea.

"Hmm. Please don't get me started thinking about that. I do agree. I can't wait to see you."

The huge sigh Kate exhaled indicated she felt the same way. "You just miss my body and the sex."

"Yes...that, too. As much as I hate to have to say this, I have to run. Otherwise I'm going to have to go change my underwear. Just thinking about having sex with you makes me wet. I'll talk to you soon. I miss you Kate."

"Ditto!"

Every day for the next week, they talked every morning and in the evening before bed. When she had any spare minutes during the day Lee would call to leave voice mail messages for Kate—never anything momentous, just small little observations that brought joy to Kate each time she listened.

Sometimes, Kate would surprise Lee by answering when she was between patients. She arranged to have one full weekend a month off starting Friday afternoon at two, and to have one additional Saturday per month off with her hours ending Friday night at six. On that weekend, they agreed that Lee would come down to spend the weekend with Kate. Kate would drive up on the weekend she finished early on Friday afternoon.

The Friday after they returned home, Lee received a box from Kate delivered to her office. She slit open the box to find a neatly wrapped present inside. Too excited to be neat about it, she tore the paper away in huge pieces like a child would. Her gift was a new state-of-the-art smartphone. The note from Kate read: *I added you to my plan. When you get this call me. Instructions are below. Can't wait to 'see' you.*

Lee placed the call to Kate after reviewing the instructions. Like magic, Kate's face appeared. Her ear-to-ear grin indicated her pleasure that the devices worked seamlessly. "Hello there. It's good to see you. This makes it more like we're really together, even though, if you kiss me goodbye it might lose a little in translation!"

"Very funny." Kate made a face that caused Lee to laugh.

"Speaking of kissing, when are we going to be able to do that?"

Kate gave Lee the dates she would be off that month. She was scheduled to make the first trip up to visit Lee in two weeks. They talked for a little while longer before saying goodbye. Kate didn't mention the surprise she had for Lee the following weekend.

A week before she was scheduled to travel to Lee, Kate left for Connecticut at noontime well ahead of most of the traffic, hoping to make good time. When she arrived at Lee's house, Kate unloaded the present she had for her, the table she'd bought before she left to come home from the Berkshires, the one Lee felt was too expensive to ship. She put the table on Lee's front step as quietly as she could then hid around the corner of Lee's house. She placed a call to Lee. "Hi there. You have a surprise waiting on your front step."

"A surprise, really? Are you here? That would be the best surprise."

"Go open the door. You'll find something you want there." Kate peered through the shrubs eagerly awaiting Lee opening the door.

"What I want more than anything is you. Anything less will be a disappointment."

Kate smiled. "I surely hope not, because it was a lot of trouble for me to get this thing delivered."

"Okay, here I come. Pucker up!"

"Don't get your hopes up, I'm not standing on your front porch. I swear. I hope that when you come outside, you'll like what you see."

Lee opened the door, the phone still pressed to her ear. "Oh, Kate. It's the table I wanted. You shouldn't have spent so much. How did you get it here?"

"I brought it." Kate stepped out from her hiding place.

Lee's shriek nearly deafened Kate. "Oh God, you're really here." Lee ran to Kate and grabbed her. She kissed her thoroughly and dragged her towards the front door.

"Wait, let's get the table inside." Once indoors, Kate said, "Show me your house. I want to see where you call home."

"Shall we start with a tour of my bedroom?" Lee asked as she pulled Kate down the hallway.

"If ever the Marine Biologist thing fizzles for you, I think you have a promising future as a tour guide."

Lee led Kate to her bedroom where she quickly stripped off Kate's clothes and her own. Touching each other nourished them. "Make love to me. I've missed you so much."

Kate kissed her way down Lee's body, feasting on her. She took as much pleasure from pleasing her lover as Lee did as the recipient of the affection. They both moaned as Kate entered her. Kate straddled Lee's leg and rocked against her in time with her thrusts. They moaned in release as they climaxed together.

Lee pushed against Kate to turn her onto her back. "I need my mouth on you. I want you so much." Using her lips and tongue, Lee made love to Kate as if they'd never see each other again. When they both were satisfied for the time being, Lee said, "I thought you were coming next week. Does this mean I won't see you next week?"

"No, this was a bonus week. I have to drive back tomorrow."

"I'm happy to see you, but it means more than eight hours in the car for you to spend only one day here with me."

"Are you complaining?" Kate asked.

"No, of course not. I just feel bad that you'll be driving so much for such a short visit."

"I don't care. I needed to see you. I missed you so much." Kate shifted her position so she could look in her lover's eyes. "You know, I've spent a good portion of my life alone and have rarely felt lonely, until now. Sometimes, at night, I'll be reading something and I want to share it with you, or I find myself wanting to ask your opinion about something. I miss you."

"I know exactly what you mean. I was watching that lawyer show on Sunday night last week. You know, the one we both like."

Kate nodded. "I saw it."

"I wanted to talk to you about it, unfortunately, well you were there and I was here." Lee ran her hand down Kate's chest between her breasts. It wasn't a sexual gesture as much as just a need to be in physical contact.

Kate tucked that bit of information away for future consideration.

"Do you think we're really going to be able to make this work?"

"You aren't ready to give up on us yet, are you? We're just getting started."

"I know. Let me pout, just a little." Lee traced Kate's mouth with her finger. "I miss being with you every day. The face-to-face on the phone helps. That was a really clever idea. At least I get to see your face and your expressions when we talk." Lee slid her hand down Kate's body through the soft curls covering her mound, cupping her in the palm of her hand. "I miss this, our being able to be together this way. I miss being able to touch you."

"Hmm. Well, there's always phone sex or computer sex." Kate arched an eyebrow.

"Yeah, even so, that won't keep my feet warm. Speaking of warm feet, where's our resident foot warmer?"

Kate laughed. "Cody? He's at home. I didn't know if your house was dog proof or dog friendly. I didn't want to just assume. Besides, this trip was a bit spur of the moment because I wasn't sure I could get coverage until a few days ago."

"I've never had pets." Lee paused briefly considering. "Do fish count?" Without waiting for an answer she continued. "Anyway, I always felt I traveled too much to have pets. Even so, I miss Cody. Wish you'd brought him along."

"Next week."

"If you tell me what food Cody likes I'll buy everything he needs. That way you don't have to lug it with you. And next time bring some clothes that you can leave here, so you don't have to pack much. If it's okay, I'll do the same when I come to you."

Kate grinned. "That would be perfect. I'll clear a space for you. By the way, I picked up a train schedule. I don't know that it'll save any time although it'll take less effort for sure. It'll let us nap or read during the trip, something we can't do while we're driving."

"That'll be good." Lee pulled away, preparing to stand. "By the way, I have some news to share. First, how about I fix us something to eat?"

"Sounds good." Kate watched as Lee stood up and grabbed her robe. Lee tossed her an oversized T-shirt. When Lee left, Kate got up, slipped into the shirt, and found her way to the kitchen.

While Lee fixed them some dinner, Kate strolled through Lee's house, examining pictures and artwork, looking for secrets Lee had yet to share. "That's my boss and his wife," Lee said pointing to the picture hanging on the wall.

"Fiona and Angus, right?"

"Yes." Lee came over and pointed to the photo. "That was taken in their house in the southern end of Key Largo."

"It's beautiful."

Lee nodded. "Yes, it is. My wish is to retire there some day. It would be even better if I could work there first. However, you know what they say about wishes. Still, it's been my dream for a long time."

"We're just getting started here...don't even tell me about the possibility of you moving to the Keys. That's definitely too far to commute."

Lee wrapped her arm around Kate and led her back to the kitchen. "So, how come you were able to get up here this weekend?"

"I got special dispensation. I told my partners what I wanted to do and they agreed to cover for me."

"You told them about us?"

"I told them I'd met someone special." Having a quick moment of panic related to Max's refusal to acknowledge their relationship, Kate asked, "Is that okay?"

"Why not? I'm looking forward to meeting them." Lee served the dinner.

As they ate, Kate reminded Lee she was going to tell her some news.

"Oh, yeah. You said you had picked up a train schedule and I told you that would be a good way to travel. I got a job teaching a night class. One of the biology professors had to have emergency surgery and they asked me to take over his night class. So, if I take the train, it'll give me time to prep for class and read papers, and I won't have to work on the weekend."

"You know, it won't matter if you do. We both spent time together on vacation doing work, you on your book, me catching up on my reading."

"Really? That's it? I hate to keep making comparisons, but Kendra always made me feel guilty if I brought work home with me."

"Honey, I'm not Kendra. We can do this. I promise."

"I know. I want it to work. It's just sometimes I get..."

"I get it, Lee. Sometimes you feel a little nervous, a little scared."

Lee nodded. "I'm sorry. It's just that you seem so sure this will work, while I still have that little voice that sometimes whispers doubts."

They carried their dishes to the sink. "Give me a chance to prove it can." Kate pulled Lee into her arms.

They finished the dishes and went to bed early, made love, and got up early the next morning. Lee showed Kate around her town before they stopped over to visit Angus and Fiona. They were pleased to meet the woman who had put a sparkle back in Lee's eyes.

Angus welcomed Kate with a big hug. "So, Lee tells us you two had a great time on your vacation. It was an interesting way that the two of you met."

"I guess interesting is one word to describe it." Kate looked over at Lee. "It doesn't matter to me how strange it was, only that it actually happened."

They stayed for lunch with Angus and Fiona. Kate loved Fiona's warmth and obvious regard for Lee. Angus entertained them with fascinating stories about his and Lee's adventures researching their first book, and talking about the Keys.

Angus explained a little about the project he and Lee were working on. "I've been trying to get our organization here involved in some joint projects with the facility in Largo. We've had no luck so far. Most of the work we do is grant funded through the center so some of our research is conducted here."

"Lee was explaining that to me when she was telling me details about your research. I know that in my field, grants are becoming more and more difficult to get funded."

Angus nodded. "Yes. We've been lucky to have our grant renewed each year we've been here. Maybe because our first book based on our research was successful. Whatever the reason, we were relieved to be notified that we're gainfully employed through January next year. Plus we get to spend about six weeks in the Keys this year. As soon as we return from our trip this summer, we'll file our summary report and ask to be extended again."

Fiona asked Kate, "Have you ever been there, to the Keys?"

"No, I haven't. From what I've seen of Lee's photos, it looks gorgeous."

"Maybe, if your schedule permits, while we're all down there this summer you can fly down and spend some time with us. You can stay at our house."

"Thank you," Kate responded. "That's very kind and generous of you. I've been reading up on the Key deer. They fascinate me. I'd love to see them in person. As a vet, there are many places I'd like to visit and things I'd like to see there, like bird and other sanctuaries, and the deer of course. It's definitely an interesting possibility for a vacation."

Lee and Kate were both eager to get home so they could spend some time in bed together before Kate had to leave and they made their departure as quickly as they could without being rude.

On the way back to Lee's house, Kate told Lee how much she'd enjoyed meeting her friends. "It's obvious they both love you very much."

"I love them, too."

They spent the early part of the afternoon making love. "It's time," Kate said, after checking her watch. "I'd better get on the road."

Tears welled in Lee's eyes. "I'm not ready for you to leave yet."

"I know. The sooner I get going, the sooner I'll be back."

Lee groaned. "Another whole week."

"Nope, only four days. I'll be here the fifth day. You'll be busy all week, and Cody and I will be here before you really have time to miss me."

Kate laughed when Lee told her that she missed her already.

"I haven't even left yet."

"It doesn't matter. Thank you for my table. It looks perfect."

"I'm glad you liked my surprise." Kate kissed her lover, a slow, sweet kiss filled with emotion.

"You were the best surprise. Call me when you get home?"

"You'll hear from me before you've had time to miss me," Kate promised.

Lee waved goodbye until Kate was out of sight.

Kate pulled to a stop around the corner and connected her phone to the lighter with the charger. She stuck the earpiece in her ear, dialed Lee's number, and after pushing dial she began her trip home.

Lee answered on the second ring.

"Did you have time to miss me yet?"

Lee sniffed, an indication to Kate that Lee had been crying. Lee covered by saying, "Are you home already?"

"Ha, I wish." Kate said brightly, "I was wondering if you'd like to keep me company on my ride home?"

"Really? This might not work out too badly, you know? If we spend the whole trip up and back talking, when you're here, or I'm there with you, we won't have to waste our time together talking. We can spend our time in bed making love."

Kate sighed. "I love making love with you."

"You're certainly not alone in that." Lee went to her laptop case and pulled her ear buds from the case and plugged them in.

Kate turned onto the highway. "I love talking to you almost as much."

Lee settled onto the sofa. "I loved it that you surprised me this weekend."

"I loved meeting your friends."

"I love how thoughtful you are. You got the table for me, and the phone. You work hard at making this easier for us." Lee laid the phone down on the arm of the sofa. "I love that you called me and we're making the trip home together."

"I love that you're going to buy food and supplies for Cody."

"I love Cody."

"I love you, Lee."

Lee paused. "I know. I love you, too."

Kate was grinning. "I recognize that it's only been a short time. But this, whatever it is between us, just feels so right. We feel so right."

"I know. It's true. I feel it, too." Lee sighed. "I just wish it wasn't so damned far. I don't want to be four feet away from you, let alone four hours. Are we crazy for even starting this?"

"Maybe. I just don't care. In my heart, I believe we're meant to be together and I'll do whatever it takes to make sure that happens."

"How long can we keep this up, Kate? I mean—you have a practice there, so you can't relocate here. I have a job here. And what would a marine biologist do in a farming community in the middle of Pennsylvania?"

"Well, technically, I'm closer to the edge of Pennsylvania." Kate exhaled slowly. "Look, I'm not saying this is or will be easy for either of us. And maybe, in six months or more, we'll agree there is no future for us. Or maybe, we'll figure something out that will work if we agree this relationship is what we want. Right now, I'm not ready to throw in the towel before we've even given us a chance."

"I'm glad. I'm not either."

"So, you love me too, huh?" Kate changed lanes, a huge grin on her face.

"Absolutely."

Kate set the cruise control. "I know I'm in love with you because I'm already sacrificing big time for you."

"How so?"

"I'm going to miss The Good Wife."

Lee checked the time. "If you don't hit traffic, you might make it home in time."

"Yeah, I might. The traffic is moving along." Kate bumped up her cruise control for five miles over the limit.

"Let's watch it together tonight when you get home if you're not too tired."

"Great idea!"

The rest of the trip went much quicker than it would have if Kate had to make the trip without Lee's company. They hated saying goodbye when Kate pulled into her driveway. "I'll call you back in a few, as soon as I get something to eat and get settled."

Kate parked the car and carried her bag inside. It was lighter than it was when she left home. She'd left her dirty clothes at Lee's. It was the first outfit of several that would take up permanent residence at Lee's place. Cody greeted her with wet kisses and a wagging tail. Beth, who had kept Cody for the weekend, left a note saying he'd had his dinner and his walk before she brought him home. Kate let him out so he could pee. After she'd tossed the ball for him for fifteen minutes, she came inside, made a snack, and then settled in front of the TV. She called Lee and together they watched the program commenting on developments between scenes. It was nearly as good as watching it in the same room.

That night began a tradition of shared evenings together. Every night, depending on their schedules, they talked. Sometimes they watched TV together from their separate locations. No matter what, they always had daily contact and ended each night talking in bed with each other. Although they were separated physically, emotionally they remained close, spending more quality time with each other than they ever had in any prior relationships.

Friday, Kate was due to drive up for a visit to Lee's again. She packed up her bags in the morning, loaded everything in her car, including Cody, and headed for work. She managed to get away on time and Lee was waiting for her when she pulled into her drive at four-thirty. The trip felt longer since she didn't have Lee to talk with on the way up. The length of the journey seemed inconsequential when Lee wrapped her arms around her and kissed her deeply. "I missed this part of us," she whispered. Lee greeted Cody as he danced around their legs. Once inside, she gave him a treat and fixed a drink for Kate. They sat at her kitchen bar sipping their tea. "Oh, I almost forgot. I have a gift for you." She produced a small, gift-wrapped box.

Kate carefully opened the wrapping and removed the lid. Inside, there was a keychain and a key. The keychain was a round, black and white yin and yang symbol. On the black side, in sterling, was a subtle woman's symbol, mirrored on the other side by a second woman's symbol. "It's beautiful Lee. I love it."

"It reminded me of us. I feel like you are my other half, and together we make a whole. I'm glad you like it."

"And the key?" Kate dangled it.

"To my house. In case you beat me home sometime. I left work a little early to be sure I'd beat you here today. Next time, if you're early, you can just come in."

"Thanks. I love the keychain. It's very special." Kate pulled her close and kissed her.

They took a walk that evening to give Cody a chance to work off some energy after having been in the car for so long. They turned in early, spending several hours making love and later talking about the weekend.

Saturday morning they went out for breakfast after making the short drive to Mystic. Following a fun day at the museum, they had a simple romantic dinner that Lee prepared. Afterwards they curled up on the sofa to read.

A few minutes later, Lee noticed that Kate was watching her. "What? Is something wrong?"

"No, nothing wrong, Quite the opposite, actually. I love our time together, no matter what we do—going out, staying in. Anything. I just love it. I spent every quiet moment this week thinking about this weekend and times like this."

Lee slid into Kate's arms. "Time during the week when we're apart seems to drag, and this time when we're together just seems to speed by. Our time is already half over."

Kate kissed Lee. "Maybe we should go to bed and make the best of it."

***

Kate left the next day and they followed the same routine they had the previous Sunday. While she drove they talked about the fact that it would be two weeks until Lee made her trip down to Kate's house.

"This will be the longest we've been apart since we met." Kate said.

"Think we'll ever get used to this?"

"I don't know. I have to say, I hate the time we're apart but I love when we can be together."

"Oh, I forgot to mention. I heard from Shelly and Jackie. They were wondering if we could get together."

"That would be nice. We can catch up with them. Go ahead and make the plans, Lee. Whatever you decide is fine."

On Thursday they were talking as they watched television, Kate said, "You know, I've been thinking. New York is about halfway between us. How would you feel about meeting me on Saturday night in New York? It's a little farther for you than for me."

"Really? I don't care about that. You have to work on Saturday and I don't, so I don't mind traveling a little farther than you do. I'll just be happy to see you. Why didn't we think about this before? That would be great. Where?"

"I'll check into it and make reservations for us. I'll send you the information tomorrow. This should be fun. A new adventure."

They were both excited at the unanticipated and spontaneous opportunity for them to be together. The meeting in New York was a relaxing time. They never even left the hotel. They met on Saturday evening, ordered room service, and made love. On Sunday morning, they ordered breakfast. At eleven, they checked out of the hotel. The weather was beautiful so they took a walk through the Village where they found a cute little cafe for dinner. They parted at six and drove home together, on the phone.

Lee made the trip to Kate's house the following weekend. Kate was surprised when Lee announced that she'd taken a personal day and wouldn't have to leave until Monday. Lee went with Kate as she visited two farms that morning. Later, when they left for the office, Lee was pleased to meet Beth and Kevin, Kate's partners. "Next time you come down I want you to meet Mike and Kyle. They were busy this weekend although they promised to buy us dinner next time you're here."

Thus began the pattern of their lives together. They each admitted that having a long distance romance was not what either of them wanted. Regardless, being together was what was important to them. The compromises they made seemed to make it work. Lee was the first to try the train. She decided that she liked traveling down to see Kate by train because it gave her time to work on the way. Kate preferred to drive because she could talk to Lee all the way home. Kate discovered a bus that left from a town about a half hour from her home that took her into New York. She liked that because, after a long day, she could catch a quick nap before meeting Lee in the city. They were able to spend most weekends together, at least one night, if not both.

CHAPTER 25

SPRING 2008

THEIR VISIT WITH SHELLY and Jackie was fun. They gathered on Friday night and, after greeting each other warmly, they enjoyed a wonderful meal Lee cooked. "This is great, Hon. I love the chicken."

"I agree. Thanks for slaving in the kitchen for us," Jackie added.

The next two days they toured the town, had a dinner out on Saturday evening, and worked together on Sunday morning to make a big breakfast. Kate and Shelly made the eggs and ham while Jackie and Lee squeezed the juice and made the toast. They spent the rest of the day playing cards and complaining about how fast the time was going. Shelly asked, "When can we do this again?"

Everyone agreed to a weekend later in May at Kate's house.

Kate spoke to Beth and Kevin about wanting to take off another two weeks in the summer to vacation with Lee. They began to discuss the possibility of hiring in another part time vet to take over some hours and to cover for them if any of them wanted time off. Each of them reached out to their contacts and soon found Dr. Akers, a vet from a few towns over who'd recently retired. He missed working with animals after he sold his practice. Being able to pick up a couple of regular days of work per week worked perfectly for him, and he was willing to fill in when any of them took off time to attend a conference or took a vacation. After a review of her finances, Kate decided she could afford to make ends meet on a few less hours and jumped at the opportunity to give up Saturday hours. She also booked him for an additional ten days of coverage during August. No Saturday hours meant she could be with Lee every weekend.

Lee, Angus, and Fiona were scheduled to begin working in the Keys starting the first week of July. Lee was thrilled when Kate told her, "I've arranged to have time off to visit you while you're in the Keys. It means we'll only be apart a month. And over Thanksgiving, I'll take some more vacation and come stay with you for a week."

When Jackie and Shelly came to Kate's for the Memorial Day weekend, Lee and Kate threw their first party as a couple—a cookout. Kate rented several rooms at the local motel for her guests because her house was too small to accommodate everyone staying with her. Fiona and Angus came, as did Lee's friend, Maggie, Shellie and Jackie, Mike and Kyle, Kate's partners Beth and Kevin, and Kevin's wife, Marty.

Kate and Lee set up 'ice breaker' games to play that served to mix people together. Before too long the group was joking and laughing like old friends. Kate arranged for a breakfast for everyone the next day at her favorite restaurant before they left for home.

Following breakfast Lee and Kate returned to Kate's house. Lee said, "What a great weekend. I wish I didn't have to go home."

"I know, me too. Even though it was a fun weekend, I wish we'd had more time alone together."

"Next weekend in New York?" Lee asked.

Kate nodded. "I'll see if I can find some tickets to a show or something if you'd like."

"You don't need to keep finding ways to entertain me. Just seeing you is enough for me."

"I don't want you to get bored."

"I'm never bored with you. I get sick of all the travel," Lee admitted. "Still, I'm never bored with you."

Kate had to cancel plans the following weekend when Kevin caught a cold. Beth was away visiting her parents, and Kate had to cover the office. Kate had taken on extra hours already to help cover for Beth and was tired. Although Lee was disappointed when Kate cancelled their weekend plans, she understood. "Want me to come to you instead? I can take the train."

Kate considered Lee's offer. She wanted to see her, but with all that was going on, she just didn't have the energy. "Don't get me wrong.

Despite the fact that I'd love to see you, I'm going to say no. I'm exhausted and besides, I won't be able to drive over to pick you up at the train on Friday. The office is open until eight, so I'll be working when you get in and I'll have to work most of Saturday. We'd hardly get any time together before you'd have to leave to go home. Plus, I think I'm getting Kevin's cold."

"Are you sure? I don't mind. It would be worth the trip just to be able to hold you while you sleep because I love you."

"I know. I love you, too. Don't be upset with me, Lee, please."

"I'm not upset. I totally understand. I'll just miss you." Lee hated not seeing Kate on the weekend, especially when she'd been looking forward to their getting together.

Kate finished up at the office on Friday evening. She was looking forward to getting into bed and wishing it could be with Lee instead of with Cody. Not seeing Lee for the weekend had her in a subdued mood all day. It was well after eight when she locked up the office. Knowing she didn't have the energy to cook, she grabbed a fast-food hamburger, shake, and fries, eating them in the car on the way home. At last, she arrived home. She pulled into her driveway and was surprised to see the lights on in her house.

As Kate parked in front of her garage, the front door flew open and Lee raced out to kiss her lover, excited that she was finally home. "Are you okay? You look so tired."

Kate held her tight. "I'm fine. Oh boy, am I glad to see you. This is a wonderful surprise."

Kate nodded affirmatively when Lee asked if she'd eaten. "Come on, let's get you to bed. You look done in. I'll give you a nice massage and you can go right to sleep."

"I need a shower, first." Kate frowned. "Hey, how'd you get here?"

"You mean from the train? I called Kyle this morning, explained my dilemma, and asked if he could pick me up and deliver me to you."

"He always was a hopeless romantic. And you were very resourceful, my love. I'm so glad to see you." She kissed Lee and just held her as she rested her head on her shoulder.

"Off to the shower with you. I'll let Cody out and lock up while you shower." Lee lit a scented candle in Kate's bedroom. Bathed in the soft light, Kate emerged from her shower wrapped in a towel that Lee loosened but didn't release. "Lie face down on the bed and I'll make you feel better."

"Oh, Honey, it's not that I don't want you, I just don't think I have the energy. I'm so tired."

Lee pulled Kate's towel away. "I just want you to lie there and enjoy. You don't have to move a muscle. I'm just going to give you a little massage and a back scratch until you fall asleep. Let me take care of you tonight."

Kate groaned when Lee began to knead her tired muscles. Kate mumbled, "Umm, that feels so good." It was a matter of minutes after Lee started to scratch Kate's back that her even breathing indicated she'd drifted off to sleep. Lee got up, blew out the candle, used the bathroom, and after removing her clothes, slid naked into bed with her lover. She moved closer, spooning against Kate who murmured sleepily, "Love you."

"Shh, me too. Go to sleep."

Kate slipped out of bed the next morning, careful not to wake Lee. She left a note on the counter for her saying how pleased she was that Lee had come, gathered the things she needed and headed off to work. Kate was still feeling tired although she had more energy than the night before.

Lee reached for Kate when she awoke, disappointed that she'd missed her. At least she was well rested. She padded downstairs to the kitchen where she read Kate's note saying she'd just let Cody out and hadn't walked him. Lee took Cody for a walk after breakfast, showered, and waited for Mike and Kyle to pick her up for the lunch she'd promised them the previous day.

Lee ran out and jumped into the car when the guys tooted the horn. They drove to Kyle's favorite diner where they settled in and ordered.

"Really," Kyle protested. "You didn't need to treat us for picking you up." They were lingering over the last of their lunch.

"No, it's the least I could do. Anyway, it's good to see you two." Lee stirred milk into her coffee. "Kate and I seem to always be on the run. She's always so tired now. I thought it would be better after she hired Dr. Akers. Still, we never seem to have enough time to do all we want to do including seeing you two and our friends at home. It's not that we don't ever see other people as a couple. It's just that I have to admit that we do tend to live in a bit of a vacuum when we're together on the weekends. It's kind of a schizophrenic, unnatural existence. The rest of the world gets put on hold when we come together, until Sunday, when we part to again return to the 'real', weekday world. It's not the best way to have a relationship for sure."

"And there's no end in sight, is there? Couldn't one of you relocate?"

Mike asked.

"No. I don't see that happening. Kate's got a thriving practice here. I love and am doing well in my job, have a great boss, and good benefits. As a marine biologist, with my areas of specialization, I'd be out of my element here in the middle of Pennsylvania farm country." Lee smiled. "The expense and wear and tear on us physically are major drawbacks but, so far, we're doing okay."

"Well, don't let my chatter make waves." Kyle glanced over at his partner. "We old happily married people always want our friends to join us in wedded bliss."

Instead of having the guys drop her at the house, Lee asked them to drop her at Kate's office. Soon after Lee arrived, Kate emerged from one of the treatment rooms with her last patient of the day. She bid her patient and his owner goodbye before turning to Lee. "So, what's on for tonight?"

"I don't care, really. You decide. You're the one who worked all day. You look like you're dragging."

Kate yawned and rubbed her eyes. She frowned at the form on her clipboard as she tried to decipher the small print. "I know. I am tired. I don't know what's wrong with me. I feel so weary all the time. I think I might go in for some blood work and a checkup, and I need to get my eyes checked. They seem to be making the small print much fuzzier than they used to. Do you mind if we just grab a pizza and hang out at home?"

"As long as it involves snuggling with you anything is fine with me."

The local pizza shop delivered their pizza. Kate carried it into the kitchen and set it on the counter. She and Lee functioned like a well-oiled machine as they gathered napkins, plates, knives, and forks in preparation for the meal. Lee poured them each a soft drink.

Kate drank down several large swallows of her drink. "I'm starving. Lately I've been a bottomless pit, eating non-stop. I can't believe I'm not gaining weight." She patted her trim stomach. "I actually think I've lost a couple of pounds."

Lee gave an appreciative appraisal of Kate's body as her eyes traveled down and then up to meet her lover's patient gaze. "Probably from all those calories we burn up when I chase you around the bed."

Lee noticed that Kate had consumed half of the pizza by the time she'd eaten two slices. "Wow! You weren't kidding...you went through that like it was your last meal."

"I'm still hungry. Can I have another slice?"

Lee pushed the box towards Kate. "Sure. I'm done."

"Want to watch some tube?"

"Sounds good. I'll clean up here, while you find us something to watch." Lee stood and began to break down the pizza box.

While Lee threw away the paper plates and washed up the glasses and silverware, she heard Kate flipping through the channels. She heated some water for tea, made them each a cup, and carried the mugs into the living room. Kate was sitting upright on the sofa, legs stretched out, head back, and feet propped on the coffee table, sound asleep. Lee slipped the remote from Kate's hand, sat on the chair so as not to disturb her lover, then tuned in an old movie she'd seen a dozen times before. Cody settled on her lap to keep her company. Lee shook Kate awake when the movie ended at eleven-thirty.

Kate pulled Lee onto her lap. "I'm sorry, Hon. I didn't even realize I'd dozed off. You should have awakened me. I wasted our whole evening sleeping."

"You were resting so quietly, I didn't want to wake you. I don't know how you can sleep sitting up like that."

Kate laughed. "I'm not sure either. It's a relatively new skill I've acquired."

Sliding off Kate's lap, Lee said, "I'll let Cody out. You go get ready for bed, and I'll let you make it up to me," Lee gave Kate a kiss intended to get her blood moving.

"I'll take a quick shower. Was this tea for me?"

"Yes. I'm sure it's cold by now."

"Doesn't matter...I'm really thirsty. Must be all the cheese on the pizza," Kate said downing the now cool mug of tea in a few quick swallows.

"Eew!" Lee's nose wrinkled. "How can you drink that at room temperature like that?"

"If it had a couple of ice cubes in it, you'd drink it, right?"

"I guess." Lee grabbed Cody's leash. "Come on Cody, want to go out?"

Kate took the cups into the kitchen before her shower. The sheets felt cool against her heated skin as she slid into bed naked. She was still tired despite her nearly two-hour nap. Regardless, she was looking forward to making love with Lee. She heard the shower start and knew Lee would be joining her soon.

Kate woke up, astonished to see light streaming through the slit in the curtains. A quick glance at the clock on her dresser told her it was eight o'clock. She had slept nearly ten hours, virtually straight through. Yet she still felt like if she rolled over she could go back to sleep. She hadn't even heard Lee come to bed last night.

Kate got up and dressed quickly after she visited the bathroom. Lee had a hot cup of tea waiting for her when she entered the kitchen. Kate kissed Lee, apologizing for abandoning her last night.

"You must have been really tired to not even wake up when this naked, love starved woman curled up against you last night. You never even moved. I'm concerned that I'm losing my allure." Lee's smile indicated she was teasing although it didn't lessen Kate's guilt.

"I'm so sorry, honey." Kate drained the glass of water she had filled at the sink.

"I just made you tea."

"I know. I'll drink that next. I'm still thirsty from the pizza, I guess."

"I didn't find it particularly salty and it didn't affect me that way. Funny." Lee stood behind Kate encircling her waist. "So are you finally awake and rested?"

Kate turned around, drawing Lee tighter against her. "Absolutely," she lied. "What would you like to do today?"

"Well, in addition to you making it worth my effort of coming down here this weekend by making mad, passionate love to me, maybe we should take Cody for a walk. It's a beautiful day. Let's walk in town. Maybe we can find a little outdoor cafe where we can eat lunch."

"Sounds good."

"I went to the bakery. Have a bun. You're going to need energy to make up for neglecting me last night and so far this morning."

Kate followed instructions, ate a bun, and took Lee to bed. By noontime, they'd settled at one of the cafes having sandwiches and a soft drink with Cody curled at their feet under the table.

"Kate, is everything okay with us?" Lee cocked an eyebrow. "You don't seem yourself."

"Nothing's wrong with us." Kate reached over to squeeze Lee's hand. She leaned forward to help keep their conversation private. "I don't know if it's because we've been on the go with no breaks or if there's something wrong with me. Maybe I'm just getting old." She shrugged as she took a sip of her cola. "I just don't have any energy. I've had to take to setting an alarm. Can you believe that? I was almost late for work one day, and Cody was pissed when he missed his morning walk."

Lee studied her lover. "Maybe you're tired of our weekly commutes?"

"No, not at all. By meeting in the city on the off weekends, we don't have to make the full commute each time. Plus we're able to see each other every week, which is twice as often as we originally thought we'd be together. What about you?"

Lee pursed her lips, one of the mannerisms Kate had fallen in love with their first few days in the cabin. "You know that even though I'm not crazy about the drive down here, I really don't mind taking the train." Lee paused. "So it's not that you're getting bored with me...with us?" Lee asked, her concern evidenced by the furrow between her brows.

Kate's pulse pounded in her ears. She hadn't meant to ignore Lee last night. "Tired of you? Oh God, no. No, definitely no. I didn't mean to neglect you last night, Sweetheart. I just had no energy. I'm so sorry." Kate wondered if Lee was asking because she was dissatisfied in their relationship. "Are you sick of the grind of us being involved long distance?"

Lee steepled her fingers together and rested her chin on them for a few seconds before she answered. "I won't say that I haven't wished that we could live together or at least could live closer to each other. My answer to your question is a definite no. Being with you is worth any effort we have to make to accomplish being together. And last night didn't bother me. It actually made it seem more like a normal relationship. You know, more like really living together than our visiting, which sometimes seems something less than a real relationship. Last night was more like real life." Lee smiled her eyes softening as she looked at Kate. "Sometimes I do worry that I can't visualize a future for us. Like there's no way for us to ever do anything different, no possibility to have anything other than this. I mean we've been doing this commute and long-distance relationship for about five months now. I worry that it may get old eventually if we can't see a light at the end of the tunnel."

"We knew going into this that there would be challenges. We never know what the future has in store for us. Life throws us curve balls all the time and gives us unexpected opportunities as well."

"What do you mean, Kate?"

"Well, neither of us has really explored employment opportunities that might be available to allow us to live together, or at least live closer to each other."

"And you suggest this as a possibility even though you know that neither of us wants to change our vocation. I mean, your practice is here, and I'm happy in my job."

Kate sat back in her chair and shrugged. "I know. It's just that when we were talking with Angus, he was excited that your grant was renewed. What if, in a year or two, your grant doesn't get renewed, or it gets transferred to a different agency or location. You'd be forced to look for work elsewhere...maybe you could find something in Philly, and our problem would become more manageable."

Lee, seemingly deep in thought, didn't respond. Kate continued. "Or, suppose another vet decided to open up here in town, and my business drops off. My partners and I would have a dilemma. Maybe we'd agree that we'd have to cut hours or that one of us would have to leave. It's also possible that I'd consider selling my share of the business so I could move and work wherever you are. The only thing holding me here is my practice. As a majority partner in the practice, I have multiple options open to me including selling my share, or keeping my share and working for someone else."

Lee reached over and touched Kate's hand. "Well, you've given me hope that the light at the end of the tunnel isn't necessarily the train. Would you seriously consider selling your practice?"

Kate shrugged. "Today? No, probably not. But situations change. I agree with you that our long distance love affair could become an issue that could cool our drive to be together. Let's face facts. It surely would be easier if we were together or at least lived closer. I think we have a wonderful relationship, and I'm certainly not willing to give up on us just because being together requires a little effort. Are you?"

"No, definitely not. I'm in love with you, Kate. It's as simple as that."

"Yes, it is." Kate smiled at her lover. "I've never been this happy. I think the only thing that would make me happier is if we were able to be together full time."

"There's one more option we haven't discussed. One of us could quit and become the other's love slave." Lee wiggled her eyebrows.

"Hmm. Let's give more thought to that shall we, starting with a sample of your skills when we get back to the house."

Later, as Kate drove Lee to the train they talked about Lee's upcoming trip. They would have several more weeks together before Lee left for her month and a half in the Keys. They'd planned for and agreed that it would be best if Kate came in August at the end of Lee's time there. Lee planned to take several days off at the end of her work assignment so she could spend some free time with Kate enjoying the Keys together.

***

Kate still was not feeling well. She mentioned it to Beth one day as they were eating lunch.

"I've noticed that you've been not quite yourself lately. You look tired. Are you getting enough rest?"

Kate shrugged.

"If you were Mrs. Pattingdome's pet poodle, you'd have the problem diagnosed within two minutes. What are your symptoms?"

"Hmm." Kate thought for a moment. "Well, I'm hungry all the time, my vision is blurry, I've lost a few pounds that I probably shouldn't have since I'm eating everything put in front of me and still feel ready to gnaw off the table leg. I'm tired all the time. I don't know. If I didn't know that I don't have a family history of it, and I'm not overweight, I'd suspect I have diabetes."

"Well, there's one sure way to find out."

"I know. I'll call this afternoon and get a physical set up. Thanks, Beth."

Since Lee was extremely busy finishing everything related to her job before she left, Kate made the trip to Lee's house for the next three weekends. She also made time to visit her physician and have blood tests done. A few days later, Kate showed up promptly for her Friday morning appointment with her physician. Doctor Findley kept her waiting for fifteen minutes, and Kate's toe was tapping by the time they called her name. The nurse took her blood pressure and checked her weight before the doctor hurried in.

"Hey Kate. How have the allergies been?"

"Allergies have been okay, but I'm having a few other problems." Kate had struggled with a bad bout with allergies the previous winter. None of her usual medications had any impact on her condition, which turned into a severe case of bronchitis. The doctor had given her three separate doses of cortisone and two rounds of antibiotics over the course of several months. Finally, by Christmas time, she was breathing better and her cough had abated. "I've been having a bunch of different symptoms, and I think I need a good physical and some blood tests." Kate listed her symptoms as the doctor typed into the computer.

"Okay, Kate, let's have a look and see what we can find."

The doctor finished his exam as the nurse came in to draw blood. Kate gave a urine sample after which she visited the receptionist to make another appointment for the following week to get the results of her tests.

A week later, Kate took the day off. Her anticipated appointment with Doctor Findley had her curious as well as apprehensive about her test results. The nurse ushered her into the office and took her vital signs before closing the door behind her as she left. Dr. Findley followed in shortly thereafter. After a few pleasantries, the doctor's face clouded before he said, "Kate, I have some unwelcome news. Your fasting blood sugar is quite elevated, nearly one fifty, and here are the results of your A1C. I don't have to tell you what this means."

"Is it possible there is some kind of mistake? I have no family history of diabetes and am not overweight." Kate remembered all the steroids she took when her allergies acted up. "Oh, think it's from all the cortisone I took?"

"It's possible. You may have steroid induced diabetes. Still, your levels should have dropped by now if that's what brought it on." He checked the chart. "You finished taking the steroids a while ago. What are your eating habits like? Do you eat regular meals?"

"I'm a vet, of course not. Half the time after breakfast it's grab and go, if anything. There are definitely too many pizzas, sandwiches, and too many pieces of cake at my farmers' places. In the office, things are usually so hectic that I'm lucky if I get lunch two times or maybe three times a week."

"What about exercise?"

"Well, I do walk Cody, but he stops to piddle at every post, so I can't honestly say I'm ever forced to breathe heavy on our walks. I do still lift weights, although not nearly as regularly as I used to."

"I don't have to tell you how important it is to get your sugar under control before the next test. You know the drill. Watch your carbs, get regular exercise, reduce your fat intake, eat regular smaller meals, and have small, healthy snacks twice a day. I want you to do another round of blood tests in a month."

"Okay."

"Remember two blood tests over the established guidelines and you'll be diagnosed with diabetes. Maybe we've caught things early enough you can get it under control with diet and exercise. As he talked, he wrote a number on the back of a slip of paper. If you have any questions you can contact this woman. She's a wonderful nutritionist who gives great suggestions." He slid the number across the desk to Kate. "Here are the orders for your next blood test." He handed her several sheets of paper. "Give the large sheet to the receptionist and make an appointment for five or six weeks from now. And get that sugar down."

Kate forced herself to stand and follow the doctor out of the treatment room. As a person with a medical background, Kate knew the implications of having diabetes and it frightened her. She vowed that she'd do everything she could to lower her blood sugar before her next blood test. After paying her bill, the drive home must have occurred in a fog as she barely could remember the route she took by the time she parked the car in her driveway.

CHAPTER 26

EARLY SUMMER 2012

DIABETES. WOW, I NEVER expected that. As a medical person, Kate knew the impact the disease could have on her body. Because she'd vowed to get her sugar under control, she began a new exercise routine that included daily cardio exercise in addition to her weight training, visited the nutritionist, and adjusted her diet. She packed her lunch and carried healthy snacks with her for between meal treats.

Because Lee was busy preparing for her trip Kate made the trip there the last three weekends before Lee was scheduled to leave. After making love, they lay cuddled in bed talking about how much they would miss being together.

"I wanted to surprise you by taking diving lessons before I joined you in the Keys. I had to postpone that because the doctor wants me to wait until I get my sugar stabilized. I'm sorry Sweetie. I don't know if I'll ever be able to share that part of your life with you now."

Lee wrapped Kate in her arms and pulled her closer. "You'll be able to for sure, as soon as you get your sugar under control. It used to be that if you had diabetes, you couldn't dive. You know it's now possible as long as you can maintain your numbers and don't experience low blood sugar levels. Even if we can't dive together we can still snorkel. I have so much to show you on the reef that we have a lifetime of exploration there without diving."

"Are you anxious to get back to the Keys?"

"Always." She smiled at Kate reaching up to touch her face. "I'll miss you. There are concerns about the damage to the reef from the environment that we'll be looking at this trip, and I'm anxious to see the changes on the reef since last year."

"I love how excited your work makes you." Kate squeezed Lee's hand and gave her a smile. "Sometimes I miss that in my job. It used to be exciting when I first started out. Anymore...I don't know. I think I miss the challenge of working with larger animals and learning new things. I've grown to hate the paperwork and the responsibility of running the practice. It's all part of the job I guess. It's just that it was a lot more fun when I started out."

"Why don't you take a class...or teach a class?"

Kate lifted her eyebrows. "There's an idea I hadn't entertained. It may be something I'll consider when I get my energy levels back to normal."

Their weekend ended all too soon. Kate lingered at the door holding Lee. "I hate to leave. Six weeks is such a long time to be away from you."

"Five and a half. You'll be there before you know it, and I'll call you every night to tell you how much I miss you, too."

As Kate pulled away from the curb, Lee watched until Kate was out of sight before she closed the door, her hand still covering her aching heart.

***

"How's the weather there in sunny Florida?" Kate pressed the phone closer to her ear to allow her to hear Lee better.

"Hello Sweetheart. It's great!" Lee glanced out the window at the ocean. "We're in the high eighties in the daytime and seventies at night. It's just perfect for being in the water. I can't wait for you to get down here."

"It's been really hot and sticky up here. You know the humidity we get here where I live. I can't wait to get down there to see you and experience those balmy ocean breezes."

"Angus and Fiona are looking forward to your visit, and they're not alone. How's your sugar?"

"Good. I went for my follow up visit that showed I've lowered my A1C levels substantially, but they're still above normal limits. The doctor put me on medication to help me."

"That's great, Hon. What does your doctor say?"

Kate sighed. "He's reserved but optimistic. I've been testing frequently, watching my low levels. I hope if I can keep them in normal range for the next six months he'll consider taking me off my meds for a trial. I'm doing my exercise routine everyday, bringing my meals, walking after I eat. I'm following my routine every day."

"That's great news, Kate. I know you'll get it under control."

"How's work going? Are you and Angus having fun?"

"We are. There's a lot of concern about the reef, though." Lee continued talking to Kate about what she was seeing and taking pictures of for her report. "We've recently begun working with a new task force. We're tasked with examining a number of factors all centered around determining the effect of environmental factors on marine organisms. It's very exciting. We're studying various species of fish for stressors such as DNA damage, reduced fertility, and lowered immune system function."

"You'd mentioned your concern about the reef before."

"Yes. I love it here in the Keys. I love what I do, and love working with other professionals who are as passionate about this work as I am." Lee's enthusiasm and excitement were evident in her voice.

Soon their conversation turned to Kate's travel plans. Kate conveyed all the pertinent information about her flight and projected arrival. "I'm so excited. I can't wait to see you." They hung up with a promise to call each other the next day at the usual time.

CHAPTER 27

AUGUST 2012

KATE LANDED IN MIAMI and picked up her bag before heading for the car rental window. She was fifth in line, and it took her about fifteen minutes to sign out the economy sized rental car. She threw her luggage into the trunk, squeezed into the rental car, checked her map, and was off to meet her lover.

Kate's mind wandered as she drove the seventy-five minutes. Being apart from her partner for the five week separation helped her realize how central Lee had become to her life. She decided to speak to Lee to determine if there was an option they could pursue that would allow them to be together. Although her diabetes was well under way to being in control, being diagnosed coalesced her resolve that she wanted to spend her life with Lee. They'd touched on the possibility of Lee moving, and Lee had told her that opportunities for her were limited where Kate lived. Kate had worked so hard to salvage her practice after Max left that she was initially not willing to make changes to her life. Now Kate wasn't so sure her future would include continuing there if it meant she couldn't be with Lee. Besides, her practice had changed dramatically over the years. She missed dealing with the larger animals she used to treat and had grown to dislike being cooped up in the office all day most days.

The beauty of the water and the amazing feat of engineering and construction of the bridge amazed Kate. With the ocean on the left and the Gulf on the right, the concrete thread of a road, floated and wound its way across the beautiful turquoise and aqua colored water. Kate passed many attractions including a number of places to grab a quick bite to eat. She was too eager to get to Lee and chose to snack on some nuts she had in her pocket instead of grabbing a burger, as she would have in the past. As she grew close to her destination, the sky, a blend of colors from reddish orange to purple, provided a backdrop for the clouds that were a mixture of dramatic shades of grey to fluffy white. They appeared almost close enough for Kate to touch. She soaked in the beauty of the scenery and gave the colorful sunset the awe it deserved. She could feel her heart beating faster as she neared marker 108 that Lee had directed her to watch for. Once there, Kate pulled over and checked the final steps of her directions. She called Lee. "I'm here! You told me to call you when I got here. Are you at home or work?"

"I'm home and I can't wait to see you. I'm so excited you're here. Think you'll be able to find Angus and Fiona's house from the directions I gave you?"

Kate looked around. "I think so. I've made it this far. I can't wait to see you."

"Me too. We waited dinner for you. You hungry?"

"Starved. I'll see you in a few minutes."

Lee was waiting on the porch when Kate pulled up in front of Angus and Fiona's house. She jammed the car into park, flung open the door and hurried to meet Lee halfway down the walk. They clung to each other murmuring endearments and sentiments about how much they missed each other.

"Come on in. I'm sure you want to clean up and use the restroom before we eat." Lee led Kate inside and down the hallway where she pressed her against the wall and kissed her thoroughly. "I've been missing you like fire. I can't wait to get you alone later. First we have to go make nice with Angus and Fiona and have something to eat." She kissed her again before turning her around and pushing her toward the bathroom. "Hurry," she said, after she gave Kate another quick kiss. "I'll see you at the table. The quicker we finish dinner, the sooner I can get you alone."

Angus and Fiona welcomed Kate with warm hugs when she joined them in the kitchen. They sat down to dinner and Angus asked, "How was your trip?"

"Long, although the drive from Miami to the Keys was beautiful. That bridge is amazing. It's surely something to be seen, and I can't wait to explore the area around here. Since Lee is working for the next few days, I'll wander and explore to my heart's content during the daytime when she's working. Then when she finishes work for the season, we'll have a few days together before we have to go home."

Angus smiled at his guest. "We hope you'll come tour the facility tomorrow so you can see what we've been up to for the past few weeks. Lee has some wonderful new pictures. She tells me you're great at organizing them and helping her locate what she needs. Maybe we'll hire you to do some work for us while you're here."

"Don't be silly, I'd be happy to help out. I'll feel better about freeloading on your hospitality if I can do something useful."

After dinner Lee and Kate washed the dishes. Wiping the last plate and hanging the towel on the rack, Kate said, "I'd like to take a walk, if it's okay. I usually walk after lunch and dinner. It helps my sugar levels."

"Sure. I think you'd better make that walk a bit shorter than normal to conserve some of that sugar because, after we walk, I'm going to help you burn off some more of that sugar, Sugar." Lee wrapped her arms around a chuckling Kate, kissed each cheek, and placed a long slow kiss on her lips. "Come on. The sooner we get going the earlier I can get you to bed. I have big plans for you tonight. My goal is to make love to you until you can't lift your head off the bed."

"Hmm...I think just tonight, if you kiss me like that again, I could be convinced to forego my walk, especially since I figure we'll be expending a considerable amount of energy for a good portion of the evening."

Lee and Kate waved goodnight to Fiona and Angus in the living room and headed down the hallway to Lee's room. As soon as they closed and locked the door, Lee pinned Kate to the wall. She kissed her thoroughly, sliding her hands under Kate's shirt to press her palms to Kate's willing breasts. Within seconds, she pulled Kate's shirt off over her head, unsnapped her bra, and began feasting on Kate's nipples. "Oh God, how I've missed you, missed this." She unbuckled Kate's belt and quickly stripped her pants and underwear from her.

Kate grabbed Lee's wrists and turned her around, pressing her against the door. "This isn't fair. I'm standing here naked and you're fully clothed."

Lee maintained eye contact as she pushed Kate away to arm's length and slowly unbuttoned her blouse before flirtatiously slipping it from her shoulders. She wasn't wearing a bra. When Kate reached for her, Lee stopped her with a shake of her head.

"Patience my love. There's more to come." Lee reached for her shorts and slipped them and her underwear down to the floor and stepped out of them.

Kate's hungry eyes traveled over Lee's body. "I want you so much," she whispered. They came together, their desire mutual. They entered each other and began moving together as they kissed deeply. "I can't wait," Kate gasped as she crested the wave, moaned her release and pulled Lee over the edge with her. She didn't give Lee a chance to recover before she was touching her everywhere with her hands, her lips, and her tongue driving Lee to a new high. "I need to taste you." They stumbled to the bed. Kate sucked Lee's hardness into her mouth making her moan. She soon brought Lee to another orgasm. Lee's arms fell limply at her sides.

Kate chuckled, "So, who wasn't going to be able to lift her head from the bed?"

"Your turn will come, my dear…in just a minute." Lee smiled up at her partner. "I love you."

"I love you, too." They took turns showing each other just how much late into the night.

CHAPTER 28

THEY BOTH GROANED WHEN the alarm shook them from sleep. "Ump," Lee grunted. "I've got to get my shower and get going. Why don't you sleep in a little before coming over to the Center for your tour? I'll leave directions for you on the table." She kissed Kate, got up, gathered a change of clothes, and quietly closed the door.

Two hours later Kate woke up, stretched, and smiled. She was pleasantly sore from her extended love making session with Lee. Until she was back in Lee's arms she hadn't realized the full extent of how much she missed her lover. She was sure Lee felt the same. Although in addition to a feeling of being cherished and loved, such enormous need also instilled a small tingle of fear in the back of her mind. She was fully cognizant that Lee's love of her job and of the Keys meant that eventually Lee might face having to choose between her love for Kate and her love for her job. She pushed down the fear with the recollection of their shared passion. Now showered and dressed, Kate was eager to be on her way to meet her lover. She headed for the kitchen where she found a note from Lee giving her directions to the Center and instructing her to have breakfast and to call her before she left.

Kate measured out and ate some cereal and fruit for breakfast. She texted Lee to inform her she was on her way before heading for her rental car. After only one wrong turn, she eventually pulled into the parking lot and parked in a visitor's spot. Lee came bounding around the corner of the building and jogged over to meet Kate. She greeted her with a warm hug, clasped her hand and led her toward the building talking all the way, explaining what Kate was seeing. Lee showed her the meeting and conference rooms, the lab, and the dock area. The tour ended in Lee's office.

Kate looked around at Lee's work area. "This is a really impressive facility. I can see how much you love it here and can understand why. The work being done here is very impressive."

"I'm glad you were able to come and see this. It's an important part of who I am. I'm glad you're here to share it with me."

***

Later that afternoon, Lee took Kate with her to collect some reef samples. Kate had worn her swimsuit under her clothes as Lee had directed in her note that morning. They took a motorboat out and anchored. Lee gave Kate a snorkel and mask and showed her how to use it. They swam along the reef as Lee took the samples she needed. As they swam, Lee stopped occasionally to take photos documenting what she was doing and sometimes taking pictures of various fish, always telling Kate what she was looking at. It was not long before Kate could identify several species of fish common to the reef area.

After being in the water swimming for over an hour, they climbed back into the boat. Kate opened a small bag of nuts and raisins and ate them to keep her blood sugar at an acceptable level as they motored back to the Center. Lee recorded her afternoon activities in her logbook, then bagged and tagged her samples for processing. They changed back into street clothes before Lee locked up her office.

As they walked back to the car Kate told Lee, "Tonight I'm taking you out for dinner. I left Fiona and Angus a note this morning telling them we'd be late tonight and inviting them out for dinner tomorrow night. You'll have to help me though, because I want to take you somewhere special where we can drink some wine and watch the sun go down. Tell me where and I'll make reservations before we head out. Maybe we can take a walk before dinner, and you can show me around a little."

"That sounds like a plan." Lee tapped the name of her favorite restaurant into her phone and handed it to Kate. They left Lee's car in the lot and took Kate's, parking near the restaurant. They walked several blocks, circling back to the restaurant in time for their reservation. The hostess greeted them as they entered.

"Hello. We have reservations under the name of Kate."

"Yes, right this way, please." She seated them at a window with a view of the water and left the menus. When the waitress came, they ordered salads and grilled shrimp from the cheerful server.

The wine arrived and was uncorked at the table. Kate did the honors of tasting and approving it. Kate raised her glass when the server left. She only poured it a third full with just enough wine to have a taste, and clinked it against Lee's. "To you and to us."

Lee smiled and nodded in acknowledgement of the toast. "So what do you think of Key Largo?"

"Well, if you need to buy diving or snorkeling equipment there are certainly sufficient options. Dive shops are on every corner around here." Kate laughed. "They are like pharmacies back home."

"Yes, true. There are places to get pretty much everything else you need and some great food, too."

"So what's on for tomorrow?"

"I'm off tomorrow." Lee set her glass on the table and leaned forward on her forearms. "We can travel down the Keys or we can do something fun around here. Interested in swimming with the dolphins?"

"I'll do anything you like."

"Parasailing might be fun."

Feigning horror, Kate responded, "Maybe I'll opt for the dolphins."

Lee laughed. "Coward."

"You betcha." Kate smiled and took a small sip of her wine. Alcohol raised her blood sugar, but this was a special occasion. She'd limit her intake to a half a glass. "So when do we sort photos?"

"We can do some of that in the evenings. I have to work through Wednesday. After that, we have four days before we leave to head home."

"Maybe we can drive down to Key West and do some sightseeing during that time. One day, while you're working, I want to go to the Key Deer Refuge Center on Big Pine Key. How far is that?"

"About an hour and a half."

Kate nodded. "That'll work."

Their dinner arrived and they chatted and ate their way through the meal. After sharing some fresh fruit for dessert, they walked to the car and headed back to visit with Fiona and Angus who enjoyed hearing about their day. Kate arranged for dinner the next evening with their hosts before heading to bed.

***

The weather was perfect when they awoke the next morning. After a breakfast of cereal and fresh fruit, Kate said. "It really is beautiful here, Lee. In addition to the gorgeous weather and scenery, there's so much to see and do. The reef is like having an amazing playground right at your fingertips. What do you have on the agenda today?"

Lee slid her hand up Kate's thigh, sliding her fingers under the leg of Kate's shorts. "You mean right now?"

Kate laughed. "Well, maybe not right this minute. I can probably figure that out for myself. I meant a little later."

"I arranged with a friend of mine for us to see the dolphins at the rescue center." Lee checked her watch. "As a matter of fact, our other activity has to be put on hold till later, because we're due at the pool in about forty minutes."

Three hours later they were on their way back to the house. Kate was gushing about the experience. "That was really amazing. Thank you for arranging the tour. I'm sure it was more fun for me than for you. You probably swim with wild dolphins everyday, and I'm sure you already know all the information he told us. For this novice it was a blast."

Kate was still pumped from her experience and as they ate dinner she couldn't stop talking to Angus and Fiona about the great time she'd had. Later, back at Angus and Fiona's house, Kate and Lee began sorting the photos. Progress was slow because Kate kept asking questions about everything she saw. "I can understand why you love this place so much, Lee. There's so much to see and do."

***

The following day, Kate got up early and drove to the Key Deer Refuge, arriving early enough that she saw several of the diminutive deer that were about the size of a good sized dog. By touring the refuge she learned a lot about the recovery of the deer population. In response to her question about the health care of the deer, the guide directed her to contact the Veterinary Hospital on Marathon Key. She stopped there on her way home and was lucky enough to meet the hospital owner whose responsibilities included care of the deer and many of the other wild animals on the Keys. She spent an interesting fifteen minutes with him learning about the Key deer, and any number of birds, tortoises, and other animals that received treatment from the hospital staff. She thanked the doctor and turned to leave.

"Kate?"

Surprised by hearing her name called, Kate turned just as one of her classmates from vet school pulled her into a big bear hug. "George? What are you doing here? Last I heard you were in California."

"I was. When this opened up I jumped at the chance to move here. Do you have a few minutes to grab a cup of coffee with me so we can catch up?"

"Sure. I'm eager to learn more about this facility and what you've been doing."

They went into the staff room where George got them each a cup of coffee and Kate an iced tea. "So what are you doing with your life?"

Kate stirred her sugar substitute into the tea. "I have a practice back in Pennsylvania. Started out doing large animals, but now most of the farms are gone and I'm doing mostly small animals. I still volunteer at the local animal sanctuary. It keeps me sane." She smiled to lessen the seemingly negative statement.

"I know exactly what you mean." George stirred his coffee vigorously. "I made the move here about nine months ago. I'm thrilled with the job. I love the facility and the variety of the work. Most of us here volunteer at the sanctuaries around here. I haven't learned so much since vet school. Almost everyday there is some new creature I've never dealt with before. It's exciting, Kate. I love it."

They spent the next fifteen minutes catching up, sharing where each of their classmates ended up, and listing the names of people with whom they'd been in touch recently. George and Kate exchanged contact information after promising each other they'd keep in touch. Kate left feeling good that her friend was happy and wishing just a little that she was still as excited about her practice as he seemed to be about his work.

Returning to Angus and Fiona's house, Kate was again filled with exciting tales of what she'd seen and learned that day. For the remainder of her stay, she and Lee traveled the length of the Keys stopping at various points of interest and eventually staying a couple of nights in Key West where they relaxed and watched the sunsets from the porch of their hotel.

"This is bliss," Kate said with a sigh. "It's what life should be like, but isn't."

"It could be."

"Maybe in a dream. We both have jobs elsewhere, lives elsewhere. I guess that's what makes it the perfect vacation. It's what you imagine perfection would be. In reality, there's nothing that's perfect."

Lee frowned. She was surprised to hear Kate make that statement and wondered what had caused her to make such a negative statement. "What do you mean?"

"I don't know. I look around and I see other people who seem to have it all. Jobs they love, partners they love. Like Kyle and Mike, Fiona and Angus, and my friend George for example."

"Not like us?"

"No." Kate sighed. "I mean what we have is great. It's just that our jobs keep us apart. You love yours and don't want to leave it. I guess what I mean is that I make enough money to support both of us. Would you ever consider that, so we can be together?"

Trying to process what she'd heard, Lee shook her head. "You mean quit my job and come to live with you and have you support me? No. I wouldn't be happy. What about you? You could work anywhere, you once told me."

"In theory, yes. However, I have the practice, two partners. I have an obligation to them, to there. Extricating myself from the practice would be complicated. I wouldn't sell to just anyone. I couldn't do that to my partners or my patients. If I could even find anyone who'd want to buy into the practice, I'd have to be comfortable with them and their skills and know that Beth and Kevin would be okay. Unless someone magically appeared on my doorstep seeking what I have, it could take a couple of years to find someone to buy me out."

"What about Kevin and Beth?"

"Neither of them could afford it right now. It was all they could do to come up with enough to buy their current share."

"So that leaves us where?"

Kate pulled Lee's hand into her lap. "It leaves us lucky. Lucky because we have a loving relationship and live close enough that we can see each other regularly. Right?" Kate looked over and met Lee's eyes.

Lee nodded slowly. "Yes, I guess. Right."

"Come on. Let's not waste our last night here talking about what we don't have. Let's spend the rest of the evening enjoying what we can and do have—each other."

Kate pulled Lee to her feet and led her to the bedroom. Their lovemaking was sweet and tender and they fell asleep wrapped tightly, afraid to lose contact.

The next morning, they reluctantly headed back to Key Largo to prepare for their flight home. Buckled in their seats after their plane took off, Kate lamented, "I can't believe the time went so fast."

"I feel exactly the same way every time I have to leave. I'm glad you understand now."

"It really is a different style of life, isn't it?"

Lee nodded and glanced out the window at her beloved Keys. "Definitely."

CHAPTER 29

THEIR LIFE SLOWLY RETURNED to normal following their vacation on the Keys. Kate got a good report from her doctor and Lee and Angus finished their report. Kate met Kyle for lunch the week after she got back. She was filled with details about what she had seen and done while in Florida.

"You should see the veterinary hospital down there that I visited. I ran into an old college friend while I was at the refuge. He was so happy and excited about what he's doing there."

"And you aren't happy about what you're doing here?"

"I don't know. It seems as time passes and my practice changes, I get farther and farther from what I envisioned when I did my training. I should be grateful. I'm blessed. I have a thriving practice, two great business partners, and a wonderful girlfriend who makes me incredibly happy."

"But?"

"No but. Well, maybe I just wish for what you and Mike have. You have a great business, you're doing something important, and you have a great full-time relationship. You have it all."

"And you don't?"

"I don't mean to whine. I know that I have many blessings. I should be grateful for everything I have."

"Although you're not?"

"No. I am. I'm just a selfish pig who wants more." Kate smiled at Kyle and he reached over and grasped her hand in his.

"So when are you and Lee going to tie the knot?"

"I don't know. I don't see it happening. Lee is already wedded to her work, and I have equal commitments here. Being together would be like adultery, since we're both married to our jobs. Not that I wouldn't jump at the chance to spend my life with her."

Kate had been thinking about their relationship a lot lately, especially after her diagnosis. Her health was fine now, although she knew all too well how quickly things could change. Having such a great time on their vacation caused her to realize that she wanted to enjoy spending time with Lee while she was still healthy enough to be active with her. Hopefully, if she continued to watch her diet and live a healthy lifestyle, her diabetes would never be an issue, but she knew how insidious diabetes could be.

Kyle drew Kate back to the conversation. "So what are you going to do? Just keep on keeping on?"

"I guess. I don't know what else there is."

"How does Lee feel?"

"I'm not sure." Kate ran her fingers through her hair, propped her chin in her palm and met Kyle's gaze. "That's not true. I know she loves me. I also know she loves her career. Maybe she's like the others have been. Maybe she loves her job more than she loves me."

"Does it have to come to her making a choice between you and her job? I mean it seems you're not all that happy with your job here anymore. Why does she have to come to you? Maybe you should consider making some changes, some sacrifices to get something you both want. Why should she be the one to give up something she loves?"

"I don't know. It just seems easier for her to come to me. It's so complicated for me. I have the business..."

"And she works at a job she loves," Kyle threw back.

"I know. What about Kevin and Beth? I have them to consider."

"What about them? You're in a partnership with them. You didn't promise them a lifetime. What if one of them decides to leave? God forbid, but what if you keeled over tomorrow. Don't you think the place would survive? None of us is indispensable, Kate. Not even you."

***

Before they knew it, the Thanksgiving holiday was right around the corner. They planned a dinner at Kate's house, inviting their friends and family. Lee took some time off and spent several extra days with Kate helping prepare the meal and arranging for their guests.

After the holiday, when all the guests had left, Lee still had one day to spend with Kate who had been uncharacteristically quiet during her visit. Kate drove her to the station to wait for her train. "Is something bothering you, Honey?"

"Why?"

"Because you haven't said anything all day. Did something upset you?"

"No." Lee was silent for a few seconds then said, "I'm excited and upset at the same time."

"What's up? You know you can tell me anything."

"Kate, they transferred our grant to the Keys. I leave in January. It's exciting. However, I don't want to leave you."

Kate pulled Lee to her. "Oh God, Sweetheart. What are we going to do?" They held each other as they cried.

Lee sniffed and wiped her tears. "I've never been so happy and so miserable all at the same time."

"We'll work something out." Kate promised.

"How? It's definitely too far to commute. If we get to see each other two or three times a year we'll be lucky." Lee pulled away. "Kate, I won't do a long distance relationship again. I just can't."

Lee's red-rimmed eyes focused on Kate's equally tear reddened ones. "I'm annoyed with myself that I'm...that we're in this situation. I can't believe we allowed ourselves to be duped into believing we had a future. We started out knowing long distance romances don't work out and that we'd end up miserable."

"Lee. Don't give up on us. At least give me a chance to come up with a solution."

"What solution? Didn't we just talk about this in Key West? We didn't see a solution at that time. What's changed?" Lee's eyes filled again. "Being able to work in the Keys is my lifelong dream. As much as I love you, I'm not willing to give up on my dream of living and working there, and you aren't willing to give up your practice here. So that leaves us nowhere."

"Just give me some time, Lee. Give us some time."

"Why? There's no solution. Here comes my train. I'll call you when I get home." Lee took a long look at Kate as if trying to imprint every detail of her face in her memory. She gave her lover a final kiss and ran for the train.

CHAPTER 30

"I'M HOME." LEE SAID when Kate answered her phone.

"Okay. I'll go on the computer." With their connection established, Kate stared at Lee's face on her computer screen. She looked miserable. "I miss you."

"I know. I miss you, too."

Kate frowned into the camera. "You shouldn't have told me that way. It wasn't fair to dump that on me then run away."

"I know. I debated about it, but I didn't want to ruin the time we had together over the holiday. So I decided to wait for the right time. There just wasn't a right time to tell you."

There was a long, pregnant pause between them. Kate's eyes filled with unshed tears. "I can't let our relationship end like this. There must be a way. I've been thinking...what if I get my pilot's license? If I rearrange my schedule, I could fly down for long weekends a couple of times a month."

Lee laughed and wiped her tears. "You're amazing. An idiot, but still amazing." She wiped her nose with a tissue and smiled at her lover. "Kate, be reasonable. Really, think about it."

"I have thought about it. I'm not willing to let you go. I can't. I love you."

"I love you, too. I don't see any other way, though. We have to let it go. You're rooted there in Pennsylvania, and I'm not willing to give up my dream. You know it's something I've wanted all my adult life." Lee sniffed. There was silence between them as Lee searched for the proper words. "You once told me you wanted a woman who could promise you a forever, who could put you first. I'm not willing or able to do that right now. I can't give up on something I've worked for all my life, something I've wanted all my life. I can't do that, you know, to be your wife, to quit my job and stay at home." Lee blotted her eyes with the tissue. "I don't want to be another one who leaves you, Kate. Come with me."

"How can I? I have the practice here…"

"I know. I'm about to attain a goal, no a dream, I've worked for all my life. I can't and won't give it up even though I love you. How can you expect me to do that when you're not willing or able to do the same for me? Your sense of responsibility to your practice and to your partners won't let you pursue what you want either. So we're at an impasse."

"I know it seems that way." Kate made one more try. "Can't we give it some time?"

"I can't. There's just no point. There's no answer for us." Lee's tears flowed freely now, tracking shamelessly down her face. "You know that after what happened with Kendra, I won't do that long distance thing again. I can't."

"What if I take a couple of weeks off and come up to spend some time with you before you go. Maybe…"

"No, Kate. I can't. I only have this week. Angus wants me to pack up here and head down there to set up our offices. I don't mean to sound harsh, but I won't have any time for you, for us. Just let me go. Please. This is hard enough as it is. Don't fight me anymore. Just let me go."

"Do you love me?"

"You know I do." Lee sniffed and wiped her already reddened eyes.

"Then wait for me. I'll figure something out."

"No, Kate. Let me go. Please."

And with that, she was gone. Kate sat staring at a blank screen. She cried out, her anguish startling Cody who came to her side. Kate picked him up and sobbed into his soft fur, crying until she had no more tears and the sobs were just dry whimpers. Even Cody's kisses couldn't help cheer her.

CHAPTER 31

KATE SAT WITH MIKE and Kyle in her living room late Sunday afternoon after they'd shared some takeout and watched the football game on television. The guys had been visiting Kate regularly since what she thought of as her fatal conversation with Lee nearly a month ago. She'd just barely managed to function and perform her duties at the clinic. Kevin and Beth had been supportive as well, often putting in extra time so Kate could go home to rest. She was obviously depressed. Even Cody couldn't cheer her up although he tried his best to be cute and entertaining. He'd taken to putting a paw on either of her shoulders and resting his head next to hers as they sat on the sofa at night as if he hoped his hug could placate her emptiness.

"Have you heard any more from her?" Mike asked during the halftime break.

"We had a Skype call when she first went down to the Keys. She told me she was staying at Angus and Fiona's house for the time being. Angus is finishing up with their responsibilities up here, while she gets things set up down there. She's helping to set up some sort of interagency planning committee. She seems excited about the job."

Kyle asked, "Any change in her position about your relationship?"

"No. She says she still loves me, but…" Kate glanced away and inhaled a deep breath. "You know, the same old, same old. No change in our situation, so no change in her position. I hate to admit that I take some consolation in the fact that she doesn't look any happier than I do. The circles under her eyes rival the ones under mine."

"Have you made any decisions?" Kyle slid over and put an arm around his friend.

"No. I did talk to Beth and Kevin about buying my practice. Although they'd love to, neither can afford it right now. Beth hasn't been working all that long and she has a raft of school loans still to pay off. Kevin is closer to being able to afford it, just not right now. They were nice about it, and said they'd understand if I sold my share. They did ask to be able to buy a controlling interest. If I sold them each an additional one percent, together they'd own an equal majority share. I can understand them wanting that even though it could make it harder for me to sell. Times are tough. So many people are struggling and out of work. I don't know if I could even get a buyer right now."

Kyle asked, "What about hiring someone to take your place? You retain ownership but hire someone to work with Beth and Kevin."

"I've thought about that. I'm afraid to take that chance without some sense of surety that I wouldn't get stuck down the road. You know, get established down in the Keys and have my replacement here quit and leave me stuck."

"Can't you lock someone into a contract for a set term?"

"I guess. What happens if I lock someone into a three year contract and things don't work out with Lee and me?"

Kyle slapped his knee causing everyone to jump. "Jeez, Louise! What happens if you drop dead tomorrow? You're being overly cautious, Kate. Where is your spirit of adventure?"

"You forget. I'm not a kid anymore."

"All the more reason. If you don't take a chance on being happy now, when are you going to do it?"

Kate exhaled and clenched her teeth together. She looked away, unwilling to show him her cowardice. "I don't know. I don't know if I can. Anyway, Lee obviously doesn't want me enough to come here and let me take care of her."

Kyle pushed his point home. "The same could be said of you. You're not willing to sacrifice your security to be with her either. That doesn't mean you don't love her, does it?"

Kate was silent for a long time before she quietly admitted, "No. No it doesn't."

Kyle took her hand. "You've always told me you wanted a forever love. I think you have that in Lee. Why aren't you embracing it? Why are you being so stubborn Kate? Why does she have to give up her dream?"

Kate remained silent.

"Why won't you let yourself be happy?" Kyle pushed harder. "Seriously, what is your dream? Is your dream to stay here and slog through another twenty years in this vet practice without the woman you love? Or is your dream to be with someone who loves you?" Kyle pulled Kate to him and put his arm around her. "You know I love you, right?"

Kate nodded her head that was resting on his shoulder.

"Maybe it's time for you to, just this once, to think with your heart instead of your head? Will you at least consider what I've said?"

Kate stretched up and kissed Kyle's cheek. "I promise. I will."

Mike who had been mostly quiet during the exchange between his partner and Kate spoke up. "Hey! I want in on some of this hugging and kissing action." He slid over and pulled Kate to him and gave her a hug. "Everyone should be happy, Kate. Even though you and Lee had to make that ungodly trek every weekend to be with each other, you were happy then. Are you happy without her?"

When Kate shook her head, Mike said simply, "Then you have an answer you need to give some serious consideration to, don't you?"

***

The guys headed home when the game ended a little after six. Kate had mindlessly watched the second half of the game as her thoughts raced. She did a lot of thinking about her conversation with Kyle and Mike after they'd left. Mike was right. If she was ever going to make changes in her life there was no time like the present. What did she really want and what was she willing to give up to get it? She thought about her conversation she'd had in the Keys with George and how happy he was, how excited about what he was doing. She considered what made her happy in her own life, about how much she enjoyed volunteering at the local animal sanctuary and about how little sense of fulfillment she was getting from her small animal practice. She shook her head. She needed to talk to Lee. She missed her so much. She got her laptop and pulled up the interface to place the call.

Lee's face appeared on the screen. She looked tired. "Hello there," Kate said when Lee smiled at her.

"Hi. I was just thinking about you. I miss you. I miss talking to you. I miss seeing you. I miss making love with you. This sucks!"

"Big time." Kate smiled. "I miss you, too...and all those other things as well." After a brief hesitation, she asked, "Are you seeing anyone?"

A frown appeared on Lee's brow. "Good Lord, no. Didn't you just hear me say I want you?"

"Honey, I don't even know if it's possible. I was talking with the guys tonight and they gave me a couple of ideas. How long is your grant good for?"

"Three years. Maybe more. It depends. You know how grants are."

"What if I could hire someone to take my place here? I'll have some money put aside I can live on and maybe I can find a job down there to help supplement my savings. Do you need an assistant? I have experience sorting pictures..."

"Kate. Are you sure? I'd love it if you'd come." Kate's unexpected offer brought a smile to Lee's lips. "You have many other admirable qualities, too, you know." Lee's smile disappeared. "Will your practice be okay? How will Beth and Kevin feel?"

"I don't know for sure. Sweetheart, this could take me a while to sort out. Are you willing to wait for me to move the mountain so I can come be with you?"

"I'd wait forever even though I don't want to. How long do you think?"

"Probably months, rather than weeks...maybe even six or more months. I promise that I'll do my best. I need to place a couple of ads in the Veterinary magazines and I'll reach out to some of my friends to see if anyone is looking. I'm eager to come and be with you. I'm sure you understand that I need to be selective, and not just grab the first person available."

Lee nodded. "Since Beth and Kevin are the ones who have to work with whoever you select, why not let them do the initial screening and interviewing. When they've made a selection of those they feel comfortable with, you could meet with their top two candidates to make the final decision."

"That's a good suggestion. I'll talk to them about it. Okay, let me go. I'm eager to get started."

***

Kate worked non-stop for the next several weeks. She informed her partners about her plans and about the interview process that Lee had suggested. Once the process was in place, they set about implementing it.

A month later, Beth and Kevin informed Kate that two candidates had applied. One was a new graduate and the other an experienced vet—one male and one female. Their ad had specified a minimum of five years of experience, so they decided to interview the experienced one first. They set up the interviews for Sunday when the office was closed so they would have no interruptions. The follow-up interview for Kate and the selected candidate was scheduled for the following Sunday. As a group they developed the list of questions they wanted to ask during the first series of interviews, then a list of follow-up questions for the final interviews.

Before Kate left work on Saturday afternoon, Kevin told her the male candidate had called to withdraw. "He accepted another position. It's not a problem. I think you'll find the remaining candidate is very qualified. We're set to interview her later this afternoon, and it'll be up to you if you want to hire her or re-advertise."

"Let's see what you think of her. I'll interview her next week if you think she'll be acceptable."

Later that night, relaxing at home, Kate was sitting on the couch getting ready to make her evening call to Lee. Cody curled up against her thigh. She looked around wondering what she was going to do with all her stuff. It was her hope that the new replacement vet would be interested in renting her house. She'd be willing to make the rental price attractive if she could rent it furnished. That way she wouldn't have to take all her possessions out. Worst case, she could move everything into the basement for storage. She was still debating. If she had to do that, maybe she should just get rid of most of the things she didn't need. It didn't make any sense to move all her belongings to Florida. She and Lee would probably find a small apartment. Currently Lee's furniture was in storage and she was renting her house for the time being.

Cody and Kate both jumped when her doorbell rang. She glanced at her watch. Seven o'clock. Who the heck could that be at this hour? She put Cody on the floor and stood up. The bell rang again just as she opened the door.

"Max!"

CHAPTER 32

"HELLO, KATE. HOW ARE you?"

"Why in the world would you care? Why are you here, Max?"

"Are you going to make me stand out here in the cold? Won't you at least invite me in?"

Kate stepped aside and Max entered. She set down her briefcase, took off her coat, and draped it over the coat tree next to the door. "The place looks the same. So do you. The years have been kind to you. You're still a very attractive woman."

"Thank you, I think. What do you want?"

"Don't tell me you're still pissed." Max patted Kate on the arm. "Holding a grudge this long isn't good for your blood pressure."

Kate ignored the comment and turned away leading the way into the living room, before taking a seat on the sofa. Max sat on the opposite chair and crossed her still shapely legs at the knee. She was dressed professionally, in a navy blue, tailored pinstripe suit, pale blue blouse, and three-inch heels.

"How's what's his name?"

"Long gone." Max shrugged one shoulder. "A couple of years after we got married, I discovered he was having an affair with a colleague. He begged, he whined, and I gave in and granted him a second chance. About six months after that, he began seeing a woman half his age. She's young enough to be his child. After his first affair, we sought counseling and eventually agreed to call it quits. We remained married although we lived separate lives. Now he's gotten his little bimbo pregnant and wants a divorce so he can marry her. That works for me, because I'm ready to move on. He's buying me out of the practice because he wants to stay in that pit of hellfire where we live and replace me in his life with the chippy." She looked away, glancing at the ceiling as if debating whether she should reveal more. When her gaze returned to Kate's, she leaned her cheek against her palm, resting her elbow on the arm of the chair. A smile tugged the corner of her lips. "You were right, by the way, about the temperatures there in Arizona. It's hot as blazes. I hated it. All that aside, as you're well aware from our previous experience it's not that easy to dissolve a practice. It'll take us a year or more to sort things out."

"You still haven't answered my question. Why are you here?"

"Kate, I'm here for the job. I just finished interviewing with Kevin and Beth."

"No, no, no..." Kate pushed to her feet.

"Wait, please hear me out."

Kate exhaled a long breath as she sat back down. "I don't trust you enough to hire you, Max. Last time we were in business together, if you'll recall, you didn't even give me two weeks notice. You just picked up and left. You nearly killed Kevin and me. I'm surprised Kevin even agreed to interview you."

"I'll admit it took some convincing." Max laughed. "He hung up on me twice when I first called. I finally got through to Beth, explained things to her and she convinced Kevin to at least talk to me."

"Why didn't they tell me?"

"I asked them not to, Kate. I asked them to give me a fair shot. Kevin knows me. He knows I'm a very capable vet. I'm good with both the clients and their owners."

"I have no qualms about your skills, Max. I'm sure Kevin feels the same. I can't imagine why he was willing to even consider your candidacy."

"Because I made him an offer he sort of couldn't refuse. I'll make the same one to you."

Kate tilted her head studying Max for any telltale signs of dishonesty. "And that is?"

"We all know I'm completely qualified for this position. When Kevin told me you weren't going to be here, I figured your primary reservation would be if I'd stick out the contract. So I offered to put my salary into an account in escrow for the duration of the three-year contract you're offering. You'll pay me a salary every month as you would any new hire. At the end of the first year, you'll return one year's worth of my money I'll place in escrow. We'll follow the same procedure for the remaining two years. If I don't keep my contract, you get to keep the money. You and your partners don't have to risk anything. I'll also rent your house, if you're willing, furnished if possible."

Kate sat silent for a long minute. "I need some time to think about this. I also need to talk to Kevin and Beth."

Max nodded. "I understand."

"One thing I don't understand. What's the saying? 'Of all the gin joints, blah, blah, blah...' God knows there are forty-nine other states, why pick this one?"

"Swear you won't laugh?"

Kate shook her head, smiling for the first time since Max came in. "Nope."

Max shrugged. "Ok, fair enough. I met someone. A couple of months ago at the conference."

"Oh God, not again."

Max laughed out loud. "It's not what you think. Doctor Campbell is a holistic pet food manufacturer located outside Philly. I attended the lecture and wanted to know more, so I made an appointment to discuss the product. One thing led to another and..."

"And here you are. Again Max? Didn't you learn last time?"

"Well, sort of. This time I'm taking my time. That's why I'm here, close enough, but not too close."

"So, he's a vet?"

"No, a scientist actually." Max paused. "And, by the way, Doctor Campbell is a she, not a he."

Kate's eyebrows shot up. "Oh."

"I'm sorry Kate...so, so sorry. I know you'll find this hard. I hope you'll believe that I did love you."

"Just not enough."

Max gave a quick tip of her head. "Perhaps. I blame youth and stupidity. I was too afraid to love you the way you needed me to so I did a stupid thing. I ran. I ran and I hurt you in the process. I'm so sorry Kate. Please. Do you think you can find it in your heart to forgive me?"

"We'll see." Kate softened her words with a smile. "I guess it's all water over the dam now."

"I hope so."

"So you're sure this is what you want?" Kate asked.

"The job or Doctor Campbell?"

"Both, I guess. One hinges on the other in a way."

"I'm sure about the job. I'll keep my commitment to you for three years, minimum. Maybe more if you want me to stay. If you want me gone before the three years are up, just let me know. Give me three months and I'll get out. You'll refund my escrow. It's a win for you all the way around. I know that in addition to our personal relationship, I walked away and treated you unfairly regarding the practice. I don't blame you for being leery. But I've arranged this so there's no risk for you at all."

"What about Dr. Campbell?"

"Ashley. Ash and I are still testing the waters. She knows my story and is, I think, a little wary. I honestly don't blame her. What I thought I wanted when I left you came at too high a cost. I've been in counseling and I've accepted my sexuality. I'm ready to live who I am. No more secrets."

"Really? For this new person's sake, just be sure Max."

"That's my plan."

"Too bad I won't be around to see the metamorphosis. It could be interesting."

"So what do you think, Kate? Do we have a deal?"

Kate knew Max's skills would be an asset to her practice. The offer of the escrow removed any unease she had regarding Max's willingness to stay for the duration of the contract.

"I still need to talk to Kevin and Beth. You have my promise that if they recommend you, I'll accept your deal."

Max stood up. "Thanks Kate. Thanks for accepting my apology and giving me another chance. I won't let you down this time." She pulled her phone from her pocket. "I need to call Ash. She's waiting for me at the diner. I'm sure she's full of coffee by now. We've got a bit of a drive ahead of us to get back to her place."

"Why don't you two stay here tonight in your old room. I'm up at five. You can leave early and beat the traffic into the city after a good night's sleep."

"Thank you for your offer. It's been a long and harrowing day. I'll ask her."

"While you do that, I'll call Kevin and see what his and Beth's recommendations are."

***

Max opened the door when Ash rang the bell. Kate was still in her office on the phone with Kevin.

Ash gave Max a brief hug and kiss before looking around. "So, this is the place you and Kate fixed up? Nice."

"I'll bet she's never done anything to the bedroom. She probably still has those hideous mirrors on the closet doors."

Kate's laughter caused the two of them to turn around. "You're right. Those doors keep me humble. Hello. You must be Ash." Kate extended her hand to the attractive brunette with icy green eyes and a winning smile.

"Yes, and you're Kate, I assume. It's a pleasure to meet you. I've heard many nice things about you."

"Really?"

Ash's eyes softened, her grin broad. "Surprised?"

Kate shrugged. "Perhaps a bit. Come in and sit down. Are you going to stay over?"

Ash shook her head. "No, I'm a little leery of all the traffic going into the city in the morning. I have an early appointment I can't miss. Thank you anyway for your generous offer."

"Will you at least come in for a bit and have something to eat or drink?" Kate gestured towards the kitchen.

"Okay, for a few minutes. I'll take a soda if you have one, if not water will do. I've had enough coffee to last me for at least a month."

"How about seltzer with some lemon?"

"Works for me. Thanks Kate." Ash turned to follow Kate.

As the other two women started down the hallway, Max asked, "May I use the restroom, Kate?"

"Sure. You know where it is. We'll be in the kitchen."

Ash sat at the island while Kate fixed the drinks. "Max only tells me good things about you. She also claimed full responsibility for the fact you two are no longer together. Do I need to be afraid?"

"You're very direct."

"I find I get more honest answers that way. Do I need to be concerned?"

"About me?" Kate shook her head in denial. "No. Not in the least. I have a wonderful partner. That's why the job and the house are available. I'm moving to the Keys to be with her. So by the time Max comes here I'll be leaving to go there."

She watched Ash exhale and relax. She glanced down at Cody who sat at Kate's feet, patiently watching. "Hi fella. What's your name?"

"That's Cody."

"He's beautiful. What do you feed him?"

"Don't tell me you're going to try to sell me some product?"

The sound of Ash's laughter was unexpected. "No. However, I do plan to send you some samples and ask that you let Cody be the judge."

"Fair enough. Is dog food what you really want to talk about?"

"It's as good a subject as any. You already answered the one question I had for you. As long as your relationship with Max is in the past, that's the only concern I had. She's been pretty open with me about the fact that she was, as she puts it, unfair in her treatment of you and that she hurt you a great deal with her betrayal. Max was honest about her past before we even started to date. She was concerned that once she told me what had happened and why, that I wouldn't want to get involved with her."

"And?"

Ash brushed her hair back behind her ear. "I wasn't born yesterday. There are things I've done in the past that I'm not proud of too. Everyone makes mistakes. Hopefully we learn from them and don't repeat them. Don't you agree?"

Max entered the kitchen as Ash was finishing her statement. "Don't let me stop your conversation. I'm interested in hearing your response, Kate."

"I guess. Sometimes it takes more than once to learn though." Kate glanced at Max before returning her focus to Ash. "If she won't let your and her parents know about your relationship, my advice is to run for solid ground."

The burst of laughter that sprang from the two of them surprised Kate.

"We've just done that this weekend," Ash said. "I introduced her to my parents yesterday. Hers are on our 'To Do' list."

Kate's eyes widened and her eyebrows arched. "Well, Max, you really have turned over a new leaf, haven't you? I'm impressed."

"Don't be. I have a deadline, six months to take Ash home to meet my parents. That's the time limit she's imposed." Max rested her chin on her palm. "I told you, she knows all about me, warts and all. I wanted her to take me on knowing what she faced and what a coward I've been in the past."

"So how did it feel meeting Ash's parents?"

The smile Ash and Max exchanged told Kate it had been okay. Max reached for Ash's hand. "It was nice. They are nice people."

"I've been out to them since high school," Ash said. "So it wasn't like I had to reveal to them that I'm a lesbian. I lost my first and only partner three years ago to breast cancer. I've been a mess for most of the time since then. When I met Max something just clicked. Together we seem to be better people than we are when we're apart."

Kate smiled. "Then I'm glad you found each other. Max, Ash..." she said, glancing between them, "I wish you all the happiness in the world. It seems like you're off to a good start."

Max sighed in relief. "Thank you. I hope you find everything you want in Florida, too."

"I already have. But I do appreciate the sentiment. By the way, I spoke to Kevin. The job is yours if you want it." Kate stuck out her hand.

Max took Kate's hand in both of her own and sought her former partner's eyes. "Yes, very much. Thank you for giving me a chance. It means a lot to me."

Kate released Max's hands and said, "You're welcome. Did Kevin discuss salary, hours, and duties with you?"

"Yes."

"I'll have my lawyer draw up a contract under the conditions we've discussed. If you're interested in renting the house, I'll get a realtor to give me a fair market value for rental and will let you know what she suggests. I'll even give you a friends and family discount because I know you'll leave it in as good a condition as you found it."

"Thanks, Kate. I'm sure whatever price you set will be fair."

Oh, and Max...leave the damned mirrors in my bedroom alone. I like them in some perverse way."

Max nodded, but Kate heard her stifle a laugh.

"Where do I send everything and when can you start?"

"I'm going back to close up my affairs in Arizona. I'll be back here, at Ash's house, by next weekend." Max took out a business card, turned it over, and wrote some additional information on the back before pushing it across the counter in Kate's direction. "All contact information you'll need is on there." Before she to stood up, Max asked one final question. "Will you do the orientation, or will Kevin or Beth? I like her, by the way."

Kate replied. "Yes, me too. I'm lucky to have them both. I think they can handle bringing you up to speed. Not that much is different since you left. Office procedures are pretty similar, so I don't think you'll encounter any surprises."

Ash and Max stood up. "What about the house, the furniture?"

"I'll pack anything personal into boxes and store them in the back room of the basement. All you'll really need are your clothes and your toothbrush."

Max glanced around. "That works for me. Thanks Kate. Thanks for giving me another chance. I won't let you down this time." Max pulled Kate toward her giving her a quick hug. Kate looked over Max's shoulder and was pleased to see a smile on Ash's face.

"I guess I'm next," Ash said, opening her arms to Kate. Another quick hug and they all walked towards the front door. Ash stopped to pet Cody. "I'm sending you some good grub. You'll like it, I promise."

"You're going to get my dog hooked on this food and then I'll discover I can't get it in Florida."

Ash grinned. "I'm working on it. Until that time, there's always UPS." They all laughed when Cody barked.

CHAPTER 33

KATE WAS PACKED AND ready to leave for Florida a week later, still amazed at how things had worked out. If she'd custom designed a solution it couldn't have been any better. She met Max at the clinic before office hours. They signed all the papers necessary to cement their business agreement and lease for the house.

After bidding everyone goodbye in the conference room, Kate gathered the papers into her briefcase. Her car was already packed and as she came down the hallway heading for the door she looked around for Cody. She noticed Ash sitting in the waiting room with Cody curled against her thigh.

"Hey there, that's my dog," Kate teased.

"Yes, I know. I made him a promise. I didn't think the food would get here in time by mail, so I figured I'd deliver it personally. I'll walk you out to your car." As Ash stood, Cody ran ahead of her and Kate bound for the door.

Kate opened her car trunk to accept the four cases of food Ash had brought for Cody. They had to open the last case and stuff the individual cans into nooks and crannies in the back seat when the whole case wouldn't fit intact. "Thanks Ash. Hope he eats this stuff."

"He'll like it, I guarantee it. You'll be begging me for more in a couple of weeks." Ash laughed. "Hey, good luck. I hope you find happiness where you're going."

"I already have. I wish the same to you and to Max as well."

Ash stuck out her hand. Kate used it to pull Ash into a loose hug.

"I'm almost sorry you're leaving. I think we could be friends, Kate."

"I think so, too. My dog is a better judge of character than I am, and he obviously approves of you. Take care now."

Ash nodded. "Drive safe." She waved as Kate drove away.

***

Around four o'clock Kate pulled into the parking lot of the marine center where Lee worked. Kate had texted Lee a few miles prior to her arrival so she wasn't surprised when Lee came bounding out of the front door, ran across the parking lot, and wrapped her in her arms. Cody barked an excited welcome, his tail wagging as hard as it could.

Lee released Kate. "I'm so glad you're here. I have a surprise for you, too. My colleague is in Australia teaching some course for six weeks and she's letting me use her apartment. We can bring Cody, and the best part is it's nice and private, so no one will hear the moans you'll be making later."

"Believe me, it's not only my moans we need to worry about. I have some plans of my own in that department." Kate looked around before giving Lee a quick kiss. "Are you able to leave now?"

"Yep. I took a couple of days leave, too. I don't have to be back till Monday. I figure we might not get out of bed until at least Saturday." They were both grinning. "I can't believe you're actually here."

"How about taking me home. I'm tired and hungry and need a shower, big time."

"Okay, follow me."

A short trip through town led them to the little bungalow Lee was staying in. Kate grabbed her bag and handed it and several loose cans of dog food to Lee.

"What's this?" Lee started gathering cans of dog food.

"Long story," Kate said. "I'll tell you later. I'll get the rest." She popped the trunk lid and removed the three additional cases Ash had given her. "Can you take Cody for a quick walk while I unload the rest of what I'll need?"

"Sure." Lee put her hand on her hip. "As soon as we're done, you'd better give me the kind of kiss I deserve."

Kate grabbed Lee and pulled her into the shade behind one of the bushes beside the door, kissing her until they were both breathing heavily.

Still snuggled against Kate, Lee sighed, "Now that's more like it. I've missed you."

"I've missed you, too. Come on. Let's get things sorted. I'm starving. After you feed me, I plan to make love to you until you can't stand up."

By the time Lee returned with Cody, Kate had finished unpacking the car, put out some food and water for Cody, and was taking a much-needed shower. Three long days in the car had taken their toll.

Lee quickly stripped off her clothes and slid into the shower behind Kate. She soaped her hands and began exploring Kate's body, her palms leaving a trail of bubbles in their wake. She covered Kate's mouth with her own and entered her mouth with her tongue as Kate opened for her at the same time her fingers slid inside Kate's moist opening. Kate groaned. Lee buried her head in Kate's neck, inhaling her familiar scent, and began stroking more quickly. She leaned back, seeking Kate's breast with her free hand, she rolled the responsive nipple between her fingers. Kate's breathing was coming faster now. Lee leaned in and ran her tongue up Kate's neck and gently bit the tender skin there. Kate shuddered, nearly collapsing into Lee's arms.

"Umm, I needed that. I needed you," Kate said turning Lee around and pushing her against the wall. She kissed her way down Lee's body quickly burying her tongue between her legs. Her hands slid upwards to tug her nipples as she sucked Lee's now stiff clit into her mouth. In seconds, Lee groaned and pulled Kate to her feet, kissing her soundly.

"That's a down payment on later," she whispered into Kate's neck. "How about some dinner?"

"Sounds good." They finished their showers, put on oversized T-shirts, and moved to the kitchen. Lee had a salad with strips of grilled chicken ready for them. After making quick work of the meal, they moved to the porch to watch the sunset, hands joined.

Before they turned in, Kate threw on some clothes and walked Cody for the last time that night before making a trip to the bathroom where she brushed her teeth. Finally finished, she slipped her clothes off and slid into bed curling against her lover. "Umm. I've missed you, missed this. You feel so good." They snuggled closer and wrapped around each other.

"I'm so excited that we'll be together like this every night, and that we have until Monday with no obligations."

"Starting next week, I need to start looking for a job."

"You don't have to hurry. I make enough to support us. You know that. Why don't you relax for a few months, take some time, and figure out what you want to do."

"Oh, I already know what I want to do, but I'm not sure there'll be a job there. All that remains to be seen."

"Are you going to tell me?"

"Nope, not yet."

"Well, if you're not going to talk to me, I have something else for you to do." Lee rolled over on top of Kate and began showing her how happy she was to have her there.

CHAPTER 34

KATE OPENED HER EYES, not quite believing that Lee was snuggled against her. She slipped out of bed early, started the kettle, and let Cody out, watching him until he finished his business. She called him back inside and opened a can of Ash's dog food. Ash had been right. He loved it. By the time Cody started to eat, the tea had finished brewing. Kate took the two cups and carried them back into the bedroom.

"Is that tea for me?" Lee, looking tousled and well loved, pulled herself into a more upright position against the headboard, tucking the sheet around her breasts. She held her hand out and Kate placed the cup into her eager grasp. "Umm. Good," Lee pronounced after taking a sip. "I could get used to this."

"I certainly hope so. I came a long way to assure that we could be together. I'd hate it a lot if you ever changed your mind."

Lee looked at her lover. There was vulnerability in Kate's eyes she'd never seen before. "Come here. What's going on?" She asked when Kate settled against her shoulder. "Feeling uneasy about something? You can tell me anything you know, because I love you and you love me."

"I know."

Lee waited, hoping Kate would eventually share what was on her mind. "So?"

"What makes you think something is wrong?"

"I didn't say anything is wrong. I asked if you were feeling uneasy."

Kate exhaled a long sigh. "Maybe just a little unsettled. I think that the impact of selling my practice just became real to me. I have no home, I have no business, and I have no job."

Lee took Kate's hand. "You have me."

Kate set her and Lee's cups on the night table and snuggled against her lover. "Do I? I certainly hope so. I've always wanted a lover who wanted to be with me forever."

Lee tilted Kate's chin up so she looked into her eyes. "I don't want you forever Kate. I want you for one day longer than forever." She sealed her promise with a kiss.

EPILOGUE

TWENTY-TWO MONTHS LATER

"THE LETTER'S HERE," LEE yelled from the kitchen to Kate who was sitting on the back porch. "Great! It came? Grab a beer and come let me see."

"Here." Lee handed Kate the overnight envelope and sat the beer on the table.

Kate tore open the wrapper, pulled a check from the envelope and perused the amount. She waved it in the air. "We're solvent."

"You're solvent. It's your profit from the sale of your house and your business." Lee sat in the chair opposite her lover. "I'm glad that buying the practice ended up being a positive experience for Max. And from what you've told me she's getting on well with the other partners."

Kate sat back in her chair, the check and the envelope resting on her lap. "Funny how things change. Max was so unhappy there before, when we were together. Now it seems she's really settled in. When we went up last month to get the last of my stuff from the basement, Max told me she's deliriously happy."

"Ash has something to do with that, don't you think?"

Kate chuckled. "Yeah, I do. Max told me that Ash doesn't let her get away with her usual crap."

"I really like Ash and I think she's good for Max." Lee reached for her bottle and took a swig of her beer. "Are you looking forward to their commitment ceremony this spring."

"Yes, I am. It'll be small—just Kyle and Mike, Beth and Kevin and their families, a couple of Ash's friends from Philly, Ash's family, and Max's parents. I still can't believe that Max came out to them. We had more arguments about telling both her family and mine about us. I can't believe she's actually out to everyone." Kate shook her head. Silence rested comfortably between them. Kate leaned over and rested her elbow on the arm of the chair, her chin on her hand. Her index finger tapped on her lips as she analyzed her feelings. "It might seem odd to some, but I actually like Ash a lot, and I like Max with her. Ash is doing great with her product line, and it's catching on here as well."

"You did help by introducing her to your boss at the clinic, and he's helped her get her foot in the door here in the Keys."

Kate nodded. "I know, but the credit is really hers. Ash has earned her success. She continually receives good press about her pet food line, and the mail response to her request for the stores on the Keys to carry her products has been overwhelmingly successful. We've even added a small section in the clinic here where customers can purchase her food and other items like leashes, leads, and vitamins."

The two women watched as the sun began to dip below the horizon setting the sky on fire with shades of red, orange, and purple.

Lee turned towards Kate. "It's beautiful, isn't it?

"Very." After a brief pause, Kate added. "We're lucky the way things worked out. Whoever would have thought we'd get one of those happy ever after romance novel endings to all our problems. Everyone ended up happy. Max said that Ash is traveling frequently for her work right now. When she's home, she's usually been staying with Max at the house. Ash has decided to give up her apartment and plans to move into the house with Max."

"That's really great."

Kate slipped the check from Max back into the envelope. "Oh, there's a letter from Max in here. Want me to read it to you?"

"Please."

Kate opened and began to read Max's letter. 'Hello my friends...Ash and I are finally all settled in the house. Kate, Ash says to tell you she's including a few extra cases of food in with each order she ships to the center that she has labeled for Cody. Consider it a 'friends and family' perk. She's arranged to meet with your boss as well as other pet stores and pet food suppliers up and down the Keys to introduce her new line of dry food when we're on our trip there next month.

Thanks for the invitation to stay in your and Lee's bungalow on Islamorada. Its location will make it a good base of operation for Ash as she travels the Keys demonstrating her new products and touching base with the buyers. I'll be in touch next week to make arrangements.

The practice is doing well. I love being back here and am enjoying working with Kevin and Beth. Who would ever have imagined?

We appreciate and accept your offer for a private tour of the Wildlife Preserve where you volunteer your time. As you suggested, I've been reading about the Key deer. It's a wonderful story how they've come back from the brink of extinction.

Are you sure Lee is okay with us staying with you? Ash is looking forward to seeing you both again. We had such fun on your recent visit back here when you collected the remainder of your belongings from the basement.

Okay, I've blathered on enough. I've enclosed the check for the house and the purchase of your interest in the clinic. Ash and I should be around one hundred by the time we pay everything off. I'm optimistic that it'll be worth every penny. See you both soon.' It's signed, Max and Ash."

Lee stood up and came over to where Kate sat and straddled her lap. "Of course I'm okay with them staying here. There's really nothing to worry about is there? She'd have a long wait if she ever wants another chance at you, right?"

Kate smiled and pulled Lee close for a gentle kiss. "That's right. We have no worries. She'd have to wait for one day longer than forever. It's what you promised me, and I won't settle for one day less."

The End

About AJ Adaire

Let me tell you a little about myself. Twenty years ago, I wrote my first book just to see if I could do it. The novel occupied space on my bookshelf, unread for nearly twenty years until one day, while in a cleaning frenzy, I considered disposing of the neatly stacked but now age-yellowed pages. As I began to read the long forgotten work, I was surprised to discover that the story was enjoyable! Editing and retyping the first book provided a new sense of accomplishment and additional tales followed. Completion of *This is Fitting* encouraged me to write four more romance novels. *I Love My Life* and *Sunset Island* were followed by *Awaiting My Assignment* and its sequel, *Anything Your Heart Desires*. *One Day Longer Than Forever* is now complete, and *It's Complicated* is in the hands of first readers before the first big edit.

Now retired, there is all the time in the world to write. I live on the east coast with my partner of twenty-eight years. Because we love a challenge, we provide a loving home for two spoiled cats instead of a dog. In addition to writing, any spare time is devoted to reading, mastering new computer programs, and socializing with friends.

Contact Information
E-mail: aj@ajadaire.com
Website: http://www.ajadaire.com
Facebook: http://www.facebook.com/ajadaire
Desert Palm Press: www.desertpalmpress.com

Other books by AJ Adaire

Available at Amazon, Smashwords, and CreateSpace

Friend Series

Sunset Island

ISBN: 9781301136629

Ren Madison is certain her life couldn't be more perfect. She owns a private island with an Inn off the coast of Maine. She treasures her loving relationship with her older brother Jack, his wife, Marie, and dotes on her niece Laura. She has a passionate and supportive relationship with her partner, Brooke, and a successful business that doesn't require her undivided attention allowing her ample time to pursue her true passion, painting.

Ren's idyllic world crumbles when Brooke dies. Friends and family worry that Ren may never fully recover from her loss.

Dr. Lindy Caprini, a multi-lingual professor, is looking for an artist to illustrate the book she is writing comparing fairy tales from around the world. To make working together on the book easier, Lindy takes a year sabbatical and leaves friends, home, and boyfriend in Pennsylvania and moves to Ren's island. Ren soon discovers that the beautiful and mischievous Lindy is a talented author and a witty conversationalist. Their collaboration on the book leads to a close, light hearted, and flirtatious friendship. Will their collaboration end there?

***

The Interim (a novelette)

ISBN: 9781311099051

Devastated that her partner cheated, Melanie flees to a new job in Maine, where she meets Ren Madison. Ren is dealing with issues of her own after losing her partner Brooke in a plane crash

What happens in the interim after one relationship ends and you're really ready to love again? For Ren Madison, Melanie was what happened.

The Interim fills in the details of Ren Madison's life on Sunset Island after Brooke but before Lindy.

***

Awaiting My Assignment

ISBN: 9781310825248

Bernie was a liar. Amanda learned that much when she caught her lover cheating the first time. Upon discovering a second indiscretion, Amanda vows there will never be another. She leaves the relationship, fleeing to her friend Dana in New York State. While staying at Dana's home, Amanda meets and falls in love with a wonderful woman named Mallory.

Amanda is ready to move on. However, the consistently surprising Bernie isn't finished yet. Amanda learns of Bernie's rudest betrayal yet when she receives a package from her recently deceased ex-lover. A very surprising revelation and one final request is contained therein. The favor comes with a gift that delivers dramatic and life-altering changes, not only to Amanda's life, but to the lives of her closest friends and new partner as well.

***

Anything Your Heart Desires

ISBN: 978131163912

"Whoa—lesbians!" That was Stacy Alexander's first thought as she observes the group of women in the new shop across the street kiss each other in greeting. Stacy had been staring out her apartment window trying to think of a motive for the death of the character she'd killed off in her mystery novel. Ah ha—extortion! What could be a better reason for the murder of my heroine than being blackmailed because she's a lesbian? Now all I need is a lesbian to teach me about the 'lesbian lifestyle.'

That's where policewoman Jo Martin enters the picture. Jo has two rules by which she religiously lives her life: never get involved with someone already in a relationship and never, ever date a straight woman.

As Jo and Stacy collaborate on the novel, will Stacy want to gain a more intimate knowledge of the topic, and will Jo hold steadfastly to her rules?

8010702R00137

Printed in Great Britain
by Amazon.co.uk, Ltd.,
Marston Gate.